Hooking Up WITH Mr. Wrong

HOOKING UP WITH MR WRONG

BOOK ONE

ELLOUISE LISTON

Hooking up with Mr Wrong

Contact Info: www.ellouiseliston.com

Professional Edit by: Ellie @ My Brother's Editor

Arc Cover by: Vivian Monir

Front Cover Design by: Shannon Passmore @ Shanoff Designs

ISBN: 978-0-6451119-1-0 (paperback)

978-0-6451119-0-3 (Ebook)

For Jackie & Sammie.

Never forget that dreams are possible with a little hard work.

"We're all stories in the end, so let's make it a good one, aye?"

— DOCTOR WHO

SIGN UP FOR MY AUTHOR NEWSLETTER

Be the first to learn about Ellouise Liston's new releases and receive exclusive content for both readers and writers.

WWW.ELLOUISELISTON.COM

CHAPTER 1

AVA

August 2019
Freshman Year

Fuck me!

I've been reading the same line over and over from this stupid book, so many times that Heathcliff's words will be forever burned in my brain. I had wanted to make a good impression on my professors by getting started with the reading list early, but it's hard to focus when I've got Rhianna blasting through my walls, thanks to my inconsiderate neighbor.

Go to college, everyone said. *It'll be fun,* everyone said. *It'll be a fucking experience!* Well, right now, I might as well be at home for all the education I'm getting at the moment.

But my little sister Lucy kept pushing the issue… and now here I am.

I let out a breath of relief when I finally hear Rhianna

start to die down, only for my muscles to start bunching up in irritation again when Drake starts to play.

I groan, not knowing whether I want to scream or cry when I plop my head, facedown, on the book I'm trying to read. I'm lucky enough to get a single dorm room, thinking I would be left alone to do my studying in peace, that and my best friend Mia decided that she didn't need to follow the rules by living in a dorm our first year, but instead got her parents to insist she live off campus in a nice place provided by them.

Too bad she couldn't let me come with.

My head pops up at the sound of my phone vibrating, somehow able to hear it through the noise. Mia, speak of the devil, I think as I answer the phone, running my fingers through the mass of dark brown hair on my head and start to rise from my chair to pace around the small dorm room.

"Hey, bitch."

"Hey to you too." I can't help the small smile from peeking through my mask of anger. She always has this effect, ever since first grade when she punched Tommy Hollis for calling me ugly. Then I proceeded to fight *her* for standing up for me when I can stand up for myself.

We've been friends ever since.

"What's up? You sound tense."

I glare at the wall where the music is coming from. "I'm surprised you can't hear it."

"Hear what?"

"I still don't know why I can't just stay with you."

She sighs. "Because my parents are douchebags. We both know this. The condition of getting my own place is that it is just me. *I'm not paying for your freeloading friends, Mia!* Like I said, douchebags."

I can almost hear her shrug and I want to hug her. She's always had problems with her parents, specifically her mother, but at the same time, I know she wants their approval, even if that means she doesn't get a say. I wish I could talk to her but she just clams up when I talk about it. So, I do all I can, be there for her.

There is a long pause before she says, "Do you want me to come over?"

"No, I'm actually going to—more Drake?! Really?!" I shout at the wall when another Drake song starts to play.

"What?"

"Oh, it's just my stupid neighbor. They've been playing Drake songs at full volume and I can't concentrate."

"What did Drake ever do to you?" She laughs, and I turn my glare to the phone.

"I appreciate music as much as the next person, but to play it that loud is rude."

"I know, how dare they not invite you." Mia continues to laugh at my expense.

"Ha ha, easy for you to laugh when you are in your quiet apartment."

She finally stops laughing long enough to say, "Look, Ava, if it's bothering you that much, just talk to them or get your RA."

"I'm not getting my RA. That will classify me as a snitch in the dorm."

She sighs. "Well, I guess you have to deal with it then, princess."

I roll my eyes. "Thanks for your help."

"I love you!"

"I love you too," I grumble before hanging up and throwing the phone on my bed just as the music gets a bit louder.

Did that fucker turn the music up?

The sudden pounding in my head answers that question and I growl, "No fucking way." A second later I storm out of my dorm room in my boxer shorts with little lambs on them and my white tank top, my hair in a messy pile on my head.

I storm out of my room and proceed to bang on my obnoxious neighbor's door with a closed fist until it suddenly swings open to reveal a pair of the bluest eyes I've ever seen.

The boy in front of me looks down at me, taking in my attire before I watch his eyebrows kick up to his dark hair-line. "Can I help you?"

I blink, looking beyond his broad shoulders to see the mass of people laughing and dancing in the small space behind him, with red Solo cups in their hands.

He's having a party?!

He looks at me expectantly, like I'm the rude one interrupting his *party.*

I throw my hand out to the scene behind him, scoffing, "Seriously?!"

He frowns, looking back at the party before looking back at me, still confused. "Did you want to come in? I mean, you're not exactly dressed for the occasion but I'm diggin' it."

I scoff again, my jaw hanging open at how ignorant this guy is, or maybe he just doesn't care. Every part of me wants to punch one of those blue eyes, but he is not worth me getting in shit, so I take a deep, calming breath and say in the most relaxed way I can, "No, I don't want to come in because I am trying to study and it's kind of hard to do that when you're playing your music so loud." My words almost turn into a growl near the end despite the smile I try to hold in place.

He just stands there, taking me in again before a small smile curves one side of his mouth. "You're a little fire-cracker, aren't you?"

I blink, unsure if I heard him correctly. "Excuse me?"

"You wear these cute fuzzy PJ's but underneath it, you're a fiery one."

I clench my jaw, already feeling him poke at me. "Only when someone plays music so loud it vibrates my walls."

"You can request a song if you don't like what we are playing."

"I don't want to request a song; I want silence so I can study."

"You are aware it's only the first week, right?"

"And unlike you, I care about my education," I snap before spinning on my heels to leave because it's obvious I'm not getting anywhere.

I feel him follow me to my door.

"Hey! That's a pretty big assumption to make when you've only just met me." He stops just before my door, crossing his arms over his massive chest and making the T-shirt he's wearing stretch over his broad shoulders. I make sure not to stare too long and instead focus my glare on him.

"And so far, I'm not impressed. You are loud, obnoxious, ignorant, and rude."

It's his turn to scoff. "I'm rude? You're rude, stuck up, mean, and a prude."

"A prude?"

"You seem like you would be one."

"That's a pretty big assumption there, buddy." I step into his space, poking his firm chest with each word, until a sly smile appears on his face.

"Are you going to prove otherwise?" He raises a brow in challenge and I hate that my lack of experience is so obvious to him when I feel my cheeks redden, and I hate that he is now using it against me.

I open my mouth and close it, unsure of how to respond. I could slap him but, again, didn't want to get in trouble. I could tell him to fuck off but that would only show how much he's getting to me.

Before I can even respond, his smile turns smug as he

steps back. "That's what I thought." He starts to walk back to his party, the music spilling out into the hall when he opens the door. "You're welcome over any time, little lamb."

I look back down at my lamb boxers when I hear his door close, the music still blasting through, and I know there is only one way I'm going to sleep tonight.

It's time I go into 'snitch' territory.

I'M NOT in bed for more than twenty minutes before there is a loud banging at my door. I groan and push myself up from the bed and make my way to the door, swinging it open to reveal a familiar pair of blue eyes glaring down at me as he rests his hands on both sides of my doorframe, his huge body taking up a majority of space in my doorway.

I blink and look up at him, loving the silence that surrounds us.

I cross my arms and lean on my doorframe, smiling a smug smile up at him. "Can I help you?"

"You called the RA."

Not a question because we both know I did, but that doesn't mean I'm going to admit it.

I shrug and blink up at him innocently. "I don't know what you are talking about."

"Bullshit. You complain about the party and the next thing I know, it's being shut down by a pissed-off RA."

"I am insulted that you would accuse me of such a thing."

"You are so full of shit. I know it was you."

"It could've been anyone on this floor. You were playing your music too loud."

He gives me a tense smile before he leans into me, until I can smell his woodsy scent. He smells like a nature walk, if that is possible. "This isn't over."

I raise my brows at him. "Excuse me?"

"You just started something, little lamb."

Just as he goes to walk away, I yell after him. "Stop calling me that."

"Sorry, but you didn't give me your name."

I growl before telling him, "Ava."

He smiles a mischievous smile that has me on edge as he backs into his room. "Conner. Until we meet again," he says before closing his door and leaving me with an uneasy feeling that my life is not going to get much easier, and that I will most definitely see that guy again.

* * *

Weeks later

"WELL, I'VE HAD A GREAT TIME." Vic, from my American Lit class, gives me a shy smile as he pulls his hands out of the pockets of his jeans.

I fumble with my room key, feeling the awkward silence almost smothering me as I give him my own shy smile. "Me too."

"So, should we do it again?" He looks hopeful with his big brown eyes and I instantly feel the weight of my regret for saying yes to a date, but what do I do? He's cute with floppy dark hair, big brown eyes and a lanky build. He's not mouth-watering, but he's cute, like a friend. I guess I've just read *Pride and Prejudice* too many times that all my heart wants is its own Mr. Darcy. Someone brooding and troubled, or maybe just someone who interests me. But alas, I have yet to find someone who lights my fire.

And unfortunately, that means a sad rejection for my friend here, but before I can even say a word, I distantly hear footsteps approaching behind me at the same time Vic's smile is wiped from his face and his attention is somewhere behind me.

Feeling my muscles tense, I don't need to look to know who it is.

The next second, he is beside me with a shit-eating grin. "Hey, little lamb."

I growl through gritted teeth, feeling my back straighten at the little pet name I've acquired. "I've told you—" But before I can finish, he cuts in.

"Your mom called."

I blink, thinking I misheard him because I haven't heard from my mom since she left when I was a kid. "What?"

"Yeah, she wanted to check in to make sure you're taking your medication. You know how you get? She said you were supposed to pick up a new script."

I narrow my eyes, seeing the mischievous twinkle in his eyes as I hear Vic gasp. "Medication?"

Conner cocks his head at Vic, as if just realizing he's there. "Oh yeah, it's nothing. If she takes the medication, then she's fine. But remember that one time you didn't take it and then you ran naked through the—"

Both Vic's and my eyes widen and I resist the urge to slam my hand over Conner's mouth, but instead I say too loudly, "Thank you for the message but I think you can go now." I finish with a tight smile and a look promising death to Conner.

Conner looks back at Vic, before throwing an arm casually over my shoulder and nuzzling my head. "What are friends for, right?"

Conner grunts when I elbow him in the ribs, making him drop his arm from my shoulders as I turn my red face to an uncomfortable looking Vic, slowly backing away.

"I gotta go, Ava. But I'll see you in class."

Did I just get rejected by the guy I was going to reject? I guess I should be happy, I mean, now I don't have to do it. But now, he probably thinks I'm crazy or something thanks to the grinning fool beside me who I turn to glare at, waving my finger in his face. "I was on a date, you idiot!" I poke his firm chest so hard, it may leave a bruise but he doesn't react, just continues to smile his smug smile.

"Oh come on! You weren't really going to date that guy,"

I tilt my chin up to meet his eyes. "I might have."

"Please," he scoffs. "Your keys kept inching toward your door, like all you wanted to do was to get away." Fuck, was I that obvious? Oh well, I'm not letting him get to me. No way will I let on that he is right.

"And besides, if he's that quick to walk away, I may have done you a favor," he adds, and I don't even want to argue because he's kind of right. And I hate that. "All in the act of helping you." He winks, giving me a proud smile before placing a hand on my shoulder in the act of comfort but I can smell the condescension a mile away.

So, I brush off his hand. "Do me a favor, and don't help me," I say before fumbling with my keys again and open my door to rid myself of this horror of a night.

As I close my door, I see Conner's smug face as he sings, "You're welcome." And I slam it in his face.

"WHY ARE YOU LAUGHING? This is not funny," I chastise Mia as she continues to laugh into the phone.

"Really, because it sounds funny." She continues to laugh and I sigh, waiting for her to calm down before I can continue to tell her what happened last night after my date.

As she starts to get her breath back, I ask, "Are you done?"

"Oh come on, it's not like you're interested in Vic anyway."

"That is exactly what Conner said. Am I really that obvious?"

"I don't know about him, but I just know because the last relationship you had was… never."

"I'm picky," I exclaim into the phone.

"And there is nothing wrong with that, but maybe Conner did you a favor." A point I already realize is true.

I grumble, throwing myself onto my bed with a flop. "That's also what Conner said."

"Sounds like Conner's real smart."

I roll my eyes, picturing his smug smile and twinkling blue eyes. "You wouldn't think that if you met him."

Mia sighs. "Do you want me to come over? We can watch *The Big Bang Theory*."

Even though the idea is tempting, I know I have too much work to do and don't want to stress about it later. I groan, "No, it's fine. I got a lot of homework to do anyway."

"All work. That's why you are my Leonard."

I smile a warm smile at our names for each other. "And you are my Penny."

Now even though Penny and Leonard are romantically involved, Mia and I have always resonated with them. She is the hot blonde that can talk to anyone and I am the awkward smart one. Lucky me, but to have a friend like Mia, yeah, I'm pretty lucky.

* * *

One month later

THE AIR IS KNOCKED out of me as a heavy weight plops on top of me as I sleep.

"Holy shit!"

"What the fuck?"

My eyes spring open at the groggy but familiar voice as I twist at the waist, my legs getting more tangled in the blankets as I see through the darkness a pair of blue. Fucking. Eyes.

Conner's eyes widen as he takes me in, surprise appearing on his face which makes no sense considering he is trespassing in my room.

I thought I locked the door, but obviously, I was too busy Skyping with my little sister Lucy to concentrate on basic security measures.

And now here we are.

But why is *he* here?

The scent of alcohol hitting my nose answers my question as I persist in pushing him off.

"Stop pushing me." He grunts, still hovering over me, his weight pushing down on my lower body.

I continue to push. "What are you doing here? Get off!" I give him one good push that not only sends him sailing to the floor with a loud thump but me tumbling after him, landing with a hard hit to the side and my legs still in the blankets.

We both grunt on impact, slowly wiggling out of our cocoons to glare at each other. Well, I glare at him, he just stares groggily at me as he rubs a hand over his tired face.

He is drunk.

"What the hell are you doing here?"

"Me? What are you doing here?!"

"It's my room, you jackass."

I can see a fight flaring up in his eyes but just as he opens his mouth, he quickly shuts it, finally noticing the girly shit and textbooks filling my room. "Oh."

"Yeah, oh."

"Sorry, I must've gotten our rooms confused. I had a bit too much to drink, obviously." He gives me a drunken smile, still sitting by me on my floor, leaning back on his hands.

I raise a brow. "On a Tuesday night?"

"I was celebrating."

"What?" I cock my head, genuinely curious as to what could be so amazing that he'd drink about it with class the next day.

His smile grows, and he lifts his arms, extending them out to his sides. "Being me."

I roll my eyes, disappointed that I didn't see it coming. "You are nauseating," I tell him and finally manage to free my legs enough to stand in my oversized T-shirt and my usual lamb boxers.

I notice Conner's smile when he sees them and I hate myself for even wearing them, but how was I supposed to know he would sneak attack me?

"And you would be really hot if you weren't so uptight," he tells me as he stands, a little shakier than me, and stretches his arms over his head enough to lift the bottom of his shirt to reveal a sliver of skin.

I mentally slap myself and blink, forcing my eyes to his just as he looks at me, finally recalling what he had just said. "What?"

"I'm just saying, you've got this whole hot, smart thing going. If you weren't so uptight, more guys may notice."

I roll my eyes, putting my hands on my hips. "Yes, because that is my life goal. To be noticed by a boy."

He raises his brows, catching the tone I am projecting and raises his hands in surrender. "I'm just saying," he says before walking away only to stop just as he reaches the door, turning back to me. "For the record, I like uptight." He gives me one final smile and wink before leaving me, fully awake and utterly annoyed at how much this guy thinks he's God's gift to women. He seriously thinks he can get away with murder. While the rest of us work our asses off.

This guy just drives me crazy.

* * *

Months later
Sophomore Year

THE SUN IS BEATING DOWN through the windshield of the U-Haul truck as Hunter, Mia and I fly by the ancient homes looking for one particular ancient home.

Mia is beaming in the middle seat while her twin brother, Hunter, who also acts as my brother at times, sits in the driver's seat, his short blond hair sticking to his forehead from the heat.

"You know, I'm probably going to hang out here, right?" Mia informs her brother as she plays on her phone beside him.

"Bullshit, you got your own place from Mom and Dad."

"A place I would've let you stay in, if you asked," she coos as she puts down her phone to rest her head on her brother's big shoulder, only making him shake his head at her. "Besides, you could've had a place too."

"And be in their debt? No thanks," Hunter scoffs, showing his obvious dislike for his parents. Safe to say they are not the most loving.

"Who are you rooming with?" I ask, changing the topic as I fan myself with a stray flyer I found in my purse.

"Some guys from campus, but one of them I actually know from football camp, though he doesn't play anymore.

We haven't seen each other in years, but we met at a party a few months ago and we've just been hanging out."

"Oh, is that the one that..."

"Yep, that's him." He nods, laughing to himself about some secret memory, but it makes me happy to see him so at ease.

"Well, at least there will be one familiar face."

"Hey, speaking of, when are you moving into your place, Ava?" Hunter asks, genuinely concerned. My place has been up in the air for months with an idiot landlord jerking me around but luckily all that headache is over.

Giving him a tense smile. "Next week hopefully."

Mia smiles. "You know what that means?"

Both Mia and Hunter look at each other mischievously a second before eliciting girlish screams as they cheer, "House party!"

I laugh. "No way. I'm not having strangers in my new place."

"Party pooper," Hunter grumbles, goodheartedly nudging his sister with his elbow just as we pull up to an old-fashioned two-story gray brick house with navy blue shutters on the white windows. It is beautiful with a long driveway and even a simple garden lining the driveway. If only I could afford a place like this, but either way, I'm happy for Hunter.

"PUSH IT!"

"*You're* supposed to be pushing!"

"How am I supposed to be pushing? I'm trying to bring it into the room. What are you trying to do?!"

I hear Mia and Hunter bicker from my place downstairs, the sound almost like a welcome home sign which is weird, but it's what I grew up with being around the two of them.

I shake off their shouting and continue in my journey up the stairs with a small table in my hands.

I'm too focused on the task of avoiding hitting the walls with the table that I don't hear the footsteps until they are right in front of me a second before I feel the slight impact, followed by a thud and a curse.

"Oh shit, I am so—" I stop, dropping the table and seeing who it is laying on the ground, cupping his jaw and frowning at me. "Actually, I'm not sorry at all." I give Conner a sly smile, liking seeing him on the ground, taken down a bit.

His hand still cupping his jaw, he moves to stand. "We've got to stop meeting like this."

I scoff, moving around the small table sitting in the middle of the stairway. "We've got to stop meeting at all."

Placing a hand over his heart. "That hurts, little lamb."

"Stop calling me that. And what are you even doing here? Are you stalking me or something?"

He laughs. "You wish."

We are interrupted by the heavy footfalls of Hunter, Mia following after him and when Hunter's eyes land on Conner, I can't help but hope he'll get his ass kicked for trespassing, but the universe isn't that kind.

Instead, Hunter's eyes light up as a huge smile takes over his face. "Conner!"

"Hunter!"

They collide in the middle of the stairway, sharing a bro hug and slapping each other's shoulders, while my mind works at connecting the dots only to short-circuit when I realize what is happening.

Hunter turns to me, his arm still draped over a smug-looking Conner. "Mia, Ava, this is—"

"It's you!" I exclaim loud enough to stun everyone but Conner, in the stairway, pointing an accusatory finger at him.

He shrugs sheepishly. "Guilty."

Hunter looks between us. "You guys met?"

"Oh!" Mia offers us a sly smile as she slowly checks Conner out. "So you are *the* Conner?"

Conner cuts a curious look back at me as I squirm and also think of ways to permanently mute my best friend. "You talk about me, huh?"

"Someone wanna fill me in?" Hunter demands, holding his hands out, and we all just look at each other until Conner decides to do the honors.

"You remember that chick I told you about? Well, that's her."

Hunter blinks, finally understanding when I ask, "You talk about me?"

Conner winks. "You bet."

"Well, at least we all know each other. That should make everything easier," Hunter says, trying to look on the positive side as he throws an arm over his sister's shoulder and they make their way back upstairs to fix whatever they were trying to fix, leaving Conner and I alone.

I see that same smug smile as he leans against the railing of the stairs, his ankles crossed and his hands in the pockets of his jeans. "One big happy family."

I growl as I stomp my way up the stairs, following Mia and Hunter, leaving Conner to deal with the table still there, hating that this guy can get under my skin so well and he knows it.

Yes, him living here won't be easy, but at least he's no longer my neighbor and maybe I won't ever see him again.

Maybe.

But we all know how the universe is a bitch.

"I CANNOT BELIEVE you're going to be living here." Mia scrunches up her nose at my new apartment as we bring the next lot of boxes in from her car.

She drops the box at her feet and puts her hand on her narrow hips, looking around the apartment in disgust.

"Why? It's not that bad," I say more to myself as I look around at the chipped paint on the walls, the scratched up wooden floors and the broken cupboards in the kitchen. Some walls even have holes behind the doors as if someone had banged the door open so hard, it bashed into the wall behind it.

Okay, it's a shit hole, but it's all I can afford.

"There's graffiti on the walls," Mia exclaims, throwing a hand out to the open door leading out in the hall with the flickering light.

I shrug, lowering my box to the rickety table that came with the apartment. "Just in the stairway."

She scoffs, "Yeah because that's better."

"Mia, I can't stay in the dorm another second."

"You could've lived at home, you don't live far from campus."

I give her a look. "Okay, you and I both know why I can't live at home."

Home is no better. True, the dorms gave no privacy and limited space, but home is where I'm left vulnerable to harsh words that cut deeper than any knife. I don't talk about my home life often but Mia knows from our childhood how life was for me. How cruel Father was and how he blamed me for my mother leaving. Or maybe he just hated me because I looked so much like her.

Either way, I couldn't do it, so I shake off the memories of my past as Mia sighs, knowing the truth. "I just worry about you. I don't wanna get a phone call telling me my best friend has been raped and murdered."

I laugh at the image she tried to paint, knowing I'll need to get multiple locks tonight. "Thank you for that."

"Just being honest."

Seeing the worry in her eyes, I move to stand before her, taking her small hands in mine and giving them a squeeze. "I will be fine. I promise. Besides, it's not like I can afford much better."

She nods, agreeing but still hating it until our moment is shattered by a loud shout bellowing through my doorway. "You cannot be serious!"

We both jump at Hunter's arrival as he storms through the door, taking in my new apartment with a look that matched Mia's. I look at him innocently, as if I don't see it myself. "What?"

He extends his arms out. "This place screams horror flick. You are not staying here, I won't have it."

I roll my eyes. "It is not that bad."

But as I turn to focus my attention on the box Mia dropped by her feet, I am frozen by the next figure that saunters his way into my apartment like he owns the place. "Actually it is that bad. I just got a whiff of a funky smell down the hall. I think someone may have died." He scrunches his nose in disgust at this and I say through gritted teeth, boxes forgotten. "What are you doing here?" Turning my attention to Hunter, whose eyes are shrouded with guilt. "What is he doing here?"

Hunter shrugs. "He offered to come."

"I figured you'd need an extra pair of hands."

I narrow my eyes at Conner. "Well, you figured wrong."

"Really?" Mia pipes in and I hold my breath as her next words leave her mouth. "What about the old TV or mattress sitting in the moving van downstairs?"

She just looks at me as if she didn't just put her foot, ankle, and whole leg into her mouth. I glare at her but she doesn't react, though I know she did it on purpose. Why, I didn't know, but she must have.

Before I can even think of another excuse, Hunter slaps

his hands together and gives them a rub before turning on his heel and heading out the door. "So it's settled. Come on, man, let's do some heavy lifting."

Conner throws me a knowing grin as he follows Hunter down the stairs and I can practically feel steam leaving my ears as I level a glare back at my best friend, growling, "What was that?"

She merely raises her hands in surrender. "Hey, I'm not lifting a mattress above my head just because you have a problem with him."

I resist the urge to stomp my foot. "Why is he even here?"

"He told you, he wanted to help."

I growl, glaring at the doorway they just exited from. "He wanted to annoy me."

"I think he just wanted to help."

WITH EVERYTHING almost already set up, I gather the blankets that sit in the last box. Hunter is putting the last touches on my TV unit, while Conner helps. Mia decides she is hungry and goes to get us some food, which I am grateful for because I am starving.

Gathering the blankets up in my hands, I make my way down the hall to the closet, feeling Conner's eyes on me as I go and I resist the urge to glare at him, to let him know that I know he is watching me.

I've caught him many times throughout the day but whenever I glare at him, he just flashes me a toothy smile, like he is proud to be caught. I am not looking again.

So instead, I pull open the closet and try to push the blankets on the top shelf.

Hating my height, I know this isn't going to work, so using one hand, I pull myself up and use my other hand to push the blankets onto the shelf properly.

I sigh when I finally have it in place, happy to be mostly done when my heart leaps into my chest as my sweaty hand holding the shelf slips, sending me sailing backward with a gasp.

I scrunch my eyes closed and brace to prepare for the impact of the hardwood floor but instead I hear a deep grunt and feel the firm warmth of another person beneath me.

I open my eyes, thankful to not be hurt, but that is short-lived when I glance back to see who caught me only to find myself staring into Conner's blue eyes and amused smile

No.

"Be careful there, little lamb," he says, holding my eyes with his until I register the feel of his hands on my waist.

Unsure of what else to do and knowing I need to get away, I jerk my elbow back, making him grunt when my elbow connects with his firm stomach. "Oh, I'm so sorry," I say insincerely as I get up, leaving him on the floor.

He picks himself up, smile still in place as he watches me adjust my jean shorts that had ridden so high on my legs they were starting to look like underwear. "Small price to pay for playing hero."

"You were not my hero."

"Did I not just save you from landing on your ass?"

"You should've let me fall."

"You don't mean that."

"You wanna bet?" But as I go to turn away his big hand takes my small one in his, forcing me to look at him and trapping the breath in my lungs as he closes the distance between us, standing so close that I can smell him.

"I do, actually." His voice is husky and low as he looks down at me, my lungs unable to function properly until there is some distance between us because yeah, he's cute. I'm not stupid. But he's a goddamn jackass.

With that thought in mind, I rip my wrist out of his grasp, blink, and turn away to walk back out to the living room.

"I think you kind of like me," Conner calls out to me, stopping me in my tracks, and I turn back around to laugh.

"Really?" Putting my hands on my hips and cocking my head, I ask, "What makes you think that?"

He doesn't answer at first. He just watches until he starts to take a step forward. Then another and another until he is right in front of me again. "The redness on your cheeks when I get close like this."

I steel my jaw. "I'm feeling smothered."

And before he can notice anything else, I turn away and escape to the living room, hearing him call after me, "Yeah, right. You can deny it all you want, but I think you kind of like me."

"And I think you're crazy," I call over my shoulder.

"COME ON, I'll give you the rest next week. I've got a test on Monday and I need this." I beg the young cashier at the campus bookstore. If only the bookstore I work at had the book I needed but it's only a small bookstore with limited selection. This would be so much easier. But instead, here I am with what little I have clutched in my hands and holding up the service line with my stubbornness to move on.

"Sorry, you should have got it earlier." No shit.

"I didn't have the money earlier."

The young cashier chews her gum obnoxiously and gives me a bored look as she says, "You don't have the money now."

"But I will have the rest next week!" I exclaim, feeling the muscles in my shoulders tense as I feel my irritation start to grow. I am off by twenty dollars. I was going to pay it!

But the cashier merely shrugs, not bothered by my

outburst. "I'm sorry but we don't do payment plans, now I have to ask that you move aside because other students want to make purchases."

At that moment a chorus of irritated and impatient groans sounded from behind me in the line as the students vocalized their displeasure at being held up.

I feel the sweat break out over my brow and down my neck as I feel their annoyed gazes on me and the weight of next week's test, the test that determines if I stay in the course or if I get asked to leave. It's an editing course which is seen as an advantage if you wanna go into publishing like I do. It's a competitive industry and every advantage helps.

Just as I start to search my brain for ways to get the extra twenty dollars, without asking friends, I feel a wall of warmth close in behind me at the same time a muscular arm reaches around me and hands a card to the cashier.

The students go silent behind me.

"Here, I got it." My heart stops as my brain registers that voice and without thinking I spin on my heel and find myself standing too close to Conner, the warmth of his body enveloping my front now, while the counter blocks my escape at the back.

The cashier takes the card from him and before anything else can be said, I say in his face, "What? No!"

He merely cocks his head at me, amusement touching his eyes. "No? Don't be silly, just let me get it so we can go. How much is it?"

The cashier answers, "One hundred eighty dollars."

Shooting her a quick glare over my shoulder, I turn back to Conner and tell him firmly, "I'm not letting you get this."

He smiles. "Well, it seems to me that you don't have much choice. You can either let me get it and we can let everyone else get out of here, or you don't get this book you need for a test next week. Choose," he says, crossing his huge arms over his massive chest, drawing my eyes there for a second.

I clear my throat and blink when the cashier intercepts our stare-off. "Ma'am, I'm gonna ask you again, if you're not making a purchase, you'll need to step aside."

I feel my glare intensify at Conner as I say through gritted teeth, knowing my options were limited. "Fine."

The cashier rings up the book using Conner's card. I feel his eyes burning into my head as I snatch up the book and without a backward glance, I storm out of the bookstore, hoping to not go back again.

I'm walking for a couple of seconds before I feel him walking next to me. "You know, you could say thank you."

I continue to face forward as I tell him a quick thank you. "Thank you."

We continue to walk side by side without speaking before I finally stop in the middle of the courtyard, spinning to face him, my hair fanning out as I spin. "Why are you following me?" I demand, evening his surprised look with a glare as my hands rest on my hips, waiting.

He looks around momentarily before shrugging, starting to look a bit shy and it just occurred to me that I don't think I've ever seen him shy before. I didn't think he was capable of it. "I don't know. I thought we could hang out. You do kind of owe me one."

I scoff, "I don't owe you a thing! And if it's the money you want, here." I shove the money bunched in my free hand into his firm chest with a shove that doesn't move him an inch. "I'll get you the rest next week."

But before I can walk away, he blocks my path, my cash in his hand. "Whoah! I was just teasing. But I did want to hang out."

I watch as shy Conner returns, his feet shuffling where he

stands and an uncertain look on his face, it makes me curious so I ask, "Why?"

He looks at me a moment before a corner of his mouth turns up. "I kind of miss my neighbor. She was cute, especially when she got mad."

I can't help but roll my eyes. "I'm sure that happened a lot around you."

He looks at me again, this time thoughtful. "Why do you hate me so much?"

I pause at first, unsure of how to answer. I do have reasons why I hate him, but if I'm honest, those reasons change each day, so I refer to old reliable. "Because you are rude."

He raises his brows, surprised by my response. "I'm rude?"

"Yes, you have no consideration for others."

He scoffs, "I just paid for your books."

"And now I'll never live that down."

"Look, obviously we got off on the wrong foot at some point. Can we start over?"

I contemplate just walking away, so why don't I? I guess I'm curious over which Conner I'm gonna get. The drunk party boy, the flirt, or the shy boy. What else is behind that pretty face? I instantly shake that thought from my head as soon as I get it, not knowing where that came from and I ask, "Why?"

He shrugs. "I wasn't lying when I said I missed my neighbor." I search his face for amusement or laughter but all I see is a softness to his blue eyes I haven't seen. "One chance, maybe a coffee and if you still hate me by the end, I'll leave you alone."

The complexity of the man before me makes me pause in thought. What could it hurt? One coffee and he would either prove me right or wrong. And it's a free coffee, what's not to love about that?

I open my mouth, about to accept his offer, when our moment is shattered by the sound of a high-pitched voice calling from across the courtyard. "Conner!"

We both follow the voice to see a busty redhead running across the courtyard with bright eyes and a beaming smile aimed right at Conner. Her breasts are heaving as she stops before Conner, not even acknowledging me as she gasps, "So, are we still on for tonight?"

Conner gives her a tense smile. "Yeah, wouldn't miss it."

She gives a little excited bounce as she says, "Can't wait."

I watch the two as everything comes into focus and I instantly want to hit myself for letting my guard down for a second.

"Oh my god," I mumble to myself, shaking my head as I move past the couple, not believing that I was actually proved right faster than I thought. Conner doesn't consider other people, he plays them, he takes no responsibility and I can't believe I almost gave him a chance.

"Hey, wait! Ava!" I hear behind me and before I know it, he's in front of me, his hand wrapping around my arm to stop me, a look of confusion marring his face.

As soon as I feel his hand, I rip my arm out of his grasp to point a finger in his face in warning. "You know what, for just a second I thought I might be wrong, that I should give you a chance."

His brows furrow. "What are you talking about?"

"You asking me to coffee when you have a girlfriend. Now I don't know how your harem handles each other, but I will not be one of them."

He actually looks hurt. "Harem? How busy do you think I get?"

"It's not important, just go back to your girlfriend."

"Girlfriend? I think you're misunderstanding something here."

"I've got somewhere to be." And I start power walking away faster than I thought I could, hating that I allowed him to get to me, that he almost had me. So close. Never again.

"Ava?!"

CHAPTER 2

AVA

One month later

"That is so beautiful." My friend Harper cries in her place beside me on the couch as we all watch *The Fault in Our Stars.* Harper's pick for movie night and every Friday night when it's her time to pick. Safe to say, it's her favorite movie. That or any Nicholas Sparks movie. Harper is a bit of a hopeless romantic, that's how we became fast friends five months ago working at Dottie's Bookstore, a local small bookstore near campus. Many night shifts later and here we are.

A glance at Mia shows she's seconds away from calling it quits. She is not the romantic type. Give her a slasher movie and some chocolate and she's set. She sits curled up in the armchair with her cheek resting on her hand and a glazed look in her eyes. "You know he's dying, right?" Mia comments, knowing full well we all know he's dying, but it's still Harper's pick.

Harper's eyes remain locked on the screen, her eyes soft and hopeful as she watches Hazel give her eulogy for Augustus. "That's the beautiful part."

"Since when is death beautiful?" Mia scoffs, cynicism clear in her words as her phone chimes in her lap. She gratefully snatches it up.

I lean into Harper. "I like Hazel's eulogy. It's sweet and romantic."

Harper nods, a sad smile forming on her soft face.

Until suddenly, the TV goes black.

Harper and I spring up in our seats, thinking it may be a blackout but the corner lamp is still on. I'm searching the blankets for the remote when Mia leaps from her armchair, waving the black remote in her hand. "Alright bitches, we're going out," she demands, throwing her blanket on the ground like a mic drop.

Harper and I furrow our brows at her, answering at the same time.

"How did you get the remote?"

"Do you need to call us bitches?"

She waves her arms dismissively with a newly energized smile lighting up her face. "I am a ninja with much skill in stealing remotes." She looks to Harper. "And yes, I say bitches out of love."

I shake my head, and neither of us moves.

"Come on! I just got a text from Trevor in my econ class. There's a party going on at my brother's house. Don't know why I didn't hear about it from him, but I will just deal with it when I get there. Now, let's go get ready!" she urges, nudging our legs with her socked feet.

I kick my own legs back at her as I say, "No, tonight is movie night and by God, we are watching—"

"A movie we have seen a hundred times," Mia whines

before looking at Harper apologetically. "No offense, Harper."

Harper's shoulders slump forward and her head bows but she nods, mumbling it's okay. Harper was never one for confrontation and I didn't expect her to be now. But I turn, facing a gleeful Mia, my hands on my hips.

"And we will finish watching it, because even though scary movies give her nightmares, every week when it's your turn, Harper does not complain. She sits and she watches the damn movie YOU pick."

Harper pipes in with a timidly small voice, "Ava, it's really okay. She's right, maybe a party will be a good idea."

The uncertainty is clear in her words, but what can I say, *I don't want to go to a party because I'm very much likely to run into a jackass*? I didn't really want to get into that right now with Mia, not again. All this time and Conner still does everything in his power to piss me off. Taking my favorite booth at the campus diner is just one of the things he does, and it may sound small but these things matter, they matter to me. And just when you think he's an alright guy, BAM, he proves you wrong.

Mia jumps, making her small boobs bounce with her. "Then it's settled. We are going to a party!" Seeing my pained expression, she softens her face and takes a step toward me. "I will be with you the whole time. If he wants to give you any trouble, he will have me to deal with and if he messes with me, Hunter will kick his ass."

The corners of my mouth tilt up in an amused smile. "Promise?"

She smiles a devilish smile, holding up her pinkie to me. My finger hooks with hers in a pinkie swear, touching our thumbs in a lock, making it sacred.

The room is silent with both Mia and Harper looking at

me, waiting. I throw up my hands in an unenthusiastic, "Party!" cheer, making Mia laugh and Harper smile.

Harper rises to stand with us in her oversized flannel pajamas, her thick brown hair in a messy bun atop her head and her bangs askew on her forehead. Where Mia is small and petite, Harper is soft and rounded around the hips, butt, and boobs, though she always hides them under oversized frumpy clothes. She was always so shy and timid, it took her months to open up to me, months of late-night talks during night shifts at the store. She sometimes reminded me of a scared Chihuahua.

Mia must see this as well, as she scans Harper up and down, assessing. "Harper, why don't you come with me, I'm sure Ava's got some stuff you can wear." She grabs Harper by the hand, leading her down the hallway to my bedroom.

"I... I don't think anything will fit." I hear Harper stammer from down the hall.

This was going to be an interesting night, but a night Harper needs.

* * *

We arrive later when the party is in full swing. Mia leads us as she struts up the driveway in a short leather skirt she kept in the trunk of her car for some reason, and a simple tight tank top, tying the look together with a pair of black boots that go past her knees. How she is not freezing to death, I have no idea. Harper and I follow in simpler attire. Harper rocking a pair of blue jeans and a black long-sleeved top that hugs her curves. The clothes came from a distant aunt who kept getting my sizing wrong, luckily for Harper. I can tell she's uncomfortable as she continues to look down, her dark hair falling over her shoulders, and continues to pull at the bottom of the shirt.

Whereas I just opted for a simple pair of black jeans, black boots, and an off the shoulder red top that didn't allow for a bra. God, I hope my nipples aren't saying hello, I think to myself as I take in the cluster of bodies filling the once large space of the living room. The music blaring so loud, I can barely hear myself think, bodies grinding together and everyone drinking from red Solo cups.

Harper and I quickly lock arms as we follow Mia through the mass of bodies to the kitchen where there is little relief from the music.

Mia leans over the counter to talk to Logan, another roommate of Hunter's. I've only met him twice, but both times he was so busy with a video game that all I got were grunts as responses. But judging by how his lips move, it appears he is using actual words with Mia. I guess he is a human being tonight.

Logan gives us a small smile when we reach the counter and sit beside Mia on the barstools. "Ladies!" he chimes, holding a shot glass in one hand when he targets his next question to me, catching me off guard. "How did she manage to drag you out tonight?"

"She gave us the puppy dog eyes." I glare at Mia, who smiles shamelessly at me, sitting straighter on her stool.

Running his hand through his short brown wavy hair, he turns his soft brown eyes to Harper who sits in the place beside me, tapping her fingers lightly on the edge of the countertop. "Who's your friend?"

"Harper." I place a gentle hand on her shoulder, feeling her stiffen beneath my touch. "She works with me at the bookstore."

"I'm Logan." He nods thoughtfully, resting his hands on the counter in front of him. "So what are you ladies having?"

Just as I start to shake my head, Mia says, "Three shots of your best tequila," while holding up three fingers to him, as if he were stupid, but he just places three shot glasses on the counter, pulling out a half-empty bottle of tequila and starts to pour.

"Where's my brother?" Mia yells over the music, still loud, even in the kitchen.

After handing us our drinks, he looks around and shrugs. "Somewhere."

"Very helpful," she says sarcastically, as we each pick up our shot glasses, Harper and I more hesitant than Mia.

She turns in her stool to face us, bumping my knees and smiling. "To another amazing year!" Her cheer is followed by a louder cheer from everyone in the kitchen as they hold up their red Solo cups in a salute of some kind.

We each throw back the drink. I scrunch my face up as the liquid fire burns down my throat only to warm my belly. I hear Harper coughing beside me and I pat her on the back only to have her wave me off, looking up at me with watery eyes.

Mia laughs playfully. "Oh come on! You act like that is your first shot."

"Because it is," Harper gasps between bouts of coughing still, shaking her head.

Mia's jaw drops and her eyes go wide as she slams her hand on the counter. "Then we must rectify this immediately. How did I not know this?"

I turn a serious expression on Mia. "I think what she needs is water."

"But water isn't fun." Mia cocks her head in confusion, not seeing my point.

"But is spending the night with your head in a toilet fun?"

"No, but you know I can handle my liquor."

I put my hand back on Harper's tense shoulder, her cough subsiding. "But Harper's never done this before. So maybe we should just take it easy. Start her off slowly." Once understanding dawns on Mia's face, I turn to Logan as he returns with a fresh glass. "Logan? Can we get a rum and Coke for Harper?"

He nods and gets to work. "I'm on it."

A glance at Harper shows her brow is furrowed and her eyes are focused on the counter in front of her, her plump lips are pursed in thought and her eyes have a faraway look. I squeeze her shoulder, making her jump as she lifts her head, the light returning to her eyes when she meets mine.

"I got you a rum and Coke," I tell her comfortingly as it's slid in front of her.

She narrows her eyes on me. "You didn't have to do that. I can do another shot." She says, the determination clear in her words and seen in her eyes.

"It's okay if you can't. No one is forcing you. You can still get drunk off a rum and Coke," I inform her.

"Not as fast as a tequila shot though," Mia mumbles beside me loud enough for us to hear, Logan nodding.

I glare at them before returning my gaze to Harper but she is now looking at Logan.

"I want another tequila shot." She says each word so seriously and with so much determination, I don't know if she's trying to convince us or herself.

With that, I nod to Logan to make the shot, which makes Mia cheer, happily clapping her hands.

Harper holds her own for a few shots, but on the fourth shot, her face starts turning a shade of green.

"Harper, are you alright?" I ask as Mia slurs for another round.

Harper places her hand on her stomach and shakes her head.

"Here, I'll take you to the bathroom," I tell her, already struggling to get off my own stool, but she quickly shakes her head.

"No, I'll be fine," she mumbles more to herself than to me as she stumbles from her stool, eventually getting her footing and hobbles down the hallway, stumbling into some of the lovers making out against the walls and not caring.

It isn't long until I realize that she doesn't know where the bathroom is.

A FEW SHOTS later and I'm already shaky on my feet as I stumble up the stairs, I've already lost Mia and Harper, I squint my eyes trying to search for anything familiar but the house looks like another world with the lights, the music and the bodies.

It makes it hard to navigate, so when I stumble into a door, opening it and thinking it is a bathroom, I'm surprised to fall face-first into the hardwood floor of a room that is most definitely not the bathroom.

I push myself to standing, dusting off the back of my pants, pushing my hair out of my face and gasp when I see I am not the only one in the room.

"You!" I exclaim clumsily.

A pair of blue eyes look back at me, wide in surprise until recognition lights up his face, seeing me standing in his room, the surprise shifts into a cocky smile. "You? I didn't think this would be your scene." Conner sits back in his swivel chair.

I stand there and can't decide if I want to stay and argue or just walk away. But of course, I was on alcohol brain right now, making dumb decisions and starting to argue.

"I was about to say the same for you," I snip at him, putting a hand on my hip and waving my other hand to the desk he's sitting at overloaded with textbooks and papers. I hated that small, and I mean small, part of me that thought it was kinda hot. I've got problems, I think to myself as Conner simply shrugs.

"I've got a test next week."

"And the noise doesn't bother you?"

He shrugs again. "You and I are different in that way, little lamb."

I bite my lip, choosing to let that one time slide, because it's obvious he's never going to let me live that name down.

I peek over his textbooks and can't help the surprise that appears on my face. "You're a science major?"

"Veterinary science," he corrects and I then find myself plopped on his bed behind him as he wheels his chair to face me.

I should leave.

"Why veterinary science? If you're into science, you could just be a doctor. Isn't that more prestigious?"

He raises his brows. "Do I seem like someone who would be into something prestigious?"

I raise my own eyebrows at him, because yeah, it kind of seems like something he would be into, but I obviously don't know him that well, if at all.

Aside from the few times we were forced to spend together with friends or the accidental run-ins, we didn't exactly talk. We argued, but didn't talk.

He rolls his eyes. "I like animals. My family owns a farm and I was raised to care for the animals and I loved it."

"What kind of animals?" I can't help but ask, my image of him slowly shifting despite my best effort of keeping the douchebag image in my head.

"Horses mostly. Some cows. We'd produce milk and sell it, my dad's amazing at rehabilitating horses. People from all around will come by the *Lucky Charm Ranch* and ask for my dad's help."

I cock my head. "Lucky Charm Ranch?"

His smile turns genuine, softer. "My dad bought it after he proposed to my mom. Always considered her his lucky charm because she kind of saved his life when they met. Like literally. Stopped him from getting hit by a car." He shakes his head at the memory and I feel the smile on my lips and I can't for the life of me get rid of it, but it's hard to miss the sting in my chest as an image forms in my head of Conner's happy and loving family. Something I missed out on, something I rarely talk about these days.

I blink, trying to swallow the sting in my chest. "Is that what you want? To work on your dad's ranch?"

He shakes his head after some thought. "No. I'd actually like to own my own practice. But that will take years."

"I never would've guessed."

His smile turns cocky again and I brace for what's to follow. "For what? That I'd actually be smart?"

"The jury is still out on that one." I scoff, deciding that now is the time to leave as I rise from my place on the bed. His bed.

"You know, I think you're only mean to me because you like me."

I turn on my heel as I reach the door to see him smiling where I left him, his brows raised daring me to argue.

"That's very juvenile thinking," I comment.

"You didn't deny it."

I narrow my gaze at him, the alcohol already starting to dissipate enough for me to know that it is time to leave. So instead of arguing, because he's being so stupid that I'm not even going to acknowledge his archaic idea, I huff and turn away, leaving him in his room.

But as I close the door, I swear I hear the fucker chuckle and that is when I know that I won't go near that room again.

CHAPTER 3

CONNER

I rub my eyes as the words in my textbook are starting the blur together.

Listening to the heavy beat of the music vibrating my walls, I consider taking a break when the music is amplified as it filters into my room.

I sit straighter in my chair and furrow my brow at my bedroom door opening, ready to shoo away any couples looking for a hookup spot, but instead I see a familiar brunette stumbling into my room. I raise my brows at her. "You're back. You missed me, didn't you?"

I lean back in my chair and smile as she glares at me. "Shut up."

Ava then steps away from the door, shutting it behind her as she stumbles her way to my bed and flops facedown on the soft mattress before rolling over with a groan.

Looking at her now, I can't help but be concerned as I take in her wild dark hair hanging around her face, her eyes are droopy and tired and she was walking like a foal.

I distantly hear the squeak of my swivel chair as I rise

from it to make my way over to stand by my bed. "Hey, you okay?"

She turns her face enough to look at me, her dark eye makeup is already smudged around her eyes, but she's still looking sexy. "Like you care."

"Of course I care," I tell her, hating that she actually believes I don't care about her. Haven't I shown her enough? I've paid for her books when she couldn't, I've helped her get out of a bad date, yeah and at the time I push her buttons on purpose but what can I say, she's cute when she's angry.

At my response, she furrows her brow and moves to lay on her back, looking up at me. "Why?"

I plop down on my bed beside her, knowing I should probably keep my distance, but it's hard to stay away from this girl. "Because then I'd have to start taking out girls who actually like me."

"That's a line from *10 Things I Hate About You*."

My smile grows. "So you caught that? At least you're not that out of it."

She looks at me a moment. "I shouldn't be in here."

"Want me to get one of your friends? I could drive you home."

But she doesn't say anything. I consider going out to look for her friends but I also didn't like the thought of leaving her here in her condition by herself, so I stay and she just lays there, watching me, her eyes soft as they run over my face, her mind ticking away within those eyes.

"What?" I ask, when time passes and nothing is said.

At first I don't think she'll respond until she says so softly I thought I may have misheard her. "I've always liked your eyes."

I'd be lying if I said that didn't make my insides warm and fluffy, but the tired and drunk look in her eyes is enough to remind me of the truth. "Okay, that is the alcohol talking."

She shakes her head, pushing herself up on her elbows. "No, it was the first thing I noticed. So blue, so beautiful." I was so enraptured by her slurred words that I didn't see one of her hands come up to grab the back of my head and pull me to hers. I gasp on impact, taking in the taste of her and the alcohol, wishing she wasn't drunk and that this was real. But the alcohol was the constant reminder and the reason why I gathered all my willpower and pulled away.

I breathe in a deep breath and hold my hand out to keep her back. "Okay, you will hate yourself in the morning for that."

"It's not morning yet." Her voice dips in a way I didn't think it could, so sexy I felt it in my cock and cursed the alcohol. Her heated eyes roam over my face again before moving down to roam over my body. The tired girl that entered the room was no more.

Keeping my hand up, I try to reason with Ava. "Ava, you are drunk out of your mind and nothing is happening tonight."

"Not even if I told you that I didn't really hate you?"

I kinda figured she thought I was hot, but to not hate me? I guess I hoped but it was hard to tell with this girl always acting like she hated me. "You don't hate me?"

"Okay, I kind of do, but what you don't know is that I think you are so hot." Yeah, I gathered that. "Sometimes I look at your mouth and I wonder how good of a kisser you are, how it would feel to have your lips against mine." She's practically gasping the words, her eyes focused on my mouth with a hunger I know all too well after living next to this girl freshman year.

I clear my throat and my head. "Yeah, you must be drunker than I thought."

"You think I'm lying?" she asks, cocking her head.

"No, but I doubt you want me knowing this."

She bites her lip, her eyes continuing to roam over me a moment before she reaches up to run a hand over my jaw, moving her hand up to run her fingers through my hair before grabbing it in a fist. I already know I should stop this, but logic escapes me when her fist pulls on my hair a little. I grunt against the pull as I start to feel her other hand come up to my chest, placing her palm over my pecs, moving her hand lower until it reaches the button of my jeans.

I stiffen in more ways than one and move back a little out of Ava's reach. "Whoah, okay I think it's time for you to go home."

"You don't want me?" I almost want to laugh at that, when I look down at my lap before looking back up at her.

"I think it's clear I do."

"Then why stop this?"

"Because we both know you don't want this."

"You have no idea how wrong you are." She practically growls the words, closing the distance between us. I see her coming closer and I know I should stop this. I should walk away. I should get up and get my phone to call Hunter to get his sister. I could've done anything, but every cell in my body is craving the woman before me, and having her beg for me made it even harder to resist.

So when she closes the distance between us, pressing her soft lips to mine, it is impossible for me not to kiss her back. Her hand remains in my hair as she practically attacks my mouth, as if she was starving for it.

I feel the warmth of her body as she presses her soft breasts against my chest and I swear my eyes roll as I groan, trying to protest one more time. "Ava."

She moves her mouth down my neck, kissing and sucking her way back up to my earlobe and I groan as she takes it in her mouth and bites, whispering in my ear as her hands continue to explore, "Just kiss me."

And just like that, I was powerless. Any thought of resisting left me as I took Ava's beautiful face in my hands and pulled her to me, kissing her with everything I have in me, showing her how much I want her.

I know I should think about the morning, but I struggled to see past the way Ava felt against me and how perfect she seemed to fit me.

CHAPTER 4

AVA

Everything hurts.

My muscles ache as I lift my arm to put it to my aching head, wincing against the sun's rays from behind my eyelids. My hands still covering my face, I blink, opening my eyes… and I blink some more in confusion.

Despite the pain in my head, I let my eyes move over every surface of this familiar room.

A small bookshelf sits against the wall, lined with anatomy and biology textbooks, with a few novels littered throughout. The walls were bare and there was a desk against the wall with a laptop closed and papers with an open textbook. A little lamp sat off to the side. But there was something about this room that screamed familiar.

The thought makes my heart accelerate as I finally register the feel of the soft cotton sheets I'm lying under, the softness against my *bare* aching muscles. I suck in a breath, having it get stuck in my throat, my mind registering that I am in a room, naked, with no idea of how I got here.

I hear a masculine groan from beside me, my eyes widening.

No.

I almost don't want to look, don't want to know. Maybe I could just leave and never know, but a part of me will always be curious as to who I lost my virginity to.

I ball my fists in the sheets, tensing my jaw and slowly turning my head, I slam my hand over my mouth to suppress my scream.

No! Anyone but him! I want to scream. I want to punch someone. I want to punch him, because if what I see is correct, then I finally gave him what he wanted.

I mentally groan, he will not let me live this down.

Maybe I could leave. Maybe he, too, won't remember. Maybe we didn't have sex, I think to myself as I slowly sit up in the bed, watching Conner's peacefully sleeping face the entire time.

I wince at a different pain that spreads from between my legs, like a bunch of pins and needles. A glance down and there is no denying it. Blood. Maybe I got my period.

Hey, I'm grasping at straws here!

Whatever happened, I need to get out of here before Conner wakes up.

Working against my discomfort, I shuffle my way to the edge of the bed, dropping the sheet as I do so, exposing everything as I swing my legs over the edge.

One foot connects with the hardwood floor, but the other lands on something slimy. My face scrunches in disgust and I peek down, lifting my foot instantly when I see that my foot landed on a condom.

The image sent a wave of nausea through me.

I guess that's that. I had officially lost my virginity at nineteen to a guy I hated at a party I didn't even want to go to, and I was so drunk that I can't remember a thing. I search my aching brain for any recollection but still come up with nothing, the ache only intensifying the more I do.

Running my hands through my hair, I see my clothes scattered around the room. My red top hanging off the desk chair, but my jeans were a couple of feet away.

I try to rise on weak aching legs, avoiding the condom this time, using the side table for balance and glancing over my shoulder at a sleeping Conner. His breaths are even, his features smooth with calm because he is completely unaware of what happened last night, and hopefully he will remain that way.

I creep across the floor on my toes, each step slow and careful, aware of any creaks that may sound as a secret alarm. My heart does a triumphant flip when I finally reach my pants, snatching them up in my hands and turning to face Conner. I was still good.

But I knew time was of the essence so without a moment's hesitation, with my eyes still focused on Conner, I push one leg through the leg hole of my pants successfully. The other leg, however, wasn't as easy.

I silently curse myself as my toe gets stuck, making my balance waver on already shaky legs at the same time that the loud, obnoxious screeching of his alarm sounds like a siren throughout his room, the sound bashing against my skull and making me jump until I am tumbling down to the floor.

I groan in pain when my side connects with the hardwood floor, my knee hitting first, sending pain up my leg.

I distantly hear a groan, some shuffling in the sheets followed by a couple of bangs as Conner hits the alarm, finally silencing it.

If I stay down, maybe he won't notice I'm here. I mentally roll my eyes; I seriously don't know how I got into college sometimes.

"Ava?" His voice is groggy but still deep with a sexy edge to it, which I hate to admit.

I expel a breath. Time to face the music and I was going

to do it with dignity, I think to myself as I finally push my leg through my other pants hole, pulling them up my naked hips, forgoing my underwear because they were lost as far as I was concerned.

I shuffle awkwardly to my feet, not even bothering to cover my exposed breasts because to do so now was pointless. He's obviously seen everything.

Instead, I stand with my pants still unbuttoned and my breasts still out with a deer in headlights look on my face I was sure.

But Conner looks at me with heated eyes, like he's taking me in all at once, like he's hungry and wants to eat me up right here. He probably already did last night. How am I to know?

His heated blue eyes, now vacant of any sign of sleep, meet mine.

When I see him open his mouth I hold my finger up and growl, "If you have a sleazy comment to make, I suggest you stay silent."

He closes his mouth and for a moment I think he will stay silent until he says, with his hands raised in surrender, "I was going to ask if you were alright. You hit the deck pretty hard there."

I try to hide the blush of embarrassment on my cheeks by ducking my head, focusing my eyes on the shirt on his desk chair.

"I need to get out of here," I say more to myself than to him as I lunge for my shirt, pulling it over my head.

"You don't have to rush off." He reclines in his bed, stretching to expose his abs and muscular chest to me as he puts his hands behind his head and flashes me a proud grin.

"I am not staying here another minute." I hold up a firm finger, waving it at him. "Never again," I promise myself more than him, trying to push back the pang of regret I feel in my chest like a rock weighing me down. The moment I have been waiting for, a rite of passage, all gone because of a drunken one-night stand. And I don't remember a thing about it. I could pretend it didn't happen, that it doesn't count, but it does. Your hymen can't break again.

At least I don't remember the pain, though I'm feeling a bit of it right now. I wince, still feeling it between my legs.

I try to ignore the moment of hurt that flashes across Conner's face before he blinks it away with a shrug, saying, "Suit yourself."

There is no smile or laugh, not even hurt on his face now. There's just nothing and for a second, I feel guilty that I might have hurt his feelings.

"I'll still have shower material for a month," he says with a completely straight face and I almost don't register it.

And there goes any feeling of guilt I might have had, replaced with disgust. "Oh my god, you are disgusting," I exclaim, my mouth curling around the words, making him laugh.

He laughs harder and I just turn on my heel, ready to leave when he chimes in, stopping me in my tracks. "There goes Ava Daniels. Doing the walk of shame."

I hear the smile in his words and I know that he is right. I know these guys and yes there is a chance that they will all be asleep, but did I want to chance it? Did I want them to see me do the walk of shame out of the room of someone I claim to despise?

I turn to glare at Conner as I storm past the bed to the window beside him, pushing it open, welcoming the cool breeze hitting my face.

"What are you doing?" Conner asks, sitting up in the bed.

I answer him by swinging one leg over the windowsill and leaving it to hang outside as I look back at him, his eyes wide.

"You won't do it."

I don't know if it's a challenge or he seriously thinks I won't. Maybe I shouldn't. I glance down, seeing I am two stories high but conveniently for me, there is a vined ladder decorating this side of the house. I didn't know if it was stable enough to hold my weight. But what's the worst that could happen? Break my leg? Die? Seeing Conner right now, I'll take my chances.

I give him one final glare, pointing my finger at him again. "This never happened."

He gives me a disappointed nod and I start to climb out the window.

I leave the room and a naked Conner behind and any memory of last night with it.

CHAPTER 5

AVA

March 2021
Sophomore Year

Four hours into my shift and I don't know why I even turned up. I'm moving slower than normal; I can't stop sweating and my stomach is churning up a storm making me feel like I'm going to puke all over the biography section.

I place my hand on my sore stomach, taking in some deep breaths as I distantly hear Harper chatting a couple of isles away from me about the internship she's hoping to get this year at Harper Collins Publishing. It's in Australia and she's been raving about it for months since she found out.

Blinking back into focus, I catch on to the butt end of her sentence. "I cannot wait to see if I can actually go to Australia." She squeals happily, making me smile despite the nausea.

This feeling has been ongoing for the past week, and it's starting to get ridiculous.

I'm so lost in my deep breaths and my focus on not puking that I jump in surprise when Harper pops into my section, holding a couple of books in her hand. She stops short when she sees me, showing the same concerned look I got when I first turned up today. I brushed off her concerns, but I can only do that for so long.

She furrows her brows at me. "You're looking worse. You need to go home."

I shake my head. "I'm fine." I look down at the books in her arms. "What are those?" I ask, trying to find something to take the focus off of me.

She glances down at them. "They were in my section, customers probably left them there earlier. I was just returning them." Instead of handing them to me, she brushes past me, putting them away herself before turning to face me with a serious expression, her now free arms are crossed over her large chest.

"What? I'm just a little nauseous, it'll pass soon," I say defensively, returning to my own pile of books to shelve. But she still doesn't leave.

Instead, she asks in a gentle, nurturing tone, "Have you eaten? Have you had enough water?" She walks around to face me with each question.

"Yes and yes, but nothing stays down," I grumble, still not meeting her eyes. "And before you say anything, I can't go home because I still have bills to pay."

Harper is silent for a moment, understanding lingers in our silence, until she says, "It's just, you don't look too good. You look like you might drop at any minute and I'm afraid I won't be able to carry you."

I can't help the laugh that escapes my lips and I shake my

head, raising my eyes to see her small encouraging smile, her eyes soft and almost hopeful.

"I'm worried about you, Ava."

I wave off her words. "I'll be fine. Only got two more hours to go."

Two of the longest hours of my life, I inwardly groan at the same time we hear a big bellowing voice erupt from behind me.

"What is with all the talking? I don't pay you two to socialize," our manager, Helen scolds us. Helen is a big woman with a big voice and an even bigger personality. You can usually hear her coming with her heavy footsteps and her big voice, but Harper and I are so distracted that we don't even notice until it's too late and we're busted.

We both look at Helen with her heavy makeup and teased blonde hair, looking like she just stepped out of an eighties movie and not a good one either. Her face holds a displeased expression as she taps her foot, waiting for an explanation.

I'm almost too scared to speak out of fear of puke coming out instead of words, so Harper steps forward only managing to get one word out before Helen silences her with a disgusted groan. She looks at me up and down.

Okay, maybe I do look like shit, but hey I can barely stand at the moment.

"Oh jeez, what happened to you, Ava? You look like death rolled over twice."

I could say so many things to that, but Harper comes to my rescue. "She didn't sleep well last night. They're doing construction outside of her apartment."

The disgust is still clear on her face, but she nods in understanding. "Go get yourself cleaned up." She turns her nose up at me, not even caring.

I seriously don't know how Helen became a manager, I think

to myself as I meet Harper's soft comforting eyes and small gentle smile as I turn on my heel and make my way toward the bathroom with Helen barking orders at Harper behind me.

I pick up my pace when I see the staff bathroom in sight, the twisting in my stomach only getting worse with each step and I only hope that I make it to the bathroom.

SAFE TO SAY, I don't last the rest of my shift.

I BLINK AWAKE, breaking away from the hazy fog I found myself in for the past few days since leaving work. I've been given the week off to recover but it doesn't feel like this thing is letting me go anytime soon, which only makes me groan as I roll over to look up at the ceiling of my bedroom. Too scared to sit up out of fear of the twisting in my stomach intensifying.

I place a hand over my stomach and wince, eyeing the water on my dresser. I don't remember the last time I had water, but it was too long ago.

I groan again, slapping my other hand over my eyes at the same time as I hear a door close nearby.

If I am getting robbed, that would be the cherry on top of this shit cake. But I think I locked my front door and what burglar would have a key?

I almost want to laugh at the insanity of it until I hear a familiar singsong voice calling from beyond my bedroom door.

"Ava? How are you feeling?" Mia's voice grows louder as I hear her footsteps approaching my bedroom door.

I don't need to reply because she gasps when she opens the door and sees me sprawled on the bed, sweating and probably pale in my underwear. Not even nice underwear, but the underwear I wear during that time of the month.

"You look like death," she comments, taking a hesitant step inside the room, probably afraid that this is contagious. I don't blame her because I wouldn't chance it.

When she comes closer, my focus on her clears enough to see she is wearing a pair of tight jeans with a black long-sleeved bodysuit underneath and in her arms she's carrying a pile of books and papers.

I groan, eyeing the books. "Those better be for you," I say before rolling over away from her to lay on my stomach, my face unflatteringly squashed against the pillow, possible drool.

Mia sighs, walking around the bed to face me with an apologetic smile. "I know how you stress, so I thought when you get better you wouldn't want to be behind in class, so I got some notes and stuff you missed over the last few days."

I see the care behind the gesture but I'm just not thinking about school right now. I narrow my eyes at her. "Does it look like I am in any state to read through school notes? I can barely sit up without throwing up."

After a moment's pause, Mia puts the books down on my bedside table and sits on the bed beside me, putting her hand to my sweaty forehead, her forehead creased in thought. "You must've been run down to catch this bug."

"It sure doesn't feel like a bug. It feels like I'm dying," I tell her, rolling away from her again, not wanting to get her sick with whatever this is that's tearing at my insides.

At the corner of my eye, Mia lights up the dark room when she pops her phone out and starts scrolling and typing. "What are your symptoms?"

I give her waiting look a confused one of my own. "What?"

"Well, if you don't think it's a bug and you don't want to

go to the doctor, then google will be our doctor. Then maybe we can figure out how to tackle this thing."

"Maybe it's a flesh-eating parasite."

She still sits waiting with her phone at the ready, so I roll my eyes, despite the bout of nausea it causes, making me wince again.

"Tired, dizzy on occasion, nausea with the puking, obviously." I list for her.

She scrolls down the screen. "So you can't keep anything down?"

"I don't think I've eaten in the past few days."

"Were you tired before the vomiting or is the vomiting making you tired?"

"I've had a lot of things going on, so I guess I was tired before. Maybe that led to me getting sick?" I offer, but she just continues to scroll, reading from a page on her screen I can't see.

She watches the screen, her face serious for a second before she suddenly drops the phone in her lap, reaching over to me before I realize what is happening and squeezes my boob.

"Ow," I cry out and glare at her. "What the fuck was that?"

She doesn't answer, but nods to herself, looking back at her phone for a long time while I massage the sore boob she grabbed. How hard did she grab it?

She finally locks her phone screen, her face solemn as she places it on the bedside table with the books before turning to me, gnawing at her bottom lip in thought. She opens her mouth then closes it, as if reconsidering her words.

She knew something, I knew that face. "What?" I exclaim impatiently. I didn't have time to waste. I wanted to get rid of this thing.

She nods to herself again, taking a deep breath before

saying to me, her hand over mine. "I'm going to ask you a question but don't freak out."

I feel my eyes widen as panic sets in at those words. Why do people always say that? If someone tells us not to freak out, we will freak out! It's like when we are not allowed to laugh, we will laugh harder than ever before.

Her hand squeezes mine as I wait. "When are you due for your period?"

I furrow my brows at her question and cock my head at her. "What? That's a little personal."

"Just answer the question."

I think back, trying to remember when my heart drops in my stomach, making my nausea increase with so much ferocity that I place my hand over my stomach, springing from the bed with a strength I didn't know I had, only just reaching the toilet in time.

I know Mia followed me when I feel my hair being pulled back from the line of fire, her other hand stroking soothing circles on my back as the puke tears its way up my throat, tears falling down my eyes.

When I'm finally done, I fall back to lean against the wall by the toilet, using a piece of toilet paper to wipe my eyes and mouth, my breathing heavy.

I look up as Mia squats down in front of me with a cup of water which I take hesitantly, taking small sips, feeling it soothe my raw throat.

Placing my hand back over my stomach, I think of when my last period was and a new kind of panic sets in when my wide eyes meet Mia's concerned ones.

"I don't remember getting my period last month." The words feel numb on my lips, like they're not mine, but spoken by a stranger I had never met.

Mia doesn't react. She simply moves to sit against the

wall beside me, her hand squeezing mine. "Do you think you could be? Is there even a slight chance?"

My mind flashes back to my only sexual encounter and I don't even remember it. I remember the condom on the floor, but maybe it broke or… I don't know. But there was only one way to find out.

I DIDN'T BOTHER with a shower, but with Mia's help, I manage to throw on a pair of sweats and a hoodie with some flip-flops. Feeling classy today!

I walk into the pharmacy with my arm locked with Mia's, using her strength to carry me forward. Maybe it would be easier to just never know, but if it's true, it'll be hard to avoid the truth when my belly starts growing.

I need to know, even if it's just to rule this out.

We look around and this place is pretty deserted so we make our way toward the aisle that holds the tests. Turning a corner we are faced with a wall of pregnancy tests, a variety of them promising accurate and fast results. But which one do I pick? Does it matter? Will each one show a different result? I mentally slap myself for the silly thought. My breathing increases and I break out in a sweat as I am faced with a wall that will determine my future.

Stupid wall!

"Hey, hey." Mia turns me to face her, placing her hands on my shoulders, making me meet her calm blue eyes. "It'll be okay."

I glance back at the tests. "There are just so many. Just a little overwhelming." I gasp.

"Well, first let's start with some deep breaths." She takes in some deep breaths, releasing them as I follow her, the panic still there, but I no longer feel dizzy from the lack of oxygen going to my brain. "I'll go get someone who works here. They will know more about this stuff than we will."

I nod more to myself than to her as she leads me over to the wall for me to lean against, before she leaves to locate someone to help.

I'm not standing there for more than a minute before a deep masculine voice calls to me from behind, sounding close so I know I can't run even if I could. "Ava! Hey, I heard you weren't feeling well, how you feeling now?"

I turn to face Hunter, Mia's twin brother, and am met with a smile that shifts into a look of disgust and shock when he sees me, taking a step back before continuing on his walk toward me.

Do I really look that bad?

"Wow, Ava, you look like death."

I guess I do look that bad. "That's what your sister said."

"So what are you doing here? Getting some meds?" I can't help but notice his eyes moving from the wall behind me then back to me, his pretty face creasing in thought. I can see the question forming in his mind. What was I doing standing by the pregnancy tests which is nowhere near the anti-nausea tablets?

I quickly stammer out, "I have a bug, so Mia is just getting my medication for me. She told me to wait here."

He nods at this, accepting at the same time when Mia returns with no salesperson, thankfully, but a huge pack of tampons she waves in her hand, grinning. "I got them!" she chimes in a singsong voice.

Hunter's brows crease at his sister. But before either of us can say anything, Mia says to Hunter with a smile. "Hey bro, what are you doing here?"

He holds up a pack of large Trojans, explaining, "I ran out."

My nausea returns the same time Mia cries out, "Ew, too much! Too much!" Only making Hunter laugh.

"You asked." He shrugs before nodding to us. "So our Ava is sick?"

I go to nod, but Mia pipes in first, waving the tampons in her hand again. "She got her period, so we were just getting supplies."

I see the confusion on Hunter's face the same time I see my secret being exposed.

"I thought you said you had a bug?" Hunter says to me.

I stammer out my words in a rush. "I do."

Mia chimes in again, throwing her arm over my shoulder. "And she has her period. Got both at the same time, poor thing."

We both nod enthusiastically at Hunter as his eyes bounce from me to his sister. After a moment's pause, the longest moment of my life, he shakes his head at us. "Okay then, well I hope you get better."

The uncertainty is clear in Hunter's words, and I have to fight the need to explain myself because I know that if I do, I will ramble and he knows that's my tell. I ramble when I lie.

So, I stay silent, smile and wave as Hunter turns to leave us, knowing how suspicious we are looking right now and not having the energy to care.

I have something I need to do, I think to myself as I snatch up a couple of tests, not caring which ones at this point and making our way to the register, careful to look out for Hunter or anyone else.

THE TEST SITS on the bathroom counter, while I sit on the cold tiled floor with my butt already going numb. But I don't focus on that, it's hard to focus on much when your fate rests on what a stick tells you.

I bite at my lip and look at my hands in my lap, picking at the chipped nail polish.

I was so caught up in doing that, that I jump a little when Mia's small hand comes over to take one of mine, giving a reassuring squeeze. I can't look at her as she sits beside me, I can't see what she is thinking because I'm more than likely thinking it myself.

Not only was my first time with someone I hated nor do I remember it, but now I might be pregnant from it.

Just my luck!

We were silent for what felt like forever, until Mia says in a small, unsure voice, "It'll be okay."

I knew she was trying to help and that she didn't know what else to say, but I just couldn't help but scoff, shaking my head. "I'll be a twenty-one-year-old mom. That doesn't sound okay."

"You don't know that yet."

I will soon.

The nausea has eased up some, my focus more on my situation than my stomach.

With that thought, I place my free hand over my stomach, thinking of what could be inside me right now, of what my future might hold. What if I was? I honestly didn't know. I can barely take care of myself, let alone another tiny human being.

But even thinking that, I can't help but stroke my thumb over my belly, stopping instantly when I realize what I'm doing.

"What are you going to do if you are?" Mia asks the big question I'll be asking myself.

I shrug. "I'm not in the right place to be a mom. I didn't exactly have a great role model."

"But you are amazing with Lucy."

"She's not my child."

She squeezes my hand again. "But she might as well be."

Snatching my hand from Mia's, turning to finally face her with a broken expression of my own, showing her every bit of pain and confusion I'm feeling. "Mia, I'm still in college, I live in a one-bedroom apartment that is falling apart." I gesture to the chipped tiles on the shower wall. "I am single and work a part-time job that just pays me enough to get by. Does it sound like I'm in the right place to be a mom?"

Mia's face mirrors my hurt, and she looks me in the eyes and says more serious than I've ever heard her. "You won't be alone. I promise you that."

I can't help but laugh. "What, you gonna be the other baby mama? We gonna raise this kid together?"

She takes my hand again. "Of course. I'll be the favorite parent." She gives me a wink but I still see the same pain and uncertainty in her eyes that I feel in my heart. We can joke all we want about this, but it doesn't change the fact that I may or may not be a mom.

She offers me a soft comforting smile at the same time a loud shrill signals the answer to my fate as our timer goes off.

Both of us look up at the counter, not able to see what it says from down here so we slowly help each other to standing. Both of us eye the stick and I decide that if I'm going to be a big girl, I've got to start now. I think this as I take slow tentative steps toward the stick and pick it up with numb shaky fingers.

My heart stops only to restart a second later, beating so hard it could be hitting my ribs. I didn't know whether to laugh, cry or scream, or maybe all of the above. But instead I just stand there, silent as I look at my answer.

"What is it?" Mia asks, coming up from behind me but she feels so far away. She gasps when she sees a single word on the stick.

Pregnant.

Well, I guess that's that, I think to myself as I place the test gently back on the counter, backing away until the back of my legs hit the toilet. I sit down, resting my elbows on my legs, seeing the word behind my eyelids every time I blink and still having no clue what to do now.

But I did know one thing.

"Don't tell him," I say the words low, but I know Mia heard me. Just like I knew she knew who I was talking about. She squats in front of me until we are at eye level.

Her brows furrow in confusion. "What?"

"Don't tell Conner. I don't want anyone knowing yet."

She simply nods, taking my hand again, but I don't feel it. I'm too numb now. "Of course." She offers me a small forced smile before asking, "So what are you going to do?"

I shrug, having absolutely no idea. Not yet, anyway.

CHAPTER 6

CONNER

I'm leaving class after a surprise test, walking out with my bag slung over one shoulder, listening to my classmate's panic over their answers. I was never one to stress, not like that. I figure stressing over something doesn't help, best to either take action or move past it. So instead of stressing with my classmates, I strut out of the room, eager to run to the library to print off the class notes for the next class when I'm stopped by a small familiar body and a mass of red curly hair, wild like that chick in *Brave*. Not like I watch that movie or anything.

Vivian's eyes light up as she shows all her big pearly teeth in a wide smile. "Hey Conner!"

"Hey." I give her a casual nod, smiling at my friend.

I've known Vivian since day one here, and we take most classes together only because she's undecided. My friends often tease me, saying she's following me around like a little puppy dog, but it's not like that with Vivian. She knows this. She must. She's cute but she isn't who I want.

My mind flashes back to that night a couple months ago with Ava, when she stumbled into my room and—no, I can't think about that here. Last thing I need is to get a boner in the middle of the hall, in front of Vivian. That would surely make things awkward.

I had told myself that I would give Ava space, but of course with similar friend circles, that makes it hard.

It isn't until then that I realize Vivian has been speaking this entire time and I haven't heard a word. Fuck.

She blinks her thick heavy lashes at me. "So what do you think?"

I cock my head. "About what?"

I instantly see her smile fade slightly as she cocks her head at me, "The study group? I'm organizing it with our classmates. You know how Professor Othman's tests can be. I figure it's best to be prepared."

She's not wrong. Professor Othman's tests are brutal and legendary. One year a student actually cried and ran out during the test. But I think that's just a rumor. I also heard some kid almost jumped off a building because of it, but that is also just another extreme rumor.

The joys of college.

But I smile at the idea, eager to sign up when a flash of green catches my eye.

I look past Vivian's red head and see her.

I haven't seen her in a while and last time I heard she wasn't coming to class. I'm not stalking her but just keeping tabs to make sure she's okay and let me tell you, I was starting to worry. Ava not coming to class is like a porn star not having sex. It just doesn't make sense. The chick lives to study. I knew that from the first moment I saw her, standing there with a cute crease between her brows and tiny shorts that showed off her shapely legs.

But looking at her, I know something is wrong.

I can see dark circles under her eyes, her face is pale and

she's wearing her dark hair in a messy bun atop her head with strands hanging limply around her face.

Ava is talking to one of her professors, who looks like they're in a hurry as she hands them a collection of papers in her hands.

"Conner!" Vivian's exclamation is enough to draw attention to us, making Ava's attention move away from her professor, allowing the professor to leave as she looks up at me with wide eyes. As if she's seeing a ghost.

For a second I think she's staring at someone behind me, but I'm standing in front of a wall, so that's unlikely.

Feeling Vivian's burning gaze as she waits for me, I raise my hand to greet Ava only to have her turn away and run.

She literally just ran away from me.

Well, that's a first, I think to myself as I drop my hand to my side.

"Look, Conner, if you don't wanna study with me…"

I finally tear my gaze from where Ava just ran from, promising to figure out what that was later. I mean, I knew she had a bit of a problem with me but I didn't think it was that bad. But I shake my head, focusing my attention on the pouting woman in front of me. Guilt growing in my chest at ignoring a friend trying to speak to me.

I nod. "Yeah, sorry. I thought I saw someone. It wasn't them." I lie with a small smile which manages to appease her when she smiles back.

"So you're in?"

"I'm in."

She instantly jumps on the spot, her large chest bouncing with her and drawing the attention of every guy passing us. I don't blame them, Vivian is beautiful with her big head of curls, fair complexion and big green eyes. But she's more of a friend to me.

She grabs my bicep. "Great, I'll text you the details."

With a wave, she turns on her heel and sashays away from me, leaving me to my buzzing brain of questions on what the fuck was that with Ava?

I know who to ask.

It doesn't take me long to find Hunter. I find him leaving the library with a bag on his back and a girl on his arm. He smiles when he sees me, waving his hand in greeting as I approach before slapping the girl's ass as a sign he wants her to leave. And she doesn't slap him? No, she just smiles, giggles, and wanders off, leaving us to stand just outside the library.

"What's up, bro?" Hunter says, seeing the concern on my face but I wasn't trying to hide it.

I shake my head, not sure how to phrase my words. "Nothing, it's just something weird just happened."

"Weird? Like alien abduction weird?" He puts his hand on my shoulder. "They probe you?"

"Fuck off." I push his hand off as he lets out a loud chuckle before continuing on his walk through campus, strutting with the confidence of a celebrity as I walk beside him.

I explain to him what happened and his brows furrow.

"Hmmm… that is weird," Hunter says, before continuing. "Vivian wants to study? These are truly dark times."

"Dude, I'm serious!" I exclaim, and he finally turns serious after raising his hands in surrender.

"Okay! So, she ran away, but maybe she just forgot something." He tries to rationalize. "Anyway, you shouldn't be overthinking this or one might think you're turning into a chick." He winks and I roll my eyes. Finally letting out a sigh, Hunter relents, "Look, I admit she has been acting weird. I ran into her and my sister at the pharmacy the other week.

She didn't look good, claimed it was a bug, but my sister told me it was her 'female time'. They were just acting weird, so I get what you're saying. But I think we both know who will know what is going on."

Hunter looks at me with a knowing smile, his brows raised and I instantly know who I need to track down next.

I SEE Mia later that day on the lawn, sitting beneath a tree with her notebook in front of her, tapping her pen on her knee.

If anyone is going to know what's going on with Ava, it's her, I think to myself as I make my way over to her, dodging crowds as I go.

When she looks up to see me coming, I see her shoulders stiffen like Ava's had but Mia recovers quickly by rolling her eyes and returning to the notebook in her lap, strands of blonde hair fall from her little ponytail and hang around her face.

When I stop just before her, I am met with a snide remark. "What do you want, douche nugget?"

I give her a tight smile, squatting down but she still doesn't look up. Instead, she's writing furiously in that notebook of hers. So, I just decide to cut to the chase.

"You haven't seen Ava around, have you?"

Despite my casual tone, she pauses in her writing for a second, tensing once again before raising her head, looking suspiciously at me. "Why?"

I shrug. "I just haven't seen her around is all."

"But why do you care?"

I raise my brows, waiting. Not answering.

Mia exhales, rolling her eyes again before returning to her book. "Look, I'm not her keeper. If you have a problem, then you can talk to her when she comes back to school."

"And when will that be?"

"When she's here," she says, not looking up and I know this coy tactic isn't working. Time to get to the point, so I plop down on the grass across from Mia, making her look up in surprise. "What do you think you're doing?" I ignore her question, leaning forward and resting my elbows on my knees.

"You know, I heard she was sick but I don't know what she has."

Mia squints her eyes at me for a moment, quickly picking up on my game. "She has a bug."

"Wow, so she's contagious?"

"Very."

"Even so, I'd like to see her to check up on her."

She gives me a tight smile that doesn't meet her eyes. "No need. I checked on her this morning."

I lean farther, making sure to look her in the eyes. "Look, I know you guys were in the pharmacy a couple of weeks ago. I also know your stories didn't match up which leads me to believe that you were lying then just like how you're lying now." Mia opens her mouth to argue but I hold up a hand silencing her, continuing, "Besides, I did see Ava recently, but it was weird. She saw me and ran away from me. Now that could give a guy a complex and I just can't figure out why she would run." I tilt my head at Mia, her jaw tense as she bites her lip. "Can you fill me in?"

We stare at each other, waiting to see which one will break first. Just when I think she won't break, she blinks, her face softens as she regards me with a worried expression filled with regret.

"4436 Randolph Street. Apartment 5B." I give her a puzzled look and she elaborates. "If you have anything to ask, ask her. This is between you two. She should be home."

So, there was something.

CHAPTER 7

AVA

M*e: I need to talk to you. 911!*
Lucy: Be at the park in 5.

I SIT IN MY CAR, staring down at the phone in my shaking hand, still trying to catch my breath. Feeling the nausea start in my belly, I instantly regret my decision to run but what else could I do? It was the first time I'd seen Conner in a while and knowing that I am going to have his baby and still have no idea what I'm going to do, it all just became too much to face. All I wanted to do today was submit my classwork and get more while I 'recover' for another week. But the way I'm feeling right now, homework is the farthest thing from my mind.

When I get to my car, I snatch my phone up and send my sister a text before I know what I'm doing. But I need to talk to someone. I need to deal with this. Mia has tried to help but she can only do so much.

I need my sister. I think this at the same time as I start the car, ready to head to the park.

. . .

It takes me ten minutes to get to the park from campus. This is the same park we would play at as children. It was safe and a place that reminded us of a time of innocence. It's where we went when it felt like our world was going up in flames. Kids rarely played there anymore considering the equipment was falling apart, which was great for us, especially right now.

I see Lucy sitting on the bench near the play equipment when I pull up, her head perking up at my arrival. Her innocent smile beaming at me and she waves eagerly, her blue eyes lighting up her face as her dark blonde curls blow in the wind.

I couldn't help but smile at her, forcing myself out of the car and slamming the door closed. Her smile wavers when she sees the shame and sadness in my eyes and moves over to make room for me on the bench. "Step into my office," she says, making me want to smile and cry all at once, but I school my features, taking a seat beside her. She turns in her seat to face me, one leg tucked underneath her, waiting.

On the way here, I kept running through how I would say this, how I would talk about this to her but now it was like my mouth had gone numb and my brain was broken.

Seeing the internal struggle in me, my hands clasped in my lap, Lucy asks, "How's college?"

I could've said 'good' like a normal person but instead all I come out and say is, "I'm pregnant." Well, at least the cat's out of the bag now.

She's silent and I turn to look at her slowly. Her eyes are wide and her mouth hangs open, until it shifts into a smile. "Oh my god! Really? I'm going to be an aunt? When did this happen? I didn't even know you were seeing anyone."

Her smile evaporates when she sees my eyes start to

water, a single tear falling down my face. I wish I could be happy, but how can I be happy when I don't know what I'm going to do?

"Hey, what's wrong? Why aren't you happy?" Lucy wraps a small arm around me, pulling me close to her side.

I shake my head. "I'm not with anyone, Lucy. It was a mistake. A onetime thing and now…" I shake my head again, unable to explain, but with Lucy, I rarely needed to. Even at seventeen, she was wiser than many her age.

"And now you don't know what to do?"

I nod, another tear running down my cheek.

"I think you do."

I look up at Lucy's words, frowning. "What?"

Lucy's face softens with sympathy and understanding, she gives my shoulder a squeeze. "I think you know what to do, you just don't like it or you don't feel you can do it."

Understanding finally clicks and the pain of knowing she is right cracks in my chest, almost making me wince. "Lucy, I am in no position to keep a baby. Besides, the father doesn't even know about it. I saw him today and just ran. Does that sound like someone who's ready to have a baby?"

She shrugs. "It actually sounds normal. You're scared and that's okay, but you are not alone. You don't have to do this on your own if this is something that you want."

"It's not that I want it, but I don't think I can get rid of it." I place a hand over my stomach. I've been doing that a lot lately since finding out, like I'm protecting and comforting the baby. "Besides, I haven't had any great parenting role models, so what makes you think I can do this?"

"Because of how you are. You protect and look out for everyone. You're even protecting your unborn baby." She gestures to my hand on my stomach. "Ava, if this is what you want, you can do this. It won't be easy, but you won't be alone, so don't think for a second that you will be."

"I'm scared," I whisper the words past numb lips, tears still coming as I stroke my thumb over my belly.

Lucy is silent for a moment until she exhales a breath. "New life is a scary thing, but it can also be pretty amazing. You just need to get through the first hurdle."

After a moment, I laugh, brushing the tears off my cheeks, looking back at Lucy. "Since when are you so smart and grown up?"

She smiles lovingly at me, squeezing me once more. "I've had a good teacher."

We both smile and sit in silence.

"So, are you going to tell the father?" Lucy asks the one question that continuously pops up in my head, like an alert I need to address, but I guess I'm just procrastinating. Wondering if it's worth it to tell him, what purpose would it serve?

I shrug, still not knowing my answer. "Maybe."

MAYBE CAME FASTER than I thought when I return to my apartment, desperate for these stupid sandals to be off my feet and replaced with slippers.

He's sitting in front of the door, his knees up and his forearms resting on his knees. When he notices me, his eyes meet mine and he sits up a bit straighter and I feel my body stiffen, unable to decide if it wants to run or not.

But a part of me knew I can't continue running. I can't hide this forever, so I steel myself and fumble with the keys in my purse as he wordlessly stands, tucking his hands in the front pockets of his jeans. "I didn't know when you would be back. I thought you would be home."

My mind blank, I ask the only thing I can think of out of the blankness in my head, "What do you want?"

"We need to talk."

Those words spark a fear in me that makes my heart beat almost out of my chest and I know it's going to be hard to say anything to him. Can't I just text him? Why does he even need to know? It could be someone else's baby, he wouldn't know. "We have nothing to talk about," I say, avoiding his eyes and moving past him to unlock the door to my apartment but before I can close my door, his huge body is standing there blocking my doorway and stopping me.

I narrow my eyes and growl, "Can you please leave?"

"Just give me ten minutes," Conner begs and a part of me caves as I let the door swing open.

"I'll give you five."

I walk in, feeling him enter my apartment and a wave of nausea suddenly takes over. Not now! Putting a hand to my stomach I turn around at the sound of the door closing behind Conner and I force myself to meet his eyes as he briefly looks around at my small apartment with hand-me-down furniture and a small retro TV, before finally looking at me, waiting.

"You wanted to talk, so talk." I cross my arms over my chest, feeling the distance between us and making sure it stays that way. I apparently don't make great decisions when we are alone and close. The evidence resides in my belly.

Conner doesn't waste time. "What was your deal today?"

I blink, feigning ignorance, but I knew what he's talking about and I know I can't avoid this. "My deal? What are you talking about?"

"On campus. You saw me and ran in the opposite direction. Did I do something to piss you off?" After I give him a pointed look telling him he always pisses me off, he rephrases the question, rolling his eyes, "I mean, did I do something to make you run away from me?"

I could lie, but what would I say? The tired feeling in my muscles tells me it's time to stop running, that this was happening and a part of me knew he should know. So, I expel a tired breath and walk around to the couch and plop myself down. "No."

He walks around so that he is standing in front of me, his big arms crossing over his chest. "Then, do you want to tell me why you ran?"

"No." At least I was honest.

He blinks. "What do you mean, no? I know something is going on."

"What makes you say that?"

"Because you ran away from me! You looked me in the eyes and you ran. And you know the worse part? You looked scared. What have I ever done to you to make you scared of me?"

Nothing, he's done nothing but be a normal guy. He's a good friend to Hunter and he's never been mean to Mia or me, though he drives me nuts. I've never been scared of him and a small part of me still wants him to have that normal life because once I tell him, that will be gone. I beg, my voice starting to crack as I try to bite back the tears pushing to fall. "Conner, please just go."

"No." He squats down in front of me until we are at eye level. "Something is up, I know it."

His eyes are wide and desperate as he begs for answers and it's then I know that it is time and that nauseous feeling increases. I swallow the bile building at the back of my throat and finally say the words I've been fighting to not say to him, my watery eyes meeting his concerned ones. "I'm not sick. I'm pregnant. With your baby."

He does not stay for further information, which hurts the most.

CHAPTER 8

CONNER

The big yellow farmhouse stands tall before me as I sit in my truck, not knowing how I ended up here. The night has been a blur since Ava told me I might be a father and I guess I could've handled it differently or handled it at all. Instead, I just walked out without a word, but I didn't know what to say. It's something I never expected to hear so soon and by someone who hates me. Not exactly ideal.

But now here I am, sitting in my truck outside my parent's house, the lights from the windows shining on the driveway in the night.

My mind flashes back to Ava. How scared she looked, and sad. I wanted to hold her but my instinct to run won out. What does that say about me? And what is she going to do about it? Am I going to be a father and if so, can I? My hands tighten on the steering wheel and my head begins to ache. It's been a crazy couple of days. Hell, it's been a crazy few months and it's only going to get crazier.

I see something move out of the corner of my eye, making me jump before I see the humorous smile on my dad's face as he watches me from my side window. After quickly calming my heart, I glare at him as I wind down my window. “How long were you there?”

My dad chuckles, shaking his head. “Long enough. Your mother wants to know if you’re going to come inside. Dinner’s ready and there’s enough to go around.”

So many things go through my mind, like telling my dad about Ava or just saying no and driving away, but instead, I take my key out of the ignition and swing the door open to hop out. At this moment I need a sense of normalcy, then I can figure out a plan for how to deal with everything.

Slamming the door, Dad and I walk up the driveway I used to play on as a kid, but now it just looks different, like I’m seeing it through another person’s eyes.

Dad throws his arm over my shoulder, giving me a squeeze when we reach the door. “Your mom will be so happy to see you.”

I force a smile, stepping through the door, and am met with the smell of mixed herbs and garlic. It was warm and comforting like the home-cooked meal I was going to dig into.

We walk down the hallway with hand-painted roses on the walls, painted by my mother. Mom always loved art, always said the world is her canvas.

Before I realize it, a small woman with black curly hair launches herself into my arms, giving me a rib-breaking squeeze. “Sweetie! I’m so glad you’re here.” The smell of paint still clinging to her like always.

“Melanie, don’t break the boy.”

At that, Mom lets me go, steps back and beams up at me with big dark eyes and an even bigger smile. “Am I not allowed to be excited about my son’s visit?”

“Of course you are, Mom.” I bring her back in for another hug, needing the comfort like a child.

This time, when she pulls back, her forehead is creased

and suspicion sits on her face as she looks up at me, placing a gentle hand to my cheek. "Everything okay, sweetie?"

I want to tell her, both of them, but how can I when I don't know what to think of it myself?

I force another smile at her, waving off her concern. "Yeah, I'm fine, Mom. I just had a big week." Not a lie, but not everything either.

After a moment, she nods, the suspicion still there but she thankfully lets it go for now. "Well, why don't we come inside." She gestures down the hall to the dining room. "We have some meatloaf, potatoes, beans and gravy. Some food will make you feel better."

I LOOK DOWN at my barely eaten food, feeling the eyes of my parents on me, their food already gone. "I'm sorry, guys, I guess I'm just not hungry. I had a big lunch," I lie, still not looking up at them but I hear my mother sigh as she rises from the chair.

"It's fine, sweetie. I'll wrap it up for you to eat tomorrow."

I nod, finally looking up to smile at her when she reaches me and takes the plate away, along with my father's, giving me the softest smile full of love before she makes her way through to the kitchen.

When she is out of earshot, my father leans forward in his seat, looking at me with expectant eyes, eyes so similar to my own and his mouth hidden behind a short brown beard, the rest of his brown hair is tucked behind his ears.

"What?" I exclaim, defensively, shifting in my seat and looking down at my hands on the table in front of me.

He tilts his head at me. "You want to tell me what's got you troubled?"

"I told you, it's been a big week," I stammer out my excuse, unbelievable to my own ears.

He waves his hands at me. "Oh don't give me that bullshit."

I snap my head back up to meet his waiting eyes with my own shocked expression. "It's not bullshit."

"You've had a lot of big weeks, but not once have you lost your appetite." His accusatory tone is making my resolve waver and my anger grow as I frown at him.

"Did you ever think that maybe I wasn't hungry?"

Dad raises a doubtful eyebrow at me. "For your mother's cooking?"

He was right. When it came to mom's cooking, there was always room. One time when I was a kid, I had a stomach bug and even though I struggled to keep food down, I still managed to chow down on whatever Mom gave me, even if that meant me spending the night in the bathroom.

Worth it.

Dad still waited. "Son?"

And my resolve breaks, I let out the shaky breath I'd been holding in since I entered the house. "Can I ask you something?"

Dad nods, and I look back down at my hands, unable to see his reaction.

"You were young when you had Riley," I smile a sad smile to myself as I think of my big brother. I haven't seen him in five years but I miss him often, not that I'll admit it. But now was one of those times. "What made you think it was right?"

It's quiet for a long time and I finally look up to see not judgment or disappointment, but my dad's face wearing a soft smile full of the same love Mom had given me before.

"No time is ever right. And when we had Riley, nothing was easy. We just worked together and took it day by day."

"You got that right." Mom chimes in when she strides back into the room, wiping her hands on a dishcloth before seating herself back at the table, regarding me with a thoughtful expression.

"How long were you listening in?" I ask.

"Long enough." She smiles at Dad before she looks to me with a serious expression. "So, you want to tell me why this sudden curiosity?"

My heart breaks a bit when I think of the disappointment they will feel and how lost I'm feeling, but I need something and they are already sniffing around.

Looking back down. "Something happened. A few months ago, we were having a party and there was a girl."

I am met with silence, so I continue. "I've known the girl for a while. She's friends with Hunter's sister, Mia. We kind of had too much to drink, and now she's pregnant."

The silence that follows is so thick I could choke on it and I refuse to look up, feeling my muscles bunch up from the tension until my mother's soft voice breaks the silence. "What's her name?"

I finally allow myself to look up, surprised by the softness in her voice and I'm met with a tender smile.

"Ava." I stutter, blinking nervously.

"The girl from the dorm." Mom nods her head, remembering the many stories I would tell her in my phone calls home. "When did she tell you?"

"Today. And I was a jerk." I laugh humorlessly, shaking my head to myself.

"Sweetie, I'm sure you weren't a jerk."

I meet her eyes. "I walked out and came here."

Her face unchanging, she says, "Then you are a jerk."

I blink at her words, thinking I misheard, my father scolds her which she only waves away, looking back at me. "So, you're telling me that you walked out on a young girl who just found out she's going to be a mother? You left her alone to come here?"

"Not the smartest move, son." Dad shakes his head, sitting back in his chair.

"Look, I didn't come here to feel guilty. I know I'm a jerk, but I don't know what to do. I'm scared and you guys are supposed to help me."

They are both silent for a moment, looking at each other as if in silent conversation, until my dad finally speaks up. "Son, I know you're scared. Hell, I was too. I was a little younger than you when I found out I was going to be a dad."

"What made it easier?"

He laughs. "Nothing makes it easier. It's a hard job and those books don't teach you shit. But it helped that I wasn't alone." He smiles at Mom. "Your mom and I didn't have the approval of our families back then, or the town, but we still had each other. If we fucked up, we did it together. If we succeeded, we did it together. It's all a learning curve."

"But what if she doesn't like me?"

"It sure sounds like she does, considering you got her pregnant."

Mom pipes in, reaching over and placing her small hand over mine. "Go talk to her. You are both scared and lost. Seek comfort in each other. Be there for each other."

She releases my hand and I sag in my chair, rubbing my eyes with my hands, suddenly feeling a wave of exhaustion.

"I'll do it tomorrow. You mind if I crash here for the night? I think I might be too tired to drive back to campus."

They both offer me a small comforting smile full of understanding. "Of course. Your room is exactly how you left it." Mom points a finger at me. "But I expect to hear everything and you better bring that girl to see me."

I chuckle. "Let's just see if she wants to talk to me again first."

CHAPTER 9

AVA

The next night, I try to sleep but the uneasy feeling continues to tickle away at my stomach, making it hard to rest.

But it's not only that.

I'm pissed.

I can't shake how pissed I am, no matter how much Mia and Harper tried to help earlier. They came over with some movies, and wine for Mia because I can't have any. We talked about everything but the pregnancy, like it was just another movie night but it was hard to miss the furtive glances they both gave my stomach, or the way they wouldn't let me help clean up, offering to do it all for me which *never* happens.

They were trying to help, I get that. But if they are going to continue to act like I'm made of glass, it's going to be a long nine months.

Then there's the other thing. You know, how the father of my baby found out and just left without a word. Yeah, that sucked. Honestly, I was hurt at first though I don't know what I expected. He had never truly cared about me before, why start now? He didn't care, he just left because he could.

He can walk away from this, from me and his baby and I won't be begging him to stay.

With a frustrated groan, I look up at my alarm clock for the hundredth time and groan again when I see the numbers *1:30* beaming back at me in my darkened room.

Another restless night.

My stomach has eased somewhat but it's still unsettled at times, like now.

Placing my hand over my belly, I speak into the darkness, "How about letting me have this night, kid?"

My stomach starts to settle and I exhale a breath, silently thanking the kid.

At least they will listen to me, I smile to myself despite the fear inside.

I can do this. I think this at the same time as my phone pings with a message. I search through the sheets until I find my phone. My heart does a little flip and the unsettled stomach returns when I see who messaged me.

Conner: Hey you up?

I wait, not knowing why, after not hearing from him since he stormed out of here, he was messaging me at this hour, thinking I would be awake. I mean, I am, but that's beside the point.

My fingers move over the keys before I have time to think.

Me: What do you want?

I didn't mean to sound abrupt but I didn't have time to muck around, not with him.

Conner: We need to talk.

The three dots appear, signaling him writing something. I wait.

Conner: Meet me at Deb's Diner?

Me: Ok.

I don't know why I say yes. It might be the fact that he is

the father of my baby and in some way, I owe it to my baby to hear him out. Or maybe it has something to do with the fact that I probably won't be sleeping tonight anyway, and what else have I got planned for tonight?

Besides, I was really starting to crave their twenty-four-hour pancakes.

IT'S NOT hard to find him when I arrive at Deb's. I rush in, bundled in a big red coat and my hair in a messy ponytail. I was getting ready in the dark.

I see him hunched over a cup of coffee in a booth in the corner.

I make my way to him, feeling the nervous shake in my legs and hands but push through. I'm a big girl now, a mama and I gotta deal with big girl things, like talking to the father of my baby about said baby most likely. Why else would he want to meet me at this time?

He raises his tired eyes up to me when I reach the booth, plopping myself down across from him.

Neither of us speak for a while, but both of us shift in our seats, hearing the squeak from the plastic of the booths.

When our eyes finally meet again, he gives me an uncomfortably tense smile which I do not return. It takes a few more moments of uncertain silence until Conner finally decides to speak, his fingers still wrapped around the coffee cup before him. "I would've gotten you a coffee, but..."

"It's fine," I say, tersely, bringing back the silence, until it becomes too much for even me.

When my eyes finally reach Conner's again, I ask, "So, you said you wanted to talk?"

I school my features to hide the nerves that built within me on the way here and were currently going crazy. I know I needed to face this and talk to him, but it's hard to forget about the fact that he just walked out the second I told him about the baby. He didn't even ask how I was feeling or if I was going to be keeping it, like he didn't care. With a baby, you need to be all in or not at all and I'm not sure about Conner.

He looks up at me, shifting in his seat again. "How are you feeling?"

Now he asks that? A little slow on the uptake, but I answer anyway, my expression neutral. "I'm fine. A little queasy at times but it comes in waves these days."

He nods, considering this. "How has school been?"

"Good. I'm getting used to moving around and not running to the bathroom every five seconds, more like every ten minutes now."

He smiles at this but the smile doesn't reach his eyes.

I lean forward, my forearms resting on the cold table. "You didn't ask me here to talk about school. So, why don't you just ask me what you want to ask me."

I see a second of panic and uncertainty, a look so foreign on him that it catches me off guard, making me aware of how scary this must be for him, but he's not the one who's going to be pushing this thing out!

He nods slightly, considering his words before looking back at me, nervous. "I'm sorry about how I reacted. I got scared and panicked."

"I'm scared too."

"I know, but I didn't plan this."

"And I did? I had a plan for myself too, you know. A baby didn't factor into that and in case you forgot, making a baby takes two so it wasn't just me doing this!" I didn't realize until I had stopped and noticed the eyes of a few of the waitresses and late-night patrons, that I was now yelling. I shrink back in my chair, taking a deep calming breath and glaring at a stunned Conner.

"Look, I'm sorry, I didn't mean it like that. Fuck." He runs a frustrated hand through his already messy hair. "I'm screwing this up." He shakes his head before continuing. "I know neither of us planned for this, but if it's okay, I would like to know what you are planning to do?"

I feel my glare soften, not sure if I want to tell him or not, but it would be hard to hide and it is part his in a way, but I'm not expecting him to be involved. I never expected it of him. I resist the need to place my hand over my stomach, clasping my hands in front of me, not wanting to draw Conner's eye there and force the words out. "I'm keeping it. I know it won't be easy, but I can't get rid of it. And don't worry, I don't expect you to be involved or anything."

It isn't until I stop talking that I notice his grim expression is now looking straight at my belly, where I have unconsciously placed my hand while I was talking. Instead of dropping my hand away, I leave it there, rubbing my thumb over the surface.

Conner's deep grave voice speaks so low; I barely hear him. "What makes you think I want nothing to do with it?"

I furrow my brows at him, leaning forward again. "If you want something to do with this baby, you've got to be all in. I won't have a halfway father for my baby. Now, I don't expect us to be together. But I do expect you to be there for your child."

He nods.

"That means, every soccer game, dance recital or graduation. You have to be there. And before the baby arrives, you can start off by being there for every appointment. It will be a good trial run before the baby arrives."

He nods again.

"Because if you don't, that's it. I won't let my baby be disappointed by you."

He flinches at that, but recovers quickly, nodding again, his soft eyes looking into my firm ones.

"I'm in," he says, his voice sure and unwavering.

I can't help but notice the feeling of butterflies fluttering in my stomach at hearing that from him, like my baby was jumping for joy at knowing its father was waiting for them. *That's right, bubba. You will have everything. I promise.*

"So what do we have to do?" Conner's voice jolts me out of my baby bubble, making me shake my head back to the present, blinking.

"Oh, um, I've got my first ultrasound in a couple of weeks. I'll send you the details. It's just to check how things are going this early in the process."

He nods. "So, we are going to be parents?"

I nod. "Yep, I guess so."

In that moment, we look at each other as the lost parents we have suddenly become, confused about the world we were about to step into but at least we would probably screw up together which gave me a strange sense of comfort. We sit in silence again when I suddenly feel a wave of fatigue hitting me, making my eyelids feel heavy and my limbs weak.

"I should head home. Sleep." I'm already shuffling out of the booth awkwardly, any thought of food being replaced by thoughts of sleep.

"Of course, did you drive here?"

I shake my head, steadying my tired legs. "No, I live nearby so I just walked."

He's out of the booth in seconds, much more graceful than I was, his fingers grazing my arm as he goes to reach for it only to stop himself a second later. "Let me walk you."

I furrow my brow in confusion at him. "Why?"

He shrugs. "Why not?"

He's never once asked to walk me home and a part of me

wants to say no but instead my lips say, "Okay." Making him smile as I turn to head out the door for my short walk home with Conner.

"So, I take it you haven't told anyone yet?" I ask him as we walk in awkward silence on this deserted street, getting closer to my apartment.

He looks at me for a second in surprise, either at the question or the fact that I was the first one to break the silence, I didn't know.

He composes himself after a moment, shaking his head. "Not yet. I didn't think it was a good idea until we spoke first."

I nod in understanding, feeling his eyes on me, waiting for a reaction.

Not looking at him, I ask, "And now? What are you going to do?"

The silence that follows stirs the nerves in my stomach so much that I eventually look up at him, seeing him facing the empty path before us and his eyes so busy with rapid thoughts.

He blinks, looking back at me with an expressionless face. "I guess it'll be hard to hide, not like I'll want to, hide it I mean." He shakes his head, running his hand through his hair. I notice that's common for him when he's stressed or agitated. "I'm screwing this up. I'm sorry. I've never done this before."

I can't help but laugh. "I should hope not."

He shakes his head again, laughing to himself. "You know what I mean."

I stop when I notice my red brick apartment building up ahead and he stops next to me. We both stand in awkward silence, shuffling our feet and only meeting each other's eyes in brief increments.

I smile a small smile, but he is the one to speak first. "So, what are you doing tomorrow?"

"Probably catch up on some much-needed sleep."

"Sounds like fun."

My smile grows. "Yeah, it'll be a party."

He chuckles. "I bet."

The silence returns with the feet shuffling and I know one of us needs to make a move to go or we will probably be out here all night and with how tired I'm feeling, that is not an option. "I should probably go." I point to the building behind me, already backing away from Conner slowly.

He nods, giving me a tight smile. "Of course. Good night Ava." He looks down at my stomach. "Good night, kid."

The flipping returns to my stomach and I can't help but smile a genuine smile, placing my hand over my stomach. "Good night, Conner."

CHAPTER 10

CONNER

"I guess congratulations are in order."

"Does this mean he's getting married?"

"You are aware of what babies are like, right?"

The guys start in on me as soon as I break the news to them the next day, when I finally wake up and they ask why I got in so late. A bunch of nosy old women these guys are, I think to myself as I roll my eyes at them. "Guys, I'm right here. Thank you and no we're not getting married, I'm not even sure what we are, and yes I have an idea of what babies are like," I say to both of my housemates in turn.

Hunter slaps a hand on my shoulder and grins. "I can't believe we are going to be family!"

"Not exactly."

Logan, my other housemate, scoffs as he slumps forward to rest his elbows on the kitchen counter. "Yeah, he just said he doesn't know what they are."

Hunter cocks his head. "So does that mean she can date?"

"Fuck no!" I exclaim, feeling hot rage boil the blood beneath my skin at the idea of another guy touching her. Luckily for me, I know she has extremely high expectations of men but that doesn't mean Mr. Perfect couldn't just walk in and ruin everything.

The sudden need to go to her and hide her away hits me, which I try to shake off, because who does that?

"Well, you might wanna put a label on it somehow," Hunter comments, something I already know, but I have a plan.

I shake my head, trying to rid my brain of visions of Ava fucking some other guy. "Stop messing with my head."

"Bro." Hunter leans forward to meet my eyes, his expression serious. "How do you think this is gonna work? Raising a baby together and not being together?"

"And how is that healthy for the baby?" Logan comments.

I raise my hands to silence them. "Look, guys, I know the situation isn't ideal, but I'm telling you that we will not be raising this baby separately."

"What are you saying?" Hunter raises an intrigued brow.

"I'm saying I just need to get her to trust me, to like me. I know she does, but she's so fucking stubborn and won't admit it."

Logan grins, waggling his brows at me. "So what, you gonna lay on the charm?"

I raise my hands again, a big smile pulls at my face and a mischievous gleam twinkles in my eyes. "Guys, I think I have to woo my baby momma."

"Cheers to that."

A COUPLE NIGHTS LATER, after getting home from work, I get a text. I launch to reach my phone, excited to hear from Ava but deflated only to see it's a text from Vivian.

It's not her fault but she wasn't who I wanted to hear from. Either way, I open up the text.

Vivian: Study group tonight?

I think of my lack of plans, knowing I was gonna study anyway. It might as well be with a group to keep me from falling asleep. So I text her back.

Me: Sure.

Vivian: Library. 30 minutes?

Me: I'll meet you there.

WHEN I GET to the library, I locate the study room Vivian said to meet everyone in and it's empty. I check to make sure I'm in the right room and I am.

Huh, everyone must be running late.

I plop my stuff by my feet and take a seat, watching the door, my mind instantly going to Ava.

I think about the softness in her eyes with an edge of defense when she speaks of our baby. Fuck! *Our baby.* That's still so weird to even comprehend, yet I'm not disappointed, miserable or remotely unhappy about it. I'm nervous, but we both are and I find a strange comfort in that, a unity almost. Like a promise that we will sort it out together.

I didn't plan to have kids yet, but I won't lie and say I'm not happy it was with her. I've been interested in Ava since she first glared at me, wanting to know more about her and push her buttons to see how she ticked. Thinking of her now, all I want to do is talk to her. Hear her voice, but I also know I haven't heard from her much since the diner the other night. She said she would text me the details about the ultrasound appointment next week so I guess I could use that as my way in.

So, instead of calling her, I decide to shoot her a text, because that's not too much, right?

Me: Hey, how are you feeling? Just asking about when the ultrasound is. You said you'd send me the details ...

She replies almost instantly, making me think she was waiting for me to text. Or maybe I'm just too hopeful.

Ava: Shoot, sorry I forgot. I have an appointment next Thursday, 11am.

Me: Cool, I'll pick you up at 10:30 and drive you there. You can tell me where I'm going lol.

Ava: You don't have to do that …

Me: I don't mind. I told you, I'm in this. Besides, it would be tragic if you and our baby got kidnapped by some psycho taxi driver.

Ava: Why would you say that? Besides, I would never take a taxi … I'd take an Uber because my sister has my car at the moment.

Me: Pretty much the same thing, little lamb.

Ava: Stop calling me that! And it is NOT the same thing, it's safer.

Me: Hmm… sure …

Ava: Oh, fuck yourself!

Me: You sure you don't wanna do it for me? ;)

There is a brief pause and I worry I may have gone too far until I finally see the little bubbles pop up signaling that she is replying.

Ava: You had your go. One is all you get.

Me: You say that now.

I smirk at my phone when someone shatters my little cyber world with Ava as they strut into the room.

I stuff my phone in my pocket and look up to see Vivian dropping her books on the table in front of me, her furrowed brow aimed at me.

"What's up with you? You act as if I caught you watching porn." She pauses, raising a brow. "Were you?"

"No," I exclaim, pulling my books out as Vivian takes a seat beside me, still not looking convinced that I'm not some kind of porn addict.

"Okay, you were just holding that phone pretty close to your face."

"I was just talking to a girl," I explain without giving away too much and it was hard not to miss the tensing of Vivian's shoulders before she slowly raises her head and gives me an even more tense smile, almost making her look like she's in pain.

"A girl?"

"Yeah," I say, checking the time and looking around us. "Hey, where's everyone else? The study group?"

Vivian shrugs, opening her notes. "They couldn't make it. Something came up."

"Everyone?"

"Yep. Anyway." Vivian swivels in her chair to face me, her books and notes forgotten and I can't help but wonder if she actually asked anyone to join us, but I shake that notion off pretty quickly when she speaks, "This girl, is this the same one that was with you at Deb's Diner the other night?"

I blink in confusion, thinking I may have misheard her because how in the hell would she know that? I cock my head and ask, "Yeah, how'd you know that?"

Vivian leans in as if to tell me a secret. "I have friends."

"And your friends keep tabs on me?"

She scoffs, "Conner, believe it or not, my world doesn't revolve around you. Some friends saw you and thought it was strange you were there at that time. I ran into those friends and they mentioned it. I wasn't even going to bring it up until you mentioned a girl. I figured they would be the same." Vivian laughs, seeing my expression. "God Conner! What, you think I'm some kind of stalker?"

I laugh despite that thought coming to mind.

After her laughter starts to die down she takes a breath, putting her hand on my knee and briefly squeezing it, she says, "Now how about we get stuck in these books?"

. . .

A COUPLE OF NIGHTS LATER, I'm lying in bed after another day at work and decide to text Ava again. Missing her wit and how she always has a comeback for what I throw at her.

I check the time when I whip out my phone, seeing that it's just past eight p.m. and hoping that's not too late for her. I stare at the message thread, not knowing what to say. Well, I do know what I want to say but also know I probably shouldn't say it… yet.

I want to tell her to come over, that once was not enough and that I haven't thought of anything else since. But instead I text her what a good future father would text.

Me: Still up?

Not fancy but it works.

She replies after a couple of minutes,

Ava: Yeah, I'm at work.

Me: What?

Ava: Work, you know that thing you do to help you earn money?

Me: I know work, smart-ass. I'm wondering if you should be working in your condition.

Ava: I should be fine.

Me: Should be? That's not a definite. I need definites, woman!

Ava: Don't 'woman' me and I'm perfectly fine to work. Besides, I'm restricted to the register if it makes you feel better.

Me: You better be ….

Ava: Or what?

Me: I'll spank you.

Ava: You wouldn't!

Me: Do you really want to test me? I'm a daddy now and I must protect my young.

Ava: You are ridiculous.

Me: You know it!

Ava: Why are you texting me?

Me: I knew you were bored and craving my attention.

Ava: Idiot.

Me: Now we don't need to use that kind of language around the baby.

Ava: Idiot.

Me: You're testing me?

Ava: You bet. Because I know you're all talk.

Me: Little lamb, you have no idea who you're dealing with.

Ava: Why do you call me that?

Me: What?

Ava: Little lamb. Why do you call me that?

Me: Because of the boxers.

Ava: What?

Me: The boxers you wore when we first met, when you made that complaint to the RA, you wore boxers with little lambs on them. They were cute.

She doesn't reply for a few minutes, but I watch the screen like my life depends on it.

Ava: You remember what I was wearing?

Me: Hard not to. It's not every day a hot little thing beats down my door.

Ava: You think I'm hot?

Me: You are pregnant with my kid, Ava. Obviously!

Ava: True but I won't be for long. Soon I'll be the size of a whale.

Me: Hot.

Ava: Bullshit.

Me: Language.

Ava: Eat me.

Me: Yes please!

Ava: I guess I walked into that one.

Me: I still say yes. No take backs!

Ava: I should probably go back to work. We have the ultrasound coming up..

Me: You nervous?

Ava: A little. You still picking me up?

Me: I'll be there with bells on... and nothing else if you like ;)

Ava: Lol. Good night Conner.

Me: Good night Ava. Good night Kid.

CHAPTER 11

AVA

I am on my sixth bottle of water and I am currently sitting with my legs jumping while I fidget in my chair. My bladder close to bursting.

The waiting room only has a few couples, each of them looking middle aged which only makes me feel more uncomfortable, but I know it would've been worse if Conner wasn't here and I had to face this on my own. In fact, I'm very happy he didn't let me down and actually turned up to pick me up this morning.

My nervous internal ramblings are silenced when Conner's hand comes over to cover my small hand bunched into a fist, just a gentle touch.

I look up at him and see him giving me a small smile, but the nerves in his eyes are clear and also making me feel a bit better that I'm not the only one here freaking out and overthinking this.

I smile a tight small smile, worried that if I relax, I will piss myself.

"You two are adorable." The soft, feminine words, pulling us out of our reveries, forcing us to meet the soft green eyes of a small woman sitting across from us with a small baby bump and wild black curls. Beside her sat a big guy with a shaved head I thought would break the woman with a simple hug, but he was merely scrolling through his phone, not paying any mind to us unlike his companion who was smiling at us.

I smile at her, mumbling a thank you, unsure of what else to say.

She leans forward. "First-time parents?"

I glance at Conner before answering with a nod. "Is it that obvious?"

I say it as a joke, but I can't help feeling a little self-conscious. But the woman laughs a light laugh. "It's just the nerves. You guys look like you are about to walk death row." She pauses, looking at us before continuing, while I hold my tight smile. "I take it this wasn't planned?"

Just as the shock sets in about this nosey woman's questions, we are interrupted by a deep voice calling someone for one of the doctors. Her head perks up, her smile grows and we are saved when she nudges the man beside her and they both scurry away with a farewell to us over their shoulder.

I breathe out a big puff of air, not knowing what else to say, looking at Conner side on, but he doesn't seem annoyed. Instead, his hand is covering his mouth and I see his shoulders start to shake with suppressed laughter. I nudge him lightly. "It's not funny," I hiss at him under my breath at the same time a loud commotion sounds just outside the doctor's office main door.

We both turn as a woman, huge with her round belly, enters the waiting room with a crowd of seven children ranging in size and age. Each of them looking like they need a shower, but then again so does the woman in her stained polka dot dress and oily black hair in a messy bun. Conner and I try to avoid looking, but the image stuns me. How big she is and how many kids follow around her. Was she alone or just today? Could that have been me if Conner hadn't stepped up? Could it still be me? I shake my head, bunching my fists and feeling Conner squeeze the fist he was still holding. It was like he could see my fears and was letting me know he was here. I take a deep breath to calm my racing heart as the woman and her children take a seat across the next row of seats, pulling out a magazine from her bag and flipping to a random page. Her kids jumping, running, fighting and screaming around her, but she doesn't even bat an eye.

Great parenting right there.

God, I hope I'm better at this.

As I think this, Conner's seat squeaks under his weight when he leans down to whisper in my ear. "Do you think you will get that big?"

My eyes widen at the idea because I honestly haven't thought about how big I will get, because I'm not sure I'm ready to think about it. "I'm not sure. Maybe."

"Is it weird to say that I'm kind of hoping that you do?"

I turn a questioning look to him, our faces surprisingly close but neither of us pull back as his grin widens. "I swear if you make size jokes, I promise that I will punch you," I warn him with a glare and he holds up his hands in surrender, sitting back in his chair.

His proud grin is still on his face when an orange-like substance is tipped all over his lap from one of the sippy cups one of the kids were holding.

And I laugh and laugh and laugh... and pee a little.

CONNER IS STILL in the bathroom cleaning himself up when I'm called in, my heart picks up in speed until it's almost beating out of my chest. My steps are slow and the nurse with too much makeup on takes my arm, hooking it with hers, telling me with her southern accent that everything will be fine. But how the fuck does she know?

When she ushers me into a room with a couple of chairs, a reclining bed chair and a monitor, I know shit is getting real. Seeing the panic in my eyes, the nurse gives me a soft comforting smile, telling me to get changed and the doctor will be with me shortly. She gestures to the paper robes laid out on the reclining bed chair, promising that she will let my boyfriend know where I am.

I don't even bother to correct her because honestly it was too complicated to explain and she left the room too quickly. And I guess a part of me wants to pretend for a moment that I am a normal pregnant woman with her boyfriend in a happy relationship and this is planned.

Clenching my legs together to stop from peeing, I start to unbutton my blouse, peeling it from my body when the squeak of the door sounds as the door opens.

I pop my head up in surprise to see Conner with stained pants and wide eyes aimed at my exposed lacy white bra a second too long before he finally looks up to meet my eyes.

I don't cover up, because it wasn't like I was topless exactly, I still had a bra on. Besides, he's seen it all before, so why bother being coy now?

He slaps his hand over his eyes, shutting the door behind him. "Oh shit! I'm sorry. They told me to walk in and I just thought—" As he scrambles through the room, his foot catches on one of the chairs for companions, sending him sailing to the floor face-first. "Fuck."

I can't help but laugh as I shuffle over to him. "What the hell are you doing?"

I pull him by the arm until he is standing, his eyes still covered. He shrugs, "I don't know. Protecting your modesty? Giving you privacy? You were getting undressed."

I smile, shaking my head as I go back to the bed, pulling the gown on, leaving my panties on while he stands by the door awkwardly. "First of all, don't you think my modesty flew out the window when you and I had sex? You've seen everything, so the jig is up."

"I don't think I saw everything. It *was* dark." He mumbles, but I continue.

"And there will be no privacy after this, considering a human being is going to come sprouting out of my vagina with a whole room of people watching the show."

His face scrunches, "Thanks for the visual."

"Just being honest." I say, hopping up on the reclining bed chair, my feet dangling off the side, making me feel small.

"Okay, I think you're safe now."

He drops his hand, raising an eyebrow at me in my paper gown, which still doesn't cover much in my opinion, leaving the back exposed but he can't see that from where he is standing. He looks me up and down until a small smile pulls at the corners of his lips and I point my finger at him.

"Don't you dare laugh." I warn him, with a promise of pain in my eyes.

But his smile doesn't go, it just grows into an amused grin when he gives me a single nod. "Nice." Is all he says, and I look down at the suspicious dark stain around the crotch of his pants and I smile back.

"You too." I can't help but chuckle a little when he groans at the stain, shaking his head.

The lightness of the room shatters when the door opens behind Conner and a tall thin woman with a white coat and blonde hair pulled back in a tight bun and big blue eyes taking up most of her face, enters the room. Her eyes bounce between us, amusement in them as she closes the door behind her, a clipboard held in one arm.

"Good to know you guys are having fun." She smiles at us, making her way to me. "Ava Daniels?"

"Yes," I stammer out, feeling the nerves return as reality sets in with the presence of this doctor with her official clipboard.

Her smile widens and her eyes soften. "Nice to meet you, my name is Dr. Hardman."

A FEW QUESTIONS later and she asks me to lay down on the bed, my legs still clenched as I feel my bladder screaming for mercy.

"This will be a bit cold," she says a second before squirting some clear gel on my belly, and she was right, it was cold, making me jump in surprise despite the warning.

My reaction makes her smile, which she always seems to be doing. It was nice at first but now it was just starting to be creepy. I look over at Conner, who stands beside me, and I can tell by the look on his face that I wasn't the only one to think so.

I clench my fists at my sides and bite my lip when she starts pressing into my stomach with this contraption, rolling it around and pressing it down into my poor bladder. She wasn't even watching me, but her eyes were on the screen beside us where I saw blobs of gray and black I couldn't make out.

I search the screen for anything but only see blobs. For a second, I start to think maybe I'm not pregnant. Maybe it was all a mistake. I should be happy with that thought but a small part I won't admit out loud is really sad at that idea.

"It's still early," the doctor says, still not looking at me. "But here it is." She points to a small blob on the screen I can just barely see. I feel Conner lean in beside me, looking at the same blob I am.

Blobby.

"Is he okay?" I ask before I think and the doctor finally looks at me.

She nods. "I see no sign of any problems, but considering you are still early, we need to monitor you closely over the next several weeks."

I nod, still looking at the blob.

"I'll go print your picture." A knowing smile appears on her lips. "You're looking very uncomfortable, why don't you go to the bathroom—"

I'm out of there before she can finish that sentence, hearing their laughter behind me as I sprint in my backless paper gown without any care in the world except for where the fuck the bathroom is.

The doctor is gone when I return, tucking my hair behind my ear I glare when I see Conner's laughing smile aimed at me as he stands by the bed with his hands buried in the pockets of his jeans.

"Better?"

I don't even answer him. Instead, I just walk to where my clothes are bundled on a chair nearby. Conner doesn't close his eyes this time when I remove my gown, but he just turns away, pretending to read from the baby diagram on the wall behind him.

Quickly pulling on my jeans and blouse, I ask him. "How do you feel?"

"What do you mean?"

I shrug even though he can't see me. "You just saw your kid. Is it real for you now? Does it scare you?"

He doesn't hesitate before he answers, "It was always real for me, Ava. But yeah, it does scare me. But mostly because I'm scared I'm going to screw this up."

I smile a small smile, feeling some comfort in that knowledge in a weird way. I exhale a relieved breath. "Me too. I should be reading the baby books or joining mother groups to learn all this shit because I have no idea what I am doing either."

"We will just figure it out together. And if we screw up, we do it together."

I laugh. "That poor kid has no idea what it's gotten itself into."

I finish doing up the last button of my jeans when the door opens, signaling the return of the doctor with yet another clipboard or maybe the same one. I can't help but wonder if that's the reason some people go to medical school, just to wear a white coat and carry a clipboard, but I very much doubt it. I almost want to laugh at the idea.

Dr. Hardman signals for us to sit down and she takes the seat across from us, giving us each a smile of pearly white teeth. "Well, congratulations on your first pregnancy. I am honored to be able to experience this with you." She hands me a small square of paper, the picture. "Here is the picture of your baby. Feel free to stick that on the fridge and show all your friends."

Conner and I both look at the picture in my hands, seeing blobby, my heart warms at knowing this kid is a part of me, that my body is helping it grow and protecting it. I give the picture a soft smile as reality sets in that I am a mom.

Before any panic can set in, the doctor sits forward in her chair, tucking the clipboard on her lap. "Now, Miss Daniels, do you take vitamins?"

I shake my head, feeling silently judged as I did so.

The doctor nods, writing something down before looking back up at me. "What kind of birth are you thinking of having? Have you thought of attending Lamaze classes? You can meet a lot of people there that may help during this journey."

All the questions jumble together in my head, making me

break out in a sweat at all the unanswered questions I have to consider now.

Seeing the panic on my face, Conner's hand takes hold of mine, giving it a comforting squeeze. "We haven't really thought about it yet. This is all still new to us." He explains, sounding more calm than I feel.

Am I already screwing this up?

I expect the doctor to tell me I shouldn't even be having this baby if I can't answer some of the big questions, like I had failed some kind of test but instead, she nods. Her smile softens in understanding. "I thought that may be the case. Don't worry, it's very common. Pregnancy is very overwhelming on its own, then add in the extras and its crazy."

She laughs to herself as she pulls some pamphlets from her clipboard, handing them to me and Conner. "Why don't you read through some of these when you get a chance. Maybe start thinking about what is best for you and the baby," she says, already jotting down notes on her clipboard again.

Pregnancy and drugs

Think Bigger

Pregnancy and alcohol

I hand my bundle to Conner, not wanting to think about these things yet, at least not until I'm home away from the watchful eyes of this doctor.

Without looking up from her clipboard, Dr. Hardman says, "So, everything looks good." She smiles up at me. "Your baby is healthy, though I recommend you start taking some prenatal vitamins. Come back to see me in four weeks so we can see how you and the baby are doing."

Honestly, I wish I could go without, but considering she is the one who knows about all this, I guess I'll have to see her. I don't have a problem with her, just the fact that I have to go to the doctor's office. It's not my favorite place in the world, but I don't say that. Instead, I nod with a forced smile and Conner chimes in with a big smile. "We will be here with bells on." Making the doctor laugh.

Neither of us really want to go home. We're still buzzed from the ultrasound and everything we've seen and heard, how real it is all becoming.

Now we sit in our usual booth at Deb's Diner, busier than the other night but not so crazy we couldn't hear ourselves think. Students and waitresses bustle past our table while we both dig into our food.

Conner devours his burger in seconds, whereas I pick at my cheese fries, eating slowly. Still too busy looking at the picture that sits by my plate, hidden from passersby.

The silence lingers for a few seconds until Conner speaks, "How do you feel?"

That was the question, wasn't it? But how do I answer that? How do I feel?

I shrug, not knowing what else to do. It all just feels so surreal sitting here and looking down at a picture of the baby that is living inside of me, that was created by Conner and me. Looking at this picture, it's hard to see what Conner and I did as a mistake… even though it was.

Feeling his eyes on me, our food forgotten, I ask, "And you?"

"Strange. But good, you know?" he answers, nodding to himself as he mulls over his answer.

I nod back. "Yeah, I understand. Me too."

"I mean, not too long ago you hated me," he comments and the grin on his face makes me want to smile and slap him all at once.

"Who says I still don't?" I raise a brow at him, which only makes his grin grow.

"Because you are still here with me. I doubt you would let someone you hated help raise a baby."

"What if it was for the benefit of the baby?"

"There's nothing beneficial about parents who hate each other. Which means just one thing."

I wait. "Which is…?"

He simply reaches over and takes a fry from my plate and pops it in his mouth, chewing around his smile as he states confidently. "It means you actually like me."

I scoff, but can't find any words as I feel the weight of his blue eyes on me, making me shift in my seat as I feel the possibility of his words on my chest.

He raises his brows. "Am I wrong, Ava?"

Just as I feel the sudden urge to jump out of the window, I hear the familiar ding of a message going off in Conner's pants, giving me an out.

Without a word, Conner takes his phone out and reads the text and sighs, disappointed.

I cock my head. "Bad news?"

Tucking his phone back, he says, "No, it's just Vivian."

Who the fuck is Vivian? Why have I not heard of her before? And where did this sudden anger come from? I work as hard as I can to keep a small smile on my face as I inquire, "Vivian? Is she a girlfriend?"

He laughs. "No, I don't have one. She's just a girl in a lot of my classes. We have a study group and we help each other with studying and stuff."

And stuff? Stop it, Ava! He's not yours, you haven't claimed him so he's fair game… even though you are having his baby, but he's still not yours.

"What did she want?" I ask, playing with my plate of fries.

"Asking me what I'm doing tonight. If I want to study."

"And what are you going to do?"

He simply watches me, mulling something over in his mind before he offers me a small soft smile. "I told her I've got plans texting my baby momma." He gives me a wink and I almost want to fist bump.

I hate the gleeful feeling I have blooming in my chest, but I also can't help the smile I have pulling at my lips. I bite my lip which only makes Conner's eyes go there, the look in them changing, almost getting heated and there was something familiar about that look. Did he look at me like that when we...?

Before I can even contemplate that, his phone goes off again, and again, and again until he growls in irritation and pulls his phone out again.

Judging by how much his phone was going off, I would guess that it was Vivian and that she wasn't happy about his plans not involving her, which makes me think she definitely wanted more with him.

Something about that boiled my blood and caused a churning in my stomach, something different than the usual nausea. I bite my lip again as he reads his phone. "Vivian?" I ask, shifting in my seat again.

Looking up at me as he quickly types out a response. "Yeah, she's stressing about a test coming up."

I can't help the snark from entering my voice when I comment, "So she can't function without you?"

His head pops up, alert as he stuffs his phone back into his pocket, hopefully for good. I shift in my seat under his watchful eyes again until a small smile tugs at the corners of his mouth, amusement dancing in his blue eyes. "Is that jealousy I'm detecting?"

"No!" I say too quickly which only makes his smile grow.

"You know what, I think you like me."

I narrow my eyes. "And I think you're stupid."

He laughs, shaking his head before leveling me with a soft, genuine look that silences me and relaxes me all at once before reaching over the table to place his hand over mine, resting near our baby picture.

My breath hitches at the warmth of his touch and the sight of his hand on mine near our baby photo. Together. I internally slap myself, forcing myself to breathe when I finally meet his eyes.

I need to get a hold of myself. This situation is already a mess and we don't need to make it worse.

"I can promise you, you have nothing to worry about, Ava. I'm all in with this. Hopefully one day you'll see that."

CHAPTER 12

AVA

It's hard to get Conner's words out of my head, like a song I can't forget. In a loop over and over again they run as I tap my fingers on the front desk at work, my eyes scanning around the vacant bookstore and I can't help but wonder how this place stays afloat. I rarely see people come in here.

I try to busy myself with whatever I find on the desk and quickly get bored. Oh well, I'm getting paid to do this either way but I do miss my late-night chats with Harper as we stack shelves.

My back stiffens as the bell at the door goes off, signaling a customer, and I instantly paste a smile on my face only for it to be wiped away a second later when I see who it is. "Oh, it's just you."

Hunter's eyes widen for a second before a grin takes over his face as he approaches the desk. "Is that how you greet all your customers? I can understand the ghost town now."

Rolling my eyes, I say, "And what are you doing here? Come to say hi?"

I raise my brows as he gives me a chuckle.

"No, I'm just here for a book."

Since when? "What book?" I casually lean forward, noticing his strange behavior as he shifts his feet and constantly chuckles. Now I know I'm not that funny.

"Just one for class."

"What class?"

"Hey, I thought you weren't working tonight." Hunter changes the subject and that's when I know something is going on and that he doesn't want to tell me. Normally I'd pry but Hunter has covered for me lots of times in the past and it's because of that, I kind of owe him one, so I just sigh, letting him have his thing and answer his question, "I got called in for a few hours."

"Oh, okay." He rubs the back of his neck while casting furtive glances at the shelves of books and I can't help but think that maybe he does just want a book. But I also doubt it, so with a final smile I tell him, "You have a good night, and I hope you find what you're looking for."

His eyes widen. "What?"

"The book?" I clarify, my brow creasing as he laughs off his reaction but he is just acting weird these days. Before I can give it much thought, he makes his way among the shelves and my phone vibrates in my back pocket, signaling a text.

It doesn't take a rocket scientist to know who would be texting. I only get texts from a few people and I know Mia is at a concert tonight and will not be messaging me, Harper and Hunter are here, Lucy is at a friend's place and we talked earlier and so that leaves….

Conner's name stares back at me from the home screen and my heart warms at the memory of what he said at lunch last week. *You have nothing to worry about.* God, I wish that were true but there was so much to worry about, like the baby and how we are going to do this together and not be together. I know Conner wants to be with me but I don't know if it's just because of the baby or me and I'm terrified if we just base a relationship around a baby then what happens when that baby leaves and goes to college? It's just all a mess I need to sort out.

My phone vibrates in my hand, signaling another message.

Conner: Hey

Conner: You wanna come over? We're having a movie night.

Me: We?

Conner: Me and Logan. Hunter ditched. So, you in?

How romantic, I think to myself as I text back.

Me: Tempting but I'm at work.

Conner: *Angry Face

Me: *Annoyed Face

Conner: *Flirting Face

Me: Oh, stop that!

Conner: Hey, you started it.

Me: No, I didn't, you did!

Conner: You may be right. So, you're not lifting anything heavy, are you? They're not pushing you too hard?

Me: I'm standing behind a counter.

Conner: Good, though I'd like you better on the counter ;)

A rush of heat hits me between my legs at the imagery that enters my mind and I am all too aware of how warm the room has gotten. I should put my phone away. I shouldn't encourage it but my traitorous fingers seem to have a mind of their own as I text him back, a small devious smile curling the corners of my mouth.

Me: That's it? That's all you got? I expected better.

Conner: Are you goading me, little lamb?

Me: Stop calling me that, and yes I am goading you.

Conner: You couldn't handle it.

Me: Try me.

He doesn't respond and I instantly regret encouraging him. Maybe I shouldn't have pushed, maybe he wasn't serious and it was all a joke I took too far.

My brain is in a loop and I don't even know if Hunter is still here or left during my sexting conversation. I can't see anyone in the isle when I go to check, so I assume he didn't find what he was after.

When I return to the front desk, it isn't vacant.

My heart stops and my steps falter as I begin to run my eyes over the tall length of Conner's lean body as he leans his forearms casually on the front counter, picking at some chipped paint until he finally sees me, a slow, sexy smile, a smile so different to the others I've seen, spreads across his face as he stands to face me.

I take in his piercing blue eyes that call for attention and his hair that's a little longer on the top now, looking windswept as he starts to look me up and down in my uniform of a purple polo and black leggings with my hair pulled back in another messy bun.

I force my legs to move, carrying me forward to the other side of the counter until I'm looking at him. "Hey, what are you doing here?"

He shrugs, his eyes never leaving mine. "You said to 'try me'. I've come to collect." He starts to move, his hand gliding along the surface of the counter as he takes small steps around to my side.

"What are you talking about? What are you doing?" My voice is shaky as I start to backstep away, keeping the counter between us because I worry about what will happen once it is no longer there. More worried about what I will do.

"You shouldn't goad me, Ava." His voice is threatening but teasing all at once and it only makes me want to goad him more.

"And why is that?"

We finally stop, me standing on my side and him on his, his eyes constantly on mine and I hold my breath as he leans in enough for me to smell the mint on his breath. His hand comes down on mine on the counter and I almost expect him to grab it and kiss me, maybe I'm hoping he will, but instead he just holds my gaze, giving my hand a gentle squeeze as he whispers. "Because I will be more than happy to bend you over this counter and punish you."

I think I swallow my tongue and blink in surprise at his words. "How would you do that?" I whisper with numb lips.

He leans closer until he is in kissing distance, his eyes moving from my mouth to my eyes, showing me that he notices the same thing. He probably planned it that way, the fucker.

He rubs his thumb over the back of my hand. "First, I would stand behind you until I have your ass against my cock, until you can feel how hard I am through my pants. I'd kiss your neck, maybe right here." He touches with the lightest of touches the spot where my neck meets my shoulder, causing a shiver to run down my spine before he continues, "Then I'd move my hand down inside your pants so I can feel how wet you are. I will keep fucking you with my fingers, until you are on the brink. And only then will I stop."

A tiny moan slips past my lips and I watch as his eyes heat and move from my mouth to my eyes, and for a moment it is just us. No outside world and no baby. It's just a guy wanting to be with a girl.

The image that evolves in my head is shattered by the sound of someone clearing they're throat off to the side and I finally suck in a gasp of air when I see Helen, my manager, standing there, her eyes narrowing into slits as they move between Conner and I.

My wide eyes move back to Conner, ripping my hand

from his and taking a step back from the counter. As if that doesn't make me look guilty, and I'm just waiting to be fired for getting hot and bothered on the job.

But that doesn't happen.

Instead this does...

"So yes, I'll just be getting this book." Conner announces loud enough for my boss to hear before sliding a thin picture book across the counter.

I cock my head at the book and have to bite my lip to keep from laughing at his choice.

'Where Did I Come From?'

It was a plain white book with a cartoon stork and a cartoon baby hanging out of the 'O'. Grabbing the book, I continue to bite my lip as I feel my boss approach close enough to peek at the cover.

"Interesting choice," I comment, feeling the weight of my boss's suspecting gaze before she finally huffs and moves away. Close enough to still keep an eye on us but not close enough to hear us.

As I ring up his purchase, I look up at him through my lashes only to see him grinning back at me, the heat is gone now, replaced with his usual look of playful mischievousness. "Your parents never told you about the birds and the bees?"

He shrugs. "It's never too late to learn something new."

I scoff. "Our unborn baby may disagree with you."

"Don't hate. And remember it takes two to tango."

"And that's something you know. Maybe next time you can remember the condom."

"I did. But it must've broken."

I furrow my brow as a thought occurs to me.

"Wait, then how do you know the baby is yours?"

His own brows furrow. "What?"

"I could be a slut and you wouldn't know it. You just

believed it was yours when I told you, knowing you were using a condom. How were you sure?"

He regards me with a thoughtful expression before he finally sighs. "I knew you weren't a slut because that was your first time."

I blink, replaying his words in my head and thinking I misheard him. "What are you talking about?"

"There was blood on the bed after. Not enough to be your period, so..." He shrugs before continuing. "You were also really fucking tight."

I'm speechless. I don't know how to feel. Yes, I'm angry I never got to really experience losing my virginity, that I don't remember it. But by now, it's something I've moved past, but to hear that Conner knew and that I was drunk and he still did it.

It breaks my heart yet pisses me off all at once.

As if reading my thoughts, he raises his hands in surrender. "I didn't know for sure until after I saw the blood." He pauses, looking at me, his eyes going soft. "I can't regret that night completely because then we wouldn't be here and our baby wouldn't be here. It wasn't planned, but I wouldn't wish our baby away. But I do regret that you didn't get the first time you deserve. I can't turn back time and redo it, but I can make sure the next time is the first time you deserved."

My stupid emotions have tears fighting to pour out of my eyes until I bite my lip, itching to hear those words again. How can I be angry at a person and want to kiss them all at once? This baby is turning my emotions into a roller coaster ride I can't get off. But even though his words are beautiful, I know that I can't let there be a next time, even though that's all my body wants.

I straighten my back, looking Conner in the eyes when I say, "There won't be a next time, Conner."

He laughs at this, shaking his head. “Oh there will be. But don’t worry, it won’t happen until you ask for it.”

“That’s good because that will never happen.”

He laughs again. “Never say never, Ava.”

My feet are killing me by the time I get home from work that night.

I almost cry when I kick off my shoes in exchange for some white fluffy slippers by the door.

I check the time and know I still have a few minutes to change so I make my way to my bedroom, putting my laptop on my bed so it’s ready for me as I put on an oversized shirt and men’s boxers. Not so sexy but very comfortable. I’m pulling my hair up in a messy bun when the laptop screen lights up right on time.

Plopping myself down on the bed, I’m smiling at the screen as I answer the Skype call.

My sister’s sweet smile fills the screen as she eagerly waves at me. “Hey!!”

“Hey.” I laugh, waving back but not as enthusiastically.

“Okay, stand up. Let me see.”

I smile, standing from the bed and rotating to the side I pull the shirt tighter around my stomach so she can see the tiny bump that’s been forming over the last month.

She squeals, making my ears ring from the other side of town. “I’m going to be an aunty!” She claps to herself. “How are you feeling?”

I plop myself back down on the bed, shaking my head. “You know, everyone has been asking me that.”

“Well, you are carrying another person inside of you. It’s kind of a big deal.”

“Yeah, but before this Conner barely spoke to me. A few

flirtatious comments there, some smart-ass remarks here. But now, it's like he's playing daddy."

"So he should."

I roll my eyes. "But I don't want him to be nice to me just because of the baby."

Lucy smiles a knowing smile. "But you want him to be nice because he likes you."

"I don't want him to like me!" I say too loudly, pointing my finger at the screen which only makes Lucy's smile grow.

"I didn't say you did. I just said you would rather that be the motivation for how he's acting, not because of any obligation of him being a father."

I mentally kick myself as the silence hangs between us, feeling Lucy's watchful eyes on me as I pick at the linen on my bedsheets.

"It's okay to feel something, Ava."

"All I feel is confusion. He's only hanging out with me because we have a baby." I pause. "And I'm making sure it doesn't go further."

Lucy does a double take, blinking in confusion. "What? Why?"

I shrug, feeling defeated. "Because then we can't be forced into a relationship of circumstance. This way he can have his life and I won't be resented and neither will the baby."

"I see where you're coming from, but you're being stupid."

"What?"

"Your argument is all based on 'what if'. What does he think about it?"

I shrug again. "He doesn't say anything."

"That doesn't answer my question."

It's true, it doesn't answer many of mine either but this is how I've chosen to do this. To protect my baby and me and in some way, Conner.

"What if he meets someone else? If you don't lock that down—"

"I know!" I exclaim, the pain of what I already know burning in my chest, but how can I take a leap based on something that may only be there because of the baby and what happens when that baby grows up and leaves? Will he stay?

I run my hand through my hair when I speak again, my sister is quiet on the other end. "He's probably already met someone. There's this girl in his class and she always asks to study with him." I clench my fists as I think of her name.

Vivian.

But who am I to be jealous? Like Lucy said, I haven't locked that down.

"Is he interested?"

"I don't know. He doesn't seem to think anything of it but that could be a lie."

Lucy shrugs. "Could be. But would he be spending so much time with you, if he was interested in someone else?"

"If he felt obligated, maybe."

Lucy growls in frustration. "You are so stubborn!"

A TEXT WAKES me around two a.m. and I silently curse the sender as I roll over, checking my phone, so the luminous light shines around my dark room.

Mia: Hey! Any chance I can crash at yours tonight?

Me: Where are you?

Mia: I may have had too much to drink. I'm near your place. I just don't want to Uber home. And I haven't seen you in Forrreevverr!!!

I roll my eyes.

Me: Hard to argue with that logic. Come on over.

Mia: <3 <3 <3

I quickly fluff the pillows from both sides and decide to get another blanket from the closet. If Mia is going to be staying here, we will need it. Ever since we were kids having sleepovers, she would always hog the blankets until we learned the brilliance of having two blankets. Life changing!

I walk my way out into the hall, pulling open the closet door and seeing the blankets stacked on the top shelf. Always the way!

After a long exhale, I tuck my foot into one of the other shelves, holding the top shelf and using it to pull myself up until I am at eye level with the desired blankets.

I let go with one hand, in hopes of reaching over to grab the blanket enough to pull it down, but instead my one hand gripping the shelving slips, sending me sailing backward before I can gather any footing or reach with my other hand. The blankets just get further and further away as I fall with my last thought being of the baby in my stomach before it goes black.

How could I have been so stupid?!

CHAPTER 13

CONNER

My heart is beating out of my chest, my hands shaking as they clench into fists in my lap.

"What else did Mia say?" I demand, feeling the sweat on my forehead as I stare at Hunter, waiting for any kind of answer for what the hell happened and how the fuck Ava ended up in the hospital but Hunter's focus was on the dark winding road in front of him as he raced through back-streets, dodging late-night traffic in hope of getting us to the hospital before I break my way out of his car.

I reach up to grip the handle above my head when he answers, "Just that Ava was unconscious. She came in and saw her on the floor unconscious and she called the ambulance. I haven't heard anything since."

I check both of our phones for an update. Nothing.

Tucking my phone in my pocket, I perk up a bit when I see the lights of the hospital in sight. I'm almost there, Ava.

I don't even wait for the car to stop when I kick open the door, tripping over my feet briefly until I am sprinting toward the hospital entrance. I hear Hunter's heavy footfalls as he runs after me, quickly catching up with his long legs.

The automatic doors open to a waiting room with a few patients already waiting but I pay them no mind as I focus my gaze on the small lady behind the reception counter, a look of nervous uncertainty crosses her petite features as I approach, I suspect I look like a crazy person.

Slamming my hand on the counter, making her jump, I demand. "I'm here to see Ava Daniels. She was admitted tonight."

"Me too." I hear a familiar voice with a husky edge to it beside me, feeling the warmth of someone standing close I turn.

I furrow my brow, looking over to see one of Ava's friends. I think her name is Harper. I instantly feel guilty for not being sure of her name but that was an issue for another time. Right now, I have to get to Ava, to my baby, if I still had one. My chest aches so bad at the thought that I wince. I shake my head trying to rid myself of the thought, focusing back on the lady with her gaze dancing between us only to widen more when a giant Hunter turns up at my back.

"Um, are you family?" she stutters, her eyes still wide as she shakes, resembling a Chihuahua.

"She's the mother of my child."

"So you're her husband?" she asks with raised expectant eyebrows and I want to sink to the floor in a mix of frustration and defeat.

I open my mouth only to be cut off by a small hand on my arm, giving it a gentle pat. "Of course he is," Harper says in a high-pitched voice that sounds overly peppy.

I freeze but try to school my features, seeing the disbelief on the lady's face when she glances down at the hand still on the counter in front of her. No ring.

Fuck.

Hunter sees this and chimes in with a laugh. "They don't

believe in the whole rings thing. They are scheduled to get their rings tattooed, saying they are forever." I can almost see Hunter shake his head as he laughs behind me, slapping his hand on my tense shoulder and giving it an encouraging squeeze.

"How cute is that?" Harper beams a cheesy smile at the lady but I see the disbelief still there, until her gaze softens when she looks back at me.

After a few seconds that feel like forever, she expels a long breath before saying in a voice so small I almost don't hear her.

"Down the hall, fifth room to the left."

I don't waste another second before I'm rushing past doctors, nurses and patients to get to the room with the door already open for me, feeling the other two right behind me as I walk through the door.

At first I see Mia sitting beside the bed, biting the nails of her free hand, the nervous worry tensing her petite features. Her small hand resting on the bed and holding tightly to Ava's hand as she lay reclined in the hospital bed. Dark circles prominent under her eyes but otherwise, she looked like herself. My eyes do a quick scan of her and I see no visible damage which makes my shoulders sag with such relief I thought I'd fall to the ground, but I gain my footing when I see who she's speaking to and who everyone else is looking at.

The doctor.

He was an older man, looking close to being a grandfather with his big thick-rimmed glasses, lines marking his face and short gray hair. But the presence he held in the room showed one of strength and surety which was comforting considering he was handling my girl… I mean, the mother of my baby.

I furrow my brow at him when he pauses in what he was

saying to the girls, everyone now turning to see me standing as a sweaty mess.

I shuffle my feet where I stand, met with looks of confusion, but it was the doctor that speaks first.

"Can I help you?"

Before I can speak, Ava pipes in first, her eyes focus on me with a mix of confusion and annoyance. "He's the father."

I watch as the doctor's expression shifts, creased with confusion only to smooth out with light happy eyes and a wide welcoming smile as he moves from his place by Ava to extend his hand to me. "I'm Dr. Kowalski, glad to meet you." I shake his hand, cautious. "I was just telling your wife—"

"We are not married," Ava says loud enough for the whole room to hear, shocking the doctor at first, but the look on her face and the message it conveys cannot be mistaken. *We fucked and accidentally ended up pregnant and I just so happen to be the father.*

The message stings a bit but I push it aside, following the doctor back to where Ava is lying, both of us standing by her bed.

"How is she?" I ask, crossing my arms over my chest.

At first the doctor doesn't answer. Instead he looks at Ava until she gives a small tentative nod, her eyes going to the free hand in her lap. Only then does he tell me.

I quench the irritation at not being able to know what's going on with my own kid just because we are not married. It's the twenty-first century, damnit!

My jaw is clenched when Dr. Kowalski finally turns to me. "Your *friend* had a fall. No major damage, but she knocked her head pretty good. We're monitoring that though."

"And the baby?"

"Is perfectly fine." The three hundred pound weight sitting on my chest finally eases, allowing me to breathe. "It was lucky that your friend turned up when she did," he says, nodding his head toward Mia who gives a small smile which doesn't reach her eyes.

I can't help the anger that starts to bubble, anger at Ava, at the doctor and anger at myself for not being there. My arms still crossed over my chest, I furrow my brow at Ava, seeing a hint of guilt and irritation living there as she looks back at me. "What were you doing?"

"What?"

"When you fell?"

She doesn't answer at first. I see Mia squeeze Ava's hand in silent support as she was about to speak up but Ava's irritated and defensive tone interrupts her as she glares at me. "What does it matter? I fell, but I'm fine, the baby is fine."

The weight crushing my heart finally eases at this, when I ask the doctor, "So when can she come home?"

He hesitates. "I'd like to keep Ava overnight."

"But I thought you said she was fine?"

"Just as a precaution." He waves on my concern.

"Can we not talk about me like I'm not here?" Ava huffs from where she sits, which only makes the doctor smile.

"Sorry, but I would recommend you not be left alone. If something were to happen, I'd recommend you have someone with you."

Mia offers a small smile, raising her hand for a second before dropping it back down to Ava's hand on the bed. "I'll stay with her." She says, giving Ava's hand another squeeze and I can't help the words that come out of my mouth.

"Like hell you are." I don't mean to sound so harsh and I can feel the tension grow within the room with those words but there is a strong part of me that just needs to keep an eye on Ava and my baby. Not that I didn't trust Mia, I've never had a problem with her that I know of, but that is my kid and the rules are changing. I can feel it.

"Dude."

"Excuse me?"

Both Mia and Hunter sound their disapproval, not realizing Hunter was standing behind me. Mia sounding hurt and insulted, while Hunter remains a mix of shock and defense of his sister, but I focus on Ava's shocked expression which morphs back into a glare.

The doctor's laugh breaks a fraction of the tension, sounding a bit like that doctor from *The Simpsons*. "Aren't you popular?" he says to Ava but she doesn't acknowledge him. "Well, I'll leave you all to sort it out." With a final smile, he leaves.

Not a second later, Mia pipes in, "What makes you think I can't take care of my friend?"

Ava speaks, drawing the attention of everyone in the room. "What makes everyone think I need a babysitter? I am perfectly capable of taking care of myself. I just fell, and it was one time."

I take a step closer to the bed. "But you aren't taking care of just yourself anymore. You have a baby to think about."

Ava only laughs a humorless laugh, rolling her eyes before looking back at me. "You think I don't know that? It's kind of getting harder to miss these days."

As she gestures to the small bump on her belly, hidden by the unflattering hospital gown, I know how right she is. She is getting bigger and a part of me really likes seeing it, knowing that's mine in there. It almost gives me a sense of pride and something else I can't pinpoint yet. But it also makes me aware of how delicate she will become in the coming months and she needs to understand that I need to be there.

I get closer, standing by the bed now opposite an annoyed Mia as she stands also, as if we are preparing for a tug of war of sorts but I focus on Ava as she looks up at me. I don't even hesitate when I say my next words. "Stay with me."

"What?" All four people say the same thing in unison, in matching tones of surprise.

"Stay with me. That way I can keep an eye on you and the baby."

She's already shaking her head, her eyes moving over the room. "I'm not having you babysit me."

I shrug. "Be smart about this. It won't be just me and you. Both the guys will be there and you know they will do anything for you. Strength in numbers." I point behind me, indicating Hunter, one of the said boys.

Her voice is small now, I see her reserve wavering. "I can take care of myself."

"I know. We all know you can, but sometimes it's good to accept some help, especially when it's not just you."

At that, I watch as she places her free hand over her belly, pausing in thought when Mia gives her other hand a squeeze, grabbing her attention.

"Hon, it's a good idea." She gives me a brief annoyed glare telling me I'm still not forgiven for what I said earlier, before looking back at Ava. "I can only do so much, whereas there you will always have someone there to help you. You have to think about the babe now. We know you can take care of yourself. You are so strong." Ava chuckles for a second. "But asking for help doesn't make you weak either. It's up to you but I think you should take the help."

Ava exhales a slow breath, raising her eyes to meet mine, defenses down. "Where would I sleep?"

It wasn't a yes, but it was pretty close and I can't help the small smile that comes through. "I'll sleep on the couch. You can have my room. It has its own bathroom so that will be yours."

She thinks it over a moment before giving a small nod. "Fine, but only until the baby arrives."

I wasn't too thrilled about the last part but I had time to change her mind. I'll deal with it later.

Hunter steps forward with a smile, leaning down to place a small kiss on Ava's forehead. "Happy to know everything is okay." Harper stands awkwardly behind him, awaiting her turn. "It's going to be good having a lady in the house. It might help everyone learn to behave themselves." He offers a wide grin, making Mia scoff.

"You are just as bad as the rest, so don't play innocent."

He places his hand over his chest. "You wound me."

Mia shakes her head before returning her focus back to Ava. "I'll take you back to your apartment to gather up some stuff in the morning. We can plan when to start moving you in."

Hunter pipes in, walking over to me, slapping a hand on my shoulder. "And I'll take this one home so we can get the place ready for you."

I didn't want to leave, but I also didn't want to push my luck.

* * *

"Dude, you need to calm down," Hunter says, raising his hands with his palms out as if I was a wild animal about to attack which only made my irritation grow.

Running my hands through my hair, wanting to squeeze some of the stress out of my head, I growl back, "How can I calm down when this place looks like a dump?! I told you guys to try and keep it clean!"

"Bro, why are you stressing?" Logan walks into the kitchen, piles of dirty dishes are in the sink from just today and a jam covered knife is sitting on the counter. Logan looks at me, confused and a little worried as he stands near Hunter.

Hunter inclines his head to Logan and whispers loud enough for me to hear. "Ava's coming today."

He says this with a slight tilt to the corner of his mouth, his eyes going from Logan to myself as I stand fuming in the center of the kitchen.

"Ooohh! That's today?" Logan exclaims, slapping his hand over his forehead and wearing a look of shock as the information registers.

I give him a tight smile that doesn't meet my eyes. "Yes, that is why I'm standing in the middle of a messy kitchen. A kitchen I cleaned before I left for class this morning."

Logan's brows furrowed. "Bro, it's just Ava. She's seen the place look worse than this."

"But she wasn't living in it!" I exclaim.

"Dude, everything will be fine." Hunter comes around to me, moving a little slowly to be cautious I'm sure but slaps a big hand on my tense shoulder and gives it a reassuring squeeze. "You go upstairs, get your shit sorted up there." I open my mouth to object but he speaks over me. "And we will focus down here. It'll be sparkling," he assures me, gesturing at Logan who now frowns in disapproval, obviously not wanting to be stuck on clean-up duty but he doesn't say anything.

After a few deep breaths, I hurry upstairs, knowing I haven't got much time until Ava will be here.

It's been a week since her accident, but other than that, everything has been fine, even though I wanted her to come straight here, we agreed—she said—that she would need time to get her things in order so she took a week and now here we are, rushing to clean so Ava doesn't think I'm completely irresponsible and that I can't take care of a house. But to be fair, a baby is one thing, a house of college dudes is a whole other universe.

I'm hanging clean towels in my bathroom for her when I hear Hunter call for me downstairs. A glance at the time and I know either Ava was here or something bad happened to the house. I was hoping for door number one.

I sprint down the stairs, almost tripping a couple of times when I am met with Ava's voice. It's light but not airy, almost effortless to listen to. I never really noticed it before, but it put my nerves at ease hearing it and knowing that she was going to be safe here while pregnant with my baby, our baby. And it only makes my plans for wooing her that much easier.

A warm feeling spreads across my chest and it makes me smile when I hit the last flight of stairs and see her.

She's wearing a light blue sundress, light and willowy around her legs and a small denim jacket. Her dark hair hangs in natural waves down her back and bags line the floor of the entryway.

It takes me a second to shake myself back to the present and realize that Ava is now looking at me, as well as Logan, Hunter and Mia. Each of them wearing smiles conveying different emotions. Hunter is laughing, Logan is confused, as usual, and Mia is curious, catching on to me looking at Ava. However, Ava's smile is tight, showing evidence of displeasure.

I know she doesn't want to come here, that she feels she can do this on her own and she can, but she doesn't have to. I don't want her to. I want her to have someone, hell I want her to have heaps of people there to help if she needs it.

She will see in time that this is best for her, me and the baby.

"Happy?" Ava asks, with an attitude, putting one hand on her hip as she rotates herself to face me more, showing me the small bump on her belly where the dress falls over it. Seeing it makes me grin proudly as I make my way down to them.

"Ecstatic." I comment, picking up one of her bags. "Follow me to your new room." I hear her grumble something I can't make out as we walk up the stairs but my smile stays firm.

CHAPTER 14

AVA

I hate this.

I hate that only at the start of this year I was a college student paying her way through college and hanging out with friends. Now, because I got myself knocked up, I'm now forced to live with the father of my baby because he all of the sudden has become this overprotective pain in my ass.

On the way here, Mia told me just to give this a chance and to think of the positives: I won't be on my own and I won't be living with strangers. All good points but that didn't make this suck any less.

When we finally reach the room, Conner throws open the door and strolls in, effortlessly laying the bag he was carrying on the bed. He turns around to see me still standing in the doorway, unable to enter. My thoughts going back to that night, my foggy memories of when I last went into this room.

My eyes linger on the bed, wondering if we did it just once, was he kind and gentle? Did it hurt? All questions I've wondered since that night, but that's what happens when you don't remember anything about losing your virginity.

A throat clearing pulls me back to the present, drawing my eyes back up to Conner's. He shuffles his feet where he stands, nervous.

He looks down at his feet, putting his hands in his pockets before giving a weak unsure laugh and looking back up at me.

It was kind of cute seeing him like this. Unsure and nervous.

He shrugs. "This is your room. I'll sleep on the couch downstairs."

I finally take a step inside the room. "It's no problem, I can sleep on the couch. I don't wanna kick you out of your room."

"No it's fine. Couch is comfy anyway." Conner moves to stand off to the side, as if sensing I need my space. We stand in awkward silence, the silence feeling so thick in the air we could choke on it. We look at each other for a brief moment before looking away, repeating this a couple more times until a loud bang from the hallway makes us both jump.

Not a second later, the doorway is filled by two massive bodies as Hunter and Logan push each other through the narrow space, stumbling as they make it through, both carrying the rest of my bags. Logan is puffing and glowers at Conner who appears to be back to normal, all nerves gone.

"Why is it we carried three bags each and you only carried one? Where's the equality in this?"

Hunter shakes his head and gives Logan a playful shove. "Pussy." This only makes Logan return the shove with one of his own, one with more force behind it.

"Hey, hey!" Conner gets between the two. "Take it outside." With a final glower at each other, they exit the room both calling over their shoulders to me.

"Glad to have you here, Ava."

"Let us know if you need *anything*." Logan's comment is then followed by a slapping sound and "*ow!*"

Conner shakes his head as he makes his way toward the door, stopping to look over his shoulder. "I'll leave you to get settled. Come down when you're ready."

I give him a nod and after a moment's hesitation, he leaves me in the quiet room where everything started with all my bags to unpack.

CHAPTER 15

CONNER

The pizza guy arrives around seven that night with dinner, boxes piled in his arms so high he had to turn to the side to look at me. After paying the guy, I carry the boxes into the kitchen, making sure to put a plain cheese pizza aside for Ava for whenever she's ready to come down, if she will ever be ready.

She's been here for five hours now and she still hasn't come down yet. I hear the water start running upstairs, signaling her having a shower. At least she was making herself at home, or starting to at least.

It doesn't take long for the stampede to happen and I brace myself, one hand over Ava's pizza and the other hand over my pepperoni, ready for when both guys push past each other, running to the kitchen counter and grabbing whatever box they can get their hands on, tearing open the lids and shoving slices in their mouths like they haven't been fed in days.

Logan groans when he swallows his bite of pizza, sauce coating his mouth as he looks around, noticing someone's missing his brows furrow. "Ava not hungry?"

"She'll be down in a sec," I tell him, still guarding the pizzas.

"Is that why you're protecting those pizzas?" Hunter grins knowingly before taking another bite of pizza.

I narrow my eyes at him and they both begin to laugh at me around their mouthfuls of pizza.

I shake my head at them, but the laughter is suddenly cut short by a distressed squeal coming from upstairs where Ava is. I don't even think; I move faster than I have ever moved in my life. It's Ava and she's still screaming when I reach the stairs taking two at a time, using the banister to pull me up.

I distantly hear the others behind me but my focus is on the path ahead of me. The screaming has stopped when I reach the top of the stairs, running for my room and colliding with a wall of warmth only reaching my nose in height.

Ava is halfway out the door when she finally registers me, her eyes wide and watery in a mix of panic and fear, her breaths come out in heavy pants as her hand holds up the towel currently covering her naked body from view.

I blink, focusing on the situation at hand, placing my hand gently on Ava's warm shoulders trying to calm her. "Hey, hey, Ava. What happened? What's wrong?"

"There's a creature in my bag," she whispers this as if hiding from said creature.

"What kind of creature?"

"It was big with fur and beady eyes."

I want to roll my eyes because that description wasn't really helpful, but I hold it back, knowing it won't help.

Lightly pushing Ava aside, I slowly make my way into the room, asking over my shoulder, "Which bag?"

Before she can answer, rustling sounds emerge from the big suitcase on the far side of the room. The bag is already unzipped but remains closed, the bag rustling as the thing inside moves about its contents.

I was thinking to myself that I should've gotten something to catch it with but I was already at the bag, hand out to lift the top, bracing for what might come out.

Taking a deep breath I flip the top and take a step back expecting to see an eight-legged hairy beast come out, but instead what I find makes me smile.

"Is it still there?" I hear the fear in Ava's voice as I reach down, picking up the creature and turning to face a surprised Ava.

Cuddling the creature that she feared, I smile. It doesn't take long before she realizes what is happening. She narrows her eyes and my smile grows more. "That thing is yours?"

Looking between my furry friend and Ava, I beam. "Ava, I'd like you to meet Rasputin. He's my pet ferret." I come forward with Rasputin and I can tell that Ava wants to step back but she holds her ground, keeping an eye on the ferret in my arms.

She furrows her brow. "Since when do you have a pet ferret. I've never seen him."

"You also haven't been in this room since…" I let that hang in the air, seeing her cheeks go red. "Besides, he usually stays out of sight. Likes small spaces like cupboards, drawers or bags."

Her guard starts to waver as she looks back at Rasputin, his beady eyes watching her, his little nose twitching at her as if trying to get a sense of this new human in his space. "Does he bite?"

I chuckle. "No, he's harmless."

"You wanna deal with me, motherfucker!" Logan shouts as he rushes into the room, baseball bat in his hand, with Hunter coming in behind him with no weapon in sight.

Quickly pulling Ava behind me, I scold them. "What the fuck, dickheads! What do you think you're doing?"

"She screamed," Hunter says like that is answer enough.

"We thought you guys were being attacked or some shit." Logan says defensively, lowering his bat.

"So you were going to save us with a baseball bat?" Ava pauses in her assessment when she looks back at Hunter. "Hunter, you too good for a weapon?"

He merely grins devilishly. "I am the weapon."

Ava and I both roll our eyes when she says, "If there was someone in the house, we" —she gestures to herself and me — "would've been dead already."

I laugh. "Yeah, what took you guys so long?"

They both look equally insulted when Logan raises his bat a little. "I had a little trouble finding my bat."

"Feeling real safe right now," she comments sarcastically, giving me a pointed look.

I meet her stare with one of my own. "I got here and I won't let anything happen to you or the baby." Turning to the guys, I say, "She just got a little spooked when she saw Rasputin. I forgot to tell her about him."

"Aw, you have nothing to worry about with that little guy. He's harmless," Logan offers by way of comfort and she gives him a tight smile.

"Yeah, he's like our mascot," Hunter says with a grin.

"I thought you guys didn't like him," I say, furrowing my brows as I remember them pleading for me to get rid of Rasputin since we moved in. To be fair, we have all been equally spooked by Rasputin a time or two. He must just love to fuck with people.

Hunter rolls his eyes before admitting, "Actually, that was me. But I don't dislike him, I just don't like when he ends up in my drawers and gives me a heart attack in the morning. Nobody needs that kind of wake-up call."

Logan chuckles at this, slapping a hand on Hunter's big shoulder. "What kind of drawers are you talking about, Hunter? Should we worry?"

That only makes Logan laugh more, I merely chuckle and shake my head at the two.

Hunter rolls his eyes. "Oh, grow up, Logan." He growls before walking away, heading back downstairs to the pizza.

"Hey bro, I'm sorry." Logan can't even finish the sentence without his laughter increasing, his face is turning red from lack of oxygen, thus leaving Ava and I alone as he follows after Hunter.

I look down at her, looking smaller in my big room as she clutches her towel to her body, goose bumps starting to dance over her shoulders, making me want to rub them away. I also notice her brows crease in displeasure as she looks at where the guys just were, grumbling. "I've been here for not even a day and already I'm causing trouble."

"How so?"

"I caused a fuss over a ferret, now Hunter is upset and Logan might die of laughter." She inclines her head toward where Hunter and Logan were, where you can still hear one of them laughing.

I tuck my finger under her chin, moving her face to look up at me, looking at her earnestly. "You didn't know about Rasputin. That's on me. Hunter will get over it. He always does and I'm positive he doesn't blame you because this kind of shit happened before you got here. Besides, this is normal behavior for those two." I incline my head to the laughing chorus downstairs.

"It'll just take some getting used to," she says, giving a small shrug, still looking unsure but not as much.

"I'll leave you to get dressed. We've got pizza downstairs and don't worry, I'll take Rasputin with me."

"You don't have to. Take Rasputin, I mean." She stammers, looking nervous.

"You sure?"

She shrugs. "It'll be nice to have the company."

CHAPTER 16

AVA

"Are you sure about this? You seem a little—"

"A little what?" I cut Conner off, lifting my pelvis off the bed to grind against his hardened cock, seeking the relief my body is craving and making Conner hiss.

I watch as he closes his eyes, his jaw hard as he takes in a deep breath before finally opening his eyes above me. "I was going to say drunk. You might regret this in the morning."

"You don't want me?" I continue to grind and bite my lip, making Connor's heated eyes focus there and I slowly lift myself up so I'm leaning back on my elbows, so our faces are so close I can smell the mint on his breath. Enticing.

His eyes never leave my lips as I watch his resolve start to slip. "You know I do."

I lean in a touch closer. "Then what are you waiting for?"

With that, I finally close the distance with a kiss, my hands running through and pulling at Conner's soft hair, my legs locked around his waist pulling him closer, making us both moan into the kiss.

A beautiful pressure was building between my legs and I

heard myself begging him to never stop, just then I spring up in the bed, Conner gone.

I blink the sleep away from my eyes and try to slow my breathing as I take in the dark room and the figure standing in the doorway.

"Conner?" I wipe my eyes as he steps into the light from the window, worry lining his handsome face as he stands in a pair of boxers and a shirt.

"You were moaning."

I blink, thinking I misheard him and hoping I did. "What?"

"I heard you downstairs. I thought you might be in pain, so I came to check on you."

The dream hits me all at once. Conner on top of me, me grinding on him and practically forcing myself on him. I drop my face to hide the blush touching my cheeks at the memory of the dream and how badly I wanted it to be real. But there is no way I will ever say that out loud. "Oh, no I'm fine. I was just having a nightmare," I lie effortlessly with a nonchalant shrug.

"You said my name."

"I did?" I cock my head, trying to hide the internal embarrassment.

He nods.

"Honestly, I don't even remember now." I shrug again, as I watch his scrutinizing gaze move over my face, searching for something as his brows crease in thought.

"Are you okay?"

"Yeah, I'm fine. I'll just go back to sleep." I reiterate this by pulling the blankets up to my chest, and this appears to appease him as he gives me a single nod before leaving and the sad part is… I didn't want him to leave. That dream was so intense, so real that I thought it was. I could smell his breath, I could hear his moans when I was grinding, I felt him and what he did to me. It all felt so real that I can't help but wonder if maybe it was, that maybe it wasn't a dream but a memory. Conner mentioned I was drunk, was this a memory from that night and was this really my fault? Was I pushing myself on Conner?

Just as I felt like I was going to overflow with questions about that night, Conner returns with a pillow and a blanket, throwing them down on the ground by the door.

I raise my brows at this. "What are you doing?"

"I'm sleeping," he says without looking at me as he plops himself on his makeshift bed on the floor.

"I thought you were sleeping on the couch. You said it was comfy."

"It is, but if you're having nightmares, I want to be here."

"Well, don't sleep on the floor." The thought of Conner sleeping on that hard cold floor wracks me with so much guilt, I feel the urge to invite him to sleep in this bed with me, but then I remember that dream, it was not a good idea.

"It's fine. It's a comfy floor." He gives me a wink before tucking himself under the covers and I can't help but roll my eyes.

"You're being ridiculous."

"Please, just let me do this."

The seriousness in his voice gives me pause and I find myself agreeing. "Okay."

We both slip under our covers and stare at the ceiling, both listening to the other's breathing and knowing neither of us are asleep when Conner's soft voice cuts through the silence and darkness. "Ava?"

"Yeah?"

He doesn't speak for a while. "You're not scared of me, are you?"

I let a little laugh slip through at that. I could never be scared of him. "Of course not."

He remains serious and I wonder where the fun-loving Conner went. "You know I would never hurt you, right?"

That is untrue but I don't say it. He could hurt me if I let him. But I don't say any of this. Instead I say, "I know you're a good person. A pain in the butt, but a good person."

Silence dances between us again until Conner finally whispers, "Good night, Ava."

"Good night, Conner."

CHAPTER 17

CONNER

"You heading off?" My boss, James says as he leans against the reception desk, watching me as I shove my things in my bag. I'm well aware of how weird it is to be a male receptionist at a veterinary clinic, but this was my foot in the door, and James has been so amazing at letting me help out, I have become more of an assistant.

I love it here so much and I am so happy that James is understanding of my situation.

"Yeah, I've been here since five this morning and I have a very hungry pregnant girlfriend at home." I realize what I said, but I can't be bothered to try to explain that whole mess.

I watch as a smug smile graces James' face. "Girlfriend, huh? That developed quickly. But then again, you did get her pregnant, so…"

"You know what I mean."

I finish shoving things in my bag, eager to get home to Ava and another sleepless night on the floor. Not my finest idea but the thought of her sleeping alone, I needed to be there.

"I'm proud of you, kid."

I pop my head up at his words and feel a sense of warmth from them. "Why?"

"Well, for starters, you're a great assistant. You'll make a great vet one day. But I'm really proud of how you are handling this whole situation with your girl. You could've run and denied everything. Lord knows most people your age would."

"I'm not most people."

"That much is clear. But you stayed. I'm proud." The lines on his face crease when his smile grows and I return it, giving him a nod.

"Thank you. I should probably head off."

"Right." James steps away from the desk to retreat back to his office, saying over his shoulder, "Have fun, kid."

WITH THE LAST day of classes fast approaching and exams finally finishing up, the crowd at Deb's Diner was finally starting to thin out, though it was still a bit busy. The booths and tables were no longer filled with college students hunched over textbooks while cramming burgers in their mouths.

I walk in, making my way to the line at the counter when my phone chimes.

AVA: Don't forget the pumpkin pie!

Me: How can I? That was the only thing you asked for.

Ava: And the milkshake!

Me: You want a milkshake now?

Ava: Don't judge me! You did this to me!

Me: You're not supposed to be yelling that at me until the baby is coming.

Ava: Just shut up and get me my food!

Me: I love a woman who knows what she wants ;)

Ava: And I love a guy who brings me my food.

Me: You love me?

Ava: I never said that.

Me: You kinda did.

Ava: ... shut up.

I'M SMILING down at my phone when the door chimes, followed by the voice of someone I don't expect to see.

"Conner?" I turn around and see Vivian with a small smile on her face, her red hair is not covered and she's wearing blue jeans and a red sweater.

I blink, caught off guard to find her here. "Vivian. What are you doing here?"

"Just meeting up with the girls." She says, pointing over her shoulder to a booth of girls in the back corner. A couple of them look up from their conversation.

"Oh." I wave, not knowing what else to do, but they just shoot me vicious scowls that almost make me want to recoil. "They seem nice."

Vivian smiles at me, not understanding my sarcasm or not wanting to acknowledge it as she bobs her head in an exaggerated nod. "They are. So, how are you?"

"I'm good. You?" I nod, tucking my hands back in the pockets of my jeans and eyeing the line that refuses to move forward.

"I'm good." Her smile lessens a bit as her eyes drift down to her shuffling feet. "So how are your exams?"

"Great, had my last one yesterday."

She smiles. "So now you're a free man?"

I shrug. "Yeah, I guess."

"Great! Because I was thinking we could hang out." She takes a step closer, putting her hand on my arm and the act that always felt normal, somehow felt wrong.

So, I give Vivian a tense smile and take a step back out of her reach, making her brows furrow. "I'm still seeing Ava," I remind her, and I see the look of realization wash over her face as she nods slowly in understanding.

"That's the girl, right?"

I rub the back of my neck, knowing now is the time to tell Vivian. "Yeah, we're actually living together now."

At that, she laughs, blowing out a big breath and shaking her head. "Wow, that was fast!"

Yes, to an outsider it may appear fast but what she doesn't know is that I've been after Ava since day one. Yes, everything is happening backward, but it's been a long time coming.

"You have no idea."

"What do you know about this girl?" It was hard to miss the accusatory tone in her voice, which only makes me frown and straighten my back in defense.

"What are you talking about?"

"I mean, you just met this girl and now she's living with you?" Her accusatory tone starts to become loud enough to draw the attention of everyone in the diner.

"It's more than that, Vivian," I say, trying to calm her down.

"How?"

I watch as she stands there waiting for me to explain and I know there's only one way: with the truth. It's a truth that is hard to hide and if I'm honest, I don't want to hide it anymore. I want people to look at Ava round with my baby and know that she is mine, that I'm hers. One day she will see it, but for now, everyone else will see it. So, I straighten my back and square my shoulders before saying confidently, "She's pregnant... with my baby."

At first, Vivian doesn't react, but stands frozen and for a moment I think I may have broken her until she whispers, her voice sounding weak and small, "What?"

"Look—" But I don't get to explain.

"How do you know?" Vivian's outburst continues to draw attention from all around us, her voice turns malicious and angry, unlike I've ever seen her. She is usually smiling and easygoing, but this Vivian in front of me seems almost like a different person. "How do you know it's yours? You don't even know her!"

"Vivian!" I yell, finally having enough and needing her to calm the fuck down. My outburst makes her mouth shut and the anger from her face vanishes into thin air only to be replaced by a look of calm.

Blinking up at me, her face full of remorse, in contrast to a moment ago, she pleads, "I'm sorry. I just worry about you. I care about you Conner and I don't want to see you being taken advantage of."

I explain, "It's not like that with Ava. It wasn't planned, but I've always liked her and it would mean a lot to me if you guys could get along." Because even though she acted like a crazy person before, we are friends and she has been there for me through some stressful times. I would hate to lose a friend over this because that's what would happen. If I had to choose between Ava and Vivian, there would be no competition.

"For you, I will try," she says giving me a small smile, not reaching her eyes.

"Maybe when classes start back up?"

Her smile grows at that to show teeth. "I wouldn't miss it."

. . .

I COME HOME LATER that afternoon and am met with the popping of guns going off on the TV, signaling Logan in his spot in front of the Xbox, his hair a greasy mess and I wonder when was the last time he showered or left the house.

I drop the food on the table by the door and stand in the doorway of the living room before Logan cheers, holding up the controller. "Here's the big guy! Did you get the food?"

"It's right here." I point to the table by the door. "Where is everyone?"

Logan doesn't look up. "Ava's upstairs and Hunter's in the kitchen. Guy practically lives there."

"Ah, oka—wait, Ava is upstairs?" I stop mid-step on my way to the kitchen, finally catching on to what Logan just said.

He nods, like nothing is wrong.

"She hasn't come down?"

He shrugs. "I don't know. I haven't seen her."

"You didn't think to check on her?" I exclaim, pissed about no one telling me if anything was wrong with Ava, and anxious about the various things that fill my head of what could be wrong. Is the baby okay? Is she okay? Did she fall again?

Just as I was about to shake the answers out of him, Hunter walks through carrying a sandwich, scolding me, "Hey, lay off him. I've been checking on Ava."

"Is she okay?"

"I've called Mia, she's on her way now."

That was not an answer, and it was clear I wasn't getting answers from these guys, so I give a frustrated groan before bolting up the stairs, taking two at a time as I hear Hunter call after me, "She's okay, man."

But I don't stop, I need to see that she is okay. After the fall, I've been a wreck when I'm not with her, when I can't be there to help or protect her. Isn't that my job as the father?

I push the door open when I reach it, throwing it open and bolting inside only to stop in my tracks at what I see on the other side.

I widen my eyes and my jaw drops, my words sputter past my slack lips. "Whoa!"

"Fuck!" Ava's wide eyes meet mine and her hands go to the bra covering her breasts until she realizes it is just me.

I'm left standing there, not knowing what to do. I mean, I want to stare at Ava sitting on my bed in nothing but a black bra and panties, her thick dark hair spilling over her shoulders and down her back. "I'm sorry, I thought you were... I'll go."

But as I go to leave, I hear her scoff. "Don't worry about it. You've seen it all before. You've gotta stop getting all shy around me."

Unsure of what to do now, I shuffle my feet where I stand, scuffing my feet on the floor as I watch her dark eyes narrow on me in suspicion, a slight curl to her full lips hinting at a smile. "You were worried about me?"

I roll my eyes because yeah, I was worried. "Well, when I heard you hadn't left the room..."

"You thought something happened." She finished the sentence, nodding her head in understanding.

"Yeah." I nod, tucking my hands in the front pockets of my jeans.

"No emergency, just my hormones being a bitch." She laughs, now avoiding my eyes but I could tell the laugh was not genuine as she looks down at her hands in her lap. I guess I should do something. But do I stay or go? I couldn't bring myself to go and I wasn't sure she wanted me near her at this time, so I just stand there, closing the door behind me, leaving me standing in the middle of the room.

She looks up at me and I ask, “Anything you want to talk to me about?”

She shakes her head. “It’s okay. Mia’s coming over.”

And yet I still don’t want to leave. I shrug awkwardly. “You can talk to me until she gets here.”

Ava raises a brow as the corner of her lip pulls up in an amused half smile. “You offering to girl talk with me?”

I grin, slowly making my way toward her, careful to watch for her reaction, she doesn’t react when I plop myself down on the bed beside her, a cheesy grin aimed at her. “You bet. Does it involve a naked pillow fight?”

This makes her fully smile, shaking her head. “Sorry, not this time.”

“Damn. Okay, hit me.”

The smile is quickly replaced with concern when she asks, uncertainty coating each word, “You sure?”

I hold my hand out for her to continue.

After a moment of staring at me, she finally relaxes her shoulders and expels a long breath, looking down at her hands once again as she speaks. “I was thinking of going out with the girls today but I couldn’t find anything to wear. I tried on everything I had and everything is just too tight because of this thing.” She gestures to the bump that has grown so much over the past few months.

My eyes follow her gesture and I shrug, my brows creasing in confusion. “You’re pregnant. We knew that your body was going to change.”

“Yeah, but I guess it’s happening faster than I thought it would. It’s silly, but I guess I’m just a little self-conscious.”

“Why?” It was a genuine question because looking at her now, it was hard to find anything she could be self-conscious about. Even with the belly, I’m finding it hard to control myself around her. In fact, the belly makes me want her more, knowing a part of us is inside of her. How could I ever find that unattractive?

She shrugs, still not looking at me. "Maybe because nothing I own fits me and sometimes when I walk around campus, I have these skinny bitches shooting looks at my belly like I just won an eating competition."

I'm taken aback and would like to know who these 'skinny bitches' are, but that's something for another time.

"I guess I'm just feeling a little less like a desirable woman these days." Ava says, absently rubbing her stomach with one hand and I instantly want to join her in touching her belly, and touching more than that.

If only she could see what I see when I look at her and how could she not feel desirable? I salivate every time she's near! Can she seriously not see it? I guess I have been backing off out of respect for her but maybe it's about time I give her some insight into how I feel. At least how I physically feel about her. She doesn't feel desirable, well that I can help with.

An idea forming in my head, I hop off the bed, making her look up at me with surprised wide eyes. "Get up."

She blinks before furrowing her brow at me. "Excuse me?"

"Stand up."

"What happened to girl talk?"

I hold out my hand to her, leaning down so my face is just in front of hers. "Well, now it's my time to talk, get up."

I can tell she wants to argue, but instead, she slumps her shoulders in defeat, knowing I'm not gonna back down before taking my hand and allowing me to lead her to the floor-length mirror on the door of my closet.

She starts to resist. "No, Conner, I don't—"

I give her hand a gentle squeeze, meeting her eyes. "Trust me."

Still cautious, she lets me lead her until I have her standing in front of the mirror in her underwear as I stand just behind her, my hands resting on the curves of her hips and I can't help but rub little circles there, enjoying the contact too much.

"What do you see?" I ask her as we both look at the reflection.

"Conner—"

"Fine, I'll tell you what I see." I take a step closer to her until I am sure she can feel the warmth of my body at her back, my voice low in her ear. I know this is a risky move and that she could easily run away from me. But I want this girl, and I think it's time she really understood that.

"The most enticing breasts I've ever seen or felt in my life." Her shocked, wide eyes meet mine in the mirror and her jaw goes slack. "They spill out of my hand. And it's these breasts that will feed our baby."

She blinks, speaking in a hushed breath, "Who says I'm breastfeeding?"

"Shh, I'm talking."

I give her hips a gentle squeeze, making her gasp. "These hips are just begging me to hold them while I—" I can't finish that sentence. Not unless I want to lose control right now and right here, but I need to wait for her. I might be ready for us, but she's not yet.

"The stomach?" Ava asks, raising a questioning brow and a slight quiver is evident in her voice.

I move one hand up to rest against her stomach, holding it protectively as I continue to whisper in Ava's ear, "It's the home for our baby, protecting it. Nothing sexier, nothing sexier than you, and I dare you to say otherwise." I growl the last words, surprised when Ava turns away from the reflection to look up at me, her belly resting between us and her doe eyes meeting mine, and I am all too aware of the little to nonexistent space between us.

"And if I do? Say otherwise, I mean."

I lean down breathing in the sweet scent of her, wanting to taste it, begging her to let me as I say in a gruff voice, "I'll have to prove it to you then."

I instantly see her eyes heat up as she looks up at me, goose bumps dancing across her skin, that full bottom lip makes its way between her teeth and it's like she's punishing me, making me all too aware of what I can't have yet. All I want to do is throw caution to the wind and fuck her against this mirror, making her turn around so she can see us fucking and see how beautiful she is.

That will help her, right?

"Oh! Sorry, am I interrupting something?" Ava and I spring apart at the sound of Mia's voice as she enters my room, her eyes moving between us, a question forming there.

"Uh, no." Ava's breaths are heavy as she blushes.

"Girl talk," I explain, making my way around Mia and away from Ava, needing the distance to catch my own breath.

Mia chuckles, crossing her arms over her chest. "You? Really?" She doesn't wait for me to respond before turning back to an awkward looking Ava, still in her underwear, holding up a big bag. "Anyway, Hunter called me and I managed to snag our mom's maternity clothes that she'd stashed away. They should fit until we can go shopping."

It's clear I'm being dismissed and I should be happy that Ava will have girl time with Mia. It'll make her feel better, but a selfish part of me wants Ava all to myself.

I brush that thought aside, knowing I should get out of here, "Well, I guess my shift is over." I give them a wink as I turn to leave.

"Conner?" I hear Ava as I reach the doorway and I turn to see her small smile. "Thanks for coming to my rescue. You seem to be doing that a lot lately."

I give her a small smile of my own. "Anytime, Ava."

And I leave my girl, and she is my girl, to her crazy friend.

CHAPTER 18

AVA

"I don't think this is such a good idea, guys," I tell Mia and Harper as they both lock arms with me and practically pull me through the mall, both with mischievous smiles on their faces.

"Sure it is," Mia chirps with a grin.

"Why wouldn't it be?" Harper asks, coyly.

"I thought we were going to hang out."

"We are. We're shopping," Mia says as she continues to stroll past the stores, not stopping until we've found what she's looking for.

"We used to always do that and you never had a problem before," Harper chimes in, giving my arm a gentle squeeze.

I narrow my eyes at her. "That was before I got too big to fit in the clothes. Come on, guys. We all know that as soon as I walk into the store, a tiny sales lady will ask us to leave, out of fear of me ripping the clothes."

That makes Mia snap her head to look at me with wide eyes burning with fury. She is small but that look would make anyone shrink with fear. "Has someone done that to you? Tell me who they are. I'll cut them!" She finally slows us down to a stop as I roll my eyes.

"You will not cut them because it hasn't happened. Yet!"

Harper moves her arm to wrap it around my shoulders. "You're stressing. It's not good for the baby."

"And you decide to take me shopping?"

"Hey!" Mia snaps, waving a sassy finger in my face. "You need to calm down. Yes, we are taking you shopping because you are running out of clothes to wear. The leggings will only work for so long and even then, you need something nice to wear, something you can fit into. Yeah, it sucks that your body is changing but that doesn't make you any less gorgeous and it doesn't change who you are. You need new clothes, and we will be here every step of the way."

Harper tells us, "They have maternity stores here too, with clothes that are designed for women in your condition."

"So what do you say? Shopping?"

They both stare at me with excited eyes, begging me to say yes, they had finally given me a choice. Do I stay or do I go?

Unable to say no to those faces, I roll my eyes and slump in defeat against Harper's side as I groan, "Shopping."

They cheer and continue to lead me off to these other stores.

I MADE it to the afternoon and I now I'm starving. After the first couple stores, I was tired and hungry, but Mia insisted we check out a few more, which led to more. It wasn't until we reached the one closer to the food court and I got a whiff of burritos that I demanded we eat, insisting that I had enough.

One look at me, and Mia and Harper were rushing me to the cash register to purchase my items. They seriously underestimate how pissed I get when I don't eat. I would kill if I had to.

Now here we are, sitting outside a taco place as I shove a burrito in my mouth to alleviate the hunger pains, while Mia and Harper pick at their burrito bowls as we talk around our food.

"Guys, I have some news," Harper pipes up, shifting in her seat, looking uncomfortable under our waiting gaze before continuing, "It might not be anything."

"Just spit it out," Mia demands impatiently.

Harper sucks in a breath before speaking. "I applied for an internship."

"Where at?"

"Harper Collins... Australia."

"Australia!" Mia and I exclaim, holding onto that one word. I remember this internship and remember her mentioning her interest, but I never thought, with everything happening that she would go. It was another country and was six months. But I would've done the same thing, given the opportunity.

Harper scrambles. "It's not a definite. I might not get it, but I applied. I wasn't going to but..."

Looking at her, I see the nerves building within her and I know she's worried about what we will think. She wants our support and even though a part of me is jealous, I am happy for my friend that has always been there for me since day one. So, with that I lean forward and place my hand over hers on the table, forcing her eyes to meet mine and give her a smile. "That's amazing, and you will get it and tell me all about it."

"Especially, all the hot Australian guys." Mia winks. "Just know I will be calling you and living vicariously through you."

Harper's cheeks go red. "Oh, I don't think that will happen."

"Oh it will happen," Mia states, leaving no room for argument as she dives back into her food. "I can't believe you didn't get one piece of lingerie," Mia comments around a mouthful of food, shaking her head at me.

I swallow my food. "Because I would have no reason to wear it."

"I could think of a reason." She shoots me some bedroom eyes that freak me out as she waggles her brows seductively.

I groan, rolling my eyes. "Don't start."

"I'm not starting anything."

"Yeah." Harper puts her fork down and turns her chair to face me. "We understand your decision but don't you think, if you have feelings for Conner, that it would be even better for the baby to just embrace those feelings and see where it leads?"

I resist another eye roll because I've been getting this a lot these days. From my sister and now these two. Why not involve the guys? But with everyone making these valid points, it's making it harder for me to find reasons to keep a distance, so I decide to play stupid. "Who said I have feelings for him?"

"Okay, cut the crap. After what I walked in on yesterday, you cannot tell me there isn't anything." Mia waves her fork accusingly at me, her eyes narrowed like I'm on trial. But it is hard to be convincing after that morning. The way Conner looked at me, how he touched me and I didn't want it to stop, how I wanted his hand—Stop!

It hasn't happened again anyway!

"That's what I'm telling you." I take another bite, avoiding their knowing looks.

"Ava, you know he isn't going to be single forever." My heart stops at the thought, because I know that, but I guess I just avoid thinking it. The thought making my food stop in my throat as Harper continues, "He's a good guy and he's hot. What happens if another girl gets interested and he reciprocates? The baby will be a part of a broken family anyway."

"So you putting yourself through this will be for nothing."

I hated to admit they were right, maybe I would need to assess this whole thing again, really think about how I feel.

"Ava?" I jump in surprise at hearing my name and turn to see a beautiful girl with a mass of hair coming toward me. Do I know her? I'd seriously remember her if I saw her, wouldn't I?

"Yes?"

She holds out her hand to me with a beaming smile which looks too big. "Conner's told me so much about you. I'm Vivian."

I recognize the name instantly, but I didn't remember Vivian being so beautiful. I instantly feel like pulling at my oversized shirt to hide my belly and fix my hair which I need to wash.

"Oh, hi. Yeah, Conner's told me a lot about you too." I say, somehow finding my voice and it is obviously the right thing to say because her eyes instantly light up.

"He talks about me? He's such a sweet guy."

"Yeah, he is," I say, looking at her eyes as they soften, and I know she is thinking of him, thinking of him the way no one but me should, and I instantly dislike this girl.

"Wow, Conner told me you were pregnant but I didn't know you were showing." She emphasizes this as her eyes widen at my belly that is starting to pop out of my oversized shirt.

I resist the urge to cover my belly because it isn't like it's a potbelly from eating too much, I am fucking pregnant. There is an actual human being inside me. Now, saying it like that makes it sound really creepy.

As Vivian comes to stand beside me and lay her hands on my belly, invading my personal space, I feel Harper and Mia stiffen near me as I stiffen myself when Vivian gasps. "Wow, there's like a real baby in there!"

I can't help myself when I say, "Thank you so much for clearing that up. Now everything makes sense in the world."

Vivian withdraws her hand and frowns at me for only a second before covering it with a laugh faker than Pamela Anderson's boobs. "Oh you know what I mean. Conner said, but it's another thing to see it myself."

"Well." I hold my hands out. "Here I am," I say, the sarcasm dripping from each word when Mia, sensing my tension reaches over and gives my hand a squeeze as she beams.

"And Conner is so happy!" Mia smiles with all teeth up at Vivian, and I watch as Vivian's smile goes tense until it is a close-lipped smile. And it is then that I see what Mia is doing. She's always had my back and she senses the same thing I can. This bitch is interested in Conner and Mia is laying down my claim for me, even though I shouldn't be laying claim because technically, I'm trying not to claim him. But Vivian doesn't need to know that.

I know it's selfish but there's something off about this bitch and a protective part of me wants to keep Conner from it.

Vivian shrugs, her smile waning now. "Maybe."

The doubt in her voice makes my back stiffen and my brows furrow as I cross my arms. "Maybe?"

"It's probably nothing." She waves it off halfheartedly when Mia snaps.

"Cut the shit."

Vivian's eyes widen in response to Mia's harsh words before she quickly recovers. "It's just that Conner is a good guy," she says, looking me in the eyes as she lowers herself in the empty seat beside me.

"Yeah, I know that."

"He would never openly hurt someone."

"Okay, where are you going with this?" Mia urges her to continue as I shift in my seat.

"I say this as his friend, but the last few times we... *studied* together." I hated the smile she gave at the word 'studied' but I push that aside for now and continue to listen. "He seemed off, more stressed than usual. I've seen a change in him Ava and I'm worried. His future as a vet means everything to him and it just breaks my heart to see him struggling so much."

My brows continue to crease as I try to think back to any time he looked like he was drowning but he was always the picture of calm around me, unless he was worried about me. "But he always seemed fine. He never mentioned anything."

She shrugs. "Maybe he just doesn't want you to worry because of the baby. He's a good guy like that."

I sit, my stomach in knots as I try to think of our time together and if he was stressed, it was when I had my fall or when he thought something happened to me, but otherwise he was fine. He never implied that he was struggling to me, which only makes it sting that much more that he had confided in Vivian, a girl I know wants him. I try not to show my panic and steady my breathing when Harper finally speaks up from her place beside Mia who is currently glaring at Vivian. "Well, thank you for telling us. You have a good day."

"Well, I—"

But before Vivian could finish, Mia loses her cool and snaps.

"She said have a good day."

After momentarily glaring at Mia, she returns her attention to me with a small smile before leaving us and strutting out of the food court with a flick of her red hair.

It's not until then that I feel the tears falling down my

cheeks and I feel my shoulders start to deflate. Am I really doing this to Conner?

"Don't you dare listen to that bitch," Mia scolds me, waving a finger in my face, a look so serious I resist the need to recoil.

"But is she wrong? Is he struggling? Does he ever look like he's drowning or unhappy?"

Mia's face finally softens. "Look, it's not easy on either of you, but I can tell you that if you tried to push that boy away, he would be pushing right back. He's not going anywhere."

I scoff, wishing I had her confidence. "You sound so sure."

"For good reason. You saw Conner in the hospital that day. He wasn't letting you leave with anyone but him."

I laugh through my tears at the memory and nod when Harper reaches across to hold my hand. "You don't see the way he looks at you when you're not looking."

"How's that?" I ask, cocking my head.

Mia answers with a soft smile. "Like he doesn't see anyone else."

CHAPTER 19

AVA

A week goes by and I can't get the girl's words out of my head.

He looks at me like he doesn't see anyone else?

I brushed it off that day, but in reality, it's all I'm thinking about. Whenever I've been in the same room, I always find my eyes going to him, trying to catch this look they speak of and I never see it. He is always looking at someone else. Sometimes he'll see me looking and give me a smile but other than that, no look.

Even now, as the hot water runs over my body as I stand under the shower, all I can think about is the fact that there is no look. Do I want there to be a look? I shouldn't, but damnit I do!

This may be the hormones going crazy but I want the fucking look. I want him to be able to talk to me like he does Vivian, and I want to not hate Vivian so much. I want to be able to take a leap with this guy that used to drive me crazy but now drives me crazy for a whole other reason.

The more I think about him these days the warmer I get

in my chest and between my legs, the more I wish I could remember that night in his room.

Without even thinking, with the warmth of the spray spreading over my shoulders, I run my hands over them, moving them slowly down to my sensitive breasts, being gentle in my caresses. I imagine Conner to be gentle, at first. I imagine his hands to be the ones touching me, making my core tingle and begging for attention.

Feeling my breathing accelerate, I close my eyes and focus on the feeling of my hand gliding over my wet skin to the sensitive spot between my legs. I let a little moan slip past my lips as my fingers, Conner's fingers, move over the little nub in small circles with just the right amount of pressure, my legs starting to shake as I slap a hand out to the wall next to me. I'm almost there and my breaths come in rapid succession when I hear the door to the bathroom open.

I squeak in surprise and remove my hand from between my legs as if it had burned me when I hear a voice.

"Make way. I'm coming in!" Conner cheers as he walks in, the door closing behind him and my face instantly warms at what I was just doing and now being so close to him, naked and turned on.

I'm screwed.

"What are you doing in here?!" I scream, pulling the shower curtain back slightly to peek around it and swallow my tongue as I watch Conner pull his T-shirt over his head until he is standing there before me in nothing but running shorts and a sweaty chest, his sweaty hair sticking to his forehead.

He smiles a seductive smile as he points to his eyes. "Eyes are up here, little lamb. Not that I mind, but just letting you know." He shrugs, and I instantly force my eyes away from his chiseled glistening chest and glare at him for being caught practically ogling him. This man is going to kill me.

I huff. "What are you doing in here?!" I demand again, trying not to stomp my foot like a child.

"What do people normally do in bathrooms? I need a shower."

I roll my eyes. "Don't you think you could wait outside until I'm done?"

"Done with what? The shower or what was causing you to moan so much?" he asks, raising a brow at me and smiling a devilishly delicious smile.

My words get stuck in my throat as I recall what he just said, my eyes widening at the thought of him knowing what I was doing. Was I really that loud?

I narrow my eyes. "You're a pig."

"Well, I think it will be better if I help you. That way we both shower and get off at the same time."

I almost want to kick myself for wanting to say yes, but I glare. "I say again, you are a pig."

"I'm nothing if not efficient." He says, shrugging as his hands start to go to his pants, tucking his thumbs into the waistband.

"Woah! What do you think you are doing?!" I exclaim, hiding behind the shower curtain, despite my desire to look.

I hear his chuckle beyond the curtain. "I thought we established that I needed to shower."

"Fine, then give me my towel." I huff, throwing my hand out of the shower, waiting for my towel, only to jump when I hear Conner's voice, low and closer than I thought.

"You sure? I wouldn't mind the company. I could even give you a hand, pardon the pun."

I can almost feel his presence on the other side of the curtain and I can't help but wonder if he is fully naked now or not.

My body is urging me to say yes, everything is urging me to say yes.

It's almost to the point where I don't even know why I'm not saying yes anymore. What is holding me back again? Oh, yeah, the protruding belly housing our baby. If I were to say yes, I don't know what that would make us. A couple? A family? A physical thing? And would it last? Would it just be because of the baby or a genuine attraction?

So much uncertainty comes with saying yes. It's best to keep it simple.

So, I wave my hand, still waiting for my towel. "Towel please."

Conner chuckles again, then I feel the fluffy towel in my hand.

Turning off the water and wrapping myself in the towel, I hop out and avoid looking back at Conner out of fear of seeing him nude and not being able to say no anymore.

Once I'm dressed in a pair of boxers and an oversized shirt, I check the time and open my laptop, knowing I need to talk to someone and only one person is coming to mind right now.

It's not long until Lucy's sweet face is filling the laptop screen, her pink room showing behind her. "Hey sis!"

I can't help but smile, feeling the warmth and comfort that comes with Lucy, like being around her is like home, like *she* is home and she is. "Hey."

Hearing my lackluster greeting, her smile deflates a bit and her brows start to furrow when she asks, "What's wrong?"

I wave it off, not sure how I can say any of this to Lucy. We've always been close, but how can I bring this up? "Nothing. How's school?"

Her frown stays in place. "It's good. I'm studying for exams now. So, let me try this again. What's wrong?"

It doesn't take much from her to budge me. I let out a

tired sigh and start to play with the ends of my shirt, trying to find the best way to explain it. "It's complicated."

"Just start from the beginning."

"No, that's the thing. This whole thing is complicated. Me, Conner, the baby. I'm trying so hard to keep it simple but it just seems to get worse."

"Why are you trying to keep it simple?"

"For the baby. I don't want our child growing up in a complicated situation."

Lucy regards me for a moment. "Ava, there is nothing simple about this no matter how much you try to keep it that way. You guys are not together, but living together and pregnant."

"Plus this Vivian chick said my being pregnant is stressing Conner out and he's struggling." I can't help the growl when I say her name but I just hate how much she got to me and by the softening look on Lucy's face, she sees it too.

"Did you talk to Conner?"

"No." I shift in my spot on the bed, already seeing her point.

"Then I don't think you should worry about that until he says something. Besides, if you're worried, then maybe you should talk to him."

"Maybe." Or maybe not.

"But I do think you should be honest with yourself," Lucy says, making me furrow my brow and cock my head in confusion.

"What do you mean?"

Lucy raises a brow. "You like him and that scares you."

I almost don't react out of the shock of hearing those words said out loud. I can't think of anything to say because how can I deny it. It's true. I feel something for him but I don't really understand it yet. It's definitely physical but is it more than that? I don't even understand his side of it. Does he feel for me or does he just like to mess with me? Or am I just there?

"But there is something you need to remember when you are trying to keep things simple." Lucy continues, "Conner seems like a good guy and he will be a good father, and those guys don't stay available for long. Other women will be interested. If that's something you can accept, then keep things simple. If not, then it might be an idea to start complicating things."

I know she's right and the idea of another woman with him, with my child, kills me. I know there will be women. There already is, even though he hasn't pursued it yet; I know one day he will. But the fear is almost too much, fear of getting hurt, of my decision hurting my child. No matter what I do, I feel like I'll be hurting someone.

"When did you get so grown up?"

Before Lucy can say anything else, the creak of the door sounds, signaling someone's arrival. I turn around, and I swear I feel my mouth water.

Standing in the doorway is Conner, wet and in nothing but a towel. Droplets run down his lean chest and his dark wet hair is slicked back off his face. Looking at each droplet, I want to lick each one off his body and I hate myself for thinking it. But my hormones are so crazy right now. Yes, let's blame it on the hormones.

Conner looks at me and smiles a guilty smile as he makes his way into the room, toward the dresser. "Oh, sorry, for—hey little Daniels, how you been?" His smile grows as he sees my sister on the screen and she is smiling an even bigger smile at him. Of course she is, who wouldn't?

"Good, how's fatherhood treating you?"

"Pretty good, but I won't interrupt your talk, I'm just getting my clothes. Catch you later, Daniels. Both Daniels!"

he calls over his shoulder, giving me a wink as he takes his clothes with him out the door, and unfortunately that towel remains on.

I'm still staring at the closed door, my jaw hanging open and possibly drooling when I hear Lucy from the laptop. "Sis, I'm sorry but you are screwed living with that. I give you a month and that's being generous."

I snap my head back at her to see her laughing at my glare, but the sad thing is, she is probably right.

This pregnancy is really going to be hell.

CHAPTER 20

AVA

"Wow, I think I needed that." I sigh as I walk my way up the driveway with a big smile on my face and my two best friends on each arm. Both of them had stopped by earlier with tickets to a new chick flick and a demand that I get ready. I was a little hesitant but after that hot trailer, I thought the movie would be worth it. And it was. Best birthday ever!

"I know you did. What's not to like about a hot romantic movie?" Mia waggles her brows with a sly smile.

"I think the book was better," Harper comments, but of course she read the book. I haven't gotten around to it yet but I guess I can't now. I've never been able to read the book after watching the movie. I already know how it ends, so why bother? But I don't mind.

Mia scoffs beside me. "I don't need to read the book. I already know what happens. Plus, that guy was hot!"

"He's a bit too pretty for me, though I like the bad boy thing," I comment as we approach the front door and see no lights on in the house, no sounds beyond the door. I furrow my brow as I reach the front door and the darkness beyond it. "I don't think anyone is home."

"Well, we can stay with you. Here, take my hand, I don't want you tripping." I unlock the door, briefly fumbling with the keys until I hear the click of the door unlocking, pushing the door open as my friends lead me into the pit of darkness that is the entryway.

I'm just crossing the doorway when the lights instantly turn on, momentarily blinding me and I hear a big chorus of, "SURPRISE!!!"

Standing before me is my family, or those that I consider family anyway. Holding a bunch of balloons of various colors is Logan and he's grinning at me. Hunter holds up a big sign saying 'Happy 20th Birthday'. My best friends stay by my side, grinning like Cheshire cats.

"Oh my god!" I cry, my jaw dropping as my hands come up to my warm face. "You guys knew?" I say accusatorially, but can't take the smile off my face. I'm not one to celebrate my birthday, not that I hate it, I just never thought to do much for it and therefore all I do most years is hang out with my friends and my sister. I've never really had a big party.

"Of course we knew." My head snaps up at that voice, recognizing it from all those video chats and years of living down the hall from each other. I see my little sister with her dark blonde curls bouncing as she walks up in a lovely white knee-length dress. I can see her growing up each time I see her and it makes me happy and sad all at the same time, but seeing her here as she emerges from the crowd of boys with a smile on her face, I am too happy for words. "Hey sis."

"Luce!" I exclaim, leaving my friends and lunging for my little sister, encircling her in a death grip of a hug, holding her close and feeling home, breathing her familiar smell in and almost wanting to cry. My voice breaks when I speak into her hair. "I've missed you."

She chuckles, wiggling out of my grasp. "Missed you too."

"I can't believe it; how did you guys do this?" I ask Mia and Harper but Mia only shrugged.

"We didn't do anything but keep you distracted."

"What?"

Harper is the one that speaks next. "It was Conner's idea."

Only then do I see him, behind everyone else, leaning against the wall in the most casual way and a small smile playing across his lips.

My heart jumps in that moment, knowing he did this for me, he got my sister here, he planned this, he knew my birthday and remembered it. No one had ever done that for me and I slowly realize that I am moving through the small group to stand before Conner, his eyes watching my every move. "You did all this?"

He merely shrugs, his smile growing slightly.

I shake my head, aghast, my voice coming out in breaths. "Why?"

He looks at me a moment before looking at our audience, who I feel staring holes into my head, but I focus on the man before me as he answers, looking back at me. "You haven't been yourself. I thought a party with people you love would cheer you up."

"But how did you know it was my birthday?"

"That was me, Ava." Hunter steps away from the group with a raised hand and a guilty smile.

I bite my lip, trying to suppress the tears wanting to get out, my heart racing for each person in this room. How time has changed! It was just me and my girls, and now I pretty much have a family. "Thank you so much." My voice breaks when I speak and go to hug Hunter, his body too big for me to wrap my arms around which isn't new. "Both of you, thank you," I say as I withdraw from the hug and am met with Conner standing before me, as if waiting for his thank you hug, but I can't make my arms move now. I want to hug him. I want to do more than that, but for some reason, my body won't cooperate, so instead we are standing in an awkward standoff until some brave soul in the form of Logan exclaims, "Hey, when are we gonna start drinking?!"

"Hold your horses, dickhead!" Hunter admonishes, leaving me to continue to stand awkwardly until I finally have to step away, looking back at the group before me. "Let's party!"

THE GUYS ORDER pizza and music is blasting from the house as I stand outside on the back porch, leaning my forearms on the wooden railing. I told the girls I needed some fresh air and when they offered to come with me outside, I said I would be fine so here I am, outside the party that was thrown for me. I did get involved but you can only dance so much with a belly weighing you down before you get exhausted. Alcohol was passed around to everyone but me and Lucy, of course. I still have my red Solo cup of water in my hand as I shiver against the slight chill in the air, lost in my own thoughts so that I don't hear the sliding door open when a deep familiar voice reaches me.

"That better be water you're drinking." I turn, leaning my back against the railing as I watch Conner in his blue jeans and white T-shirt that hug his chest so well. Damn, I shouldn't be alone with this guy, not until I figure everything out.

But he stops just in front of me, with his hands tucked into the front pockets of his jeans when I answer with a smile. "It is."

He shuffles his feet. "What are you doing out here?"

"I guess I needed some air," I say, shrugging and taking another sip of water.

"Do you like your party?"

"I love it. Thank you, Conner. Seeing my sister, being able to hold her …" I stop myself, unable to find words. My sister and I don't have a normal relationship. From a young age, since our mother left, I've been caring for her, working to make sure there is food for her to eat and clothes to wear. I almost had to play mom to her and because of that, our relationship is different. I'm not saying I am her mother or I see her like a daughter, but we are closer because it was only us, we only had us to rely on. No one ever understood that.

"You really love your sister, don't you?"

I blink up at Conner, coming back to my place on the back porch with him looking down at me, his eyes soft when I nod. "Of course. Do you have any siblings?"

The mood instantly changes, I see it in his face as his jaw hardens slightly and his eyes go distant as he clears his throat and takes a step away from me. "I have a big brother."

He doesn't offer up more and I should let it go, but I don't know a lot about Conner, and the funny thing is I want to know everything about him. Maybe it's because I'm carrying his baby or something else but I want to know either way. "What's he like?"

He is hesitant but he eventually speaks, his voice more gruff than usual. "He's a musician, always quiet, used his music to express himself. He's a few years older than me. He's in England right now playing with a band that picked him up."

"You hear from him often?"

A coat of sadness washes over his face before he quickly blinks it away. "No. We aren't as close as you and Lucy."

My heart aches for him and what he is missing out on and I wonder if he craves a relationship with his brother at all. "That's too bad."

We stand in tense silence for a few moments and I

consider going back inside when I notice Conner's expression shift from serious to mischievous, his eyes darkening and there is a devilish curl to his lips as he takes a step closer, almost closing the distance between us and I feel the temperature start to rise out here as I breathe in his woodsy cologne and I'm hit with flashing images that only appear for a second before they are gone. Images of passionate kisses and touching, gentle touches.

I feel my face heat up and a breath is caught in my throat when Conner leans down so his face is just above mine when he whispers, "So, I hear your type is bad boys?"

It takes me a moment to realize what he just said and just like that, the mood is gone and I am overcome by a wave of embarrassment at him having heard what I said outside before the party. "Oh God! I can't believe you heard that." I put my face in my hands to hide my shame, he chuckles, pulling at my hands.

"No, it's okay." I let him take my hands and he holds them, pulling me closer slightly until he is almost warming my front, "I now know I need to step up my game."

"Be a bad boy?" I scoff, despite the heat between my legs at having him this close and being so alone. I don't even remember sex but now I want it, with him.

"Hell yeah. I gotta keep my woman interested."

I scoff again, looking him up and down. "I don't think you have it in you to be a bad boy." I don't believe that for a second, he can be very bad, but not the kind that treats girls like crap.

The heat returns between us when he pulls me so close that we are touching from my swollen breasts to my knees, my belly only getting in the way but Conner doesn't show it. I stop breathing for a moment, when he leans down again, his mouth inches from mine and I can practically taste him. "Oh yeah? You wanna bet?"

I only have to lean in a bit and I'll be kissing him.

"And I noticed that you didn't correct me when I referred to you as my woman." He moves away from my lips to whisper in my ear, the heat of his breath tickling down my neck and the ache between my legs is almost too much. "Are you finally admitting it?"

I let a groan slip past my lips and just when I'm about to jump this guy and finally give myself some release, the loud music from inside filters its way out to us when the door opens again.

"Hey, oh sorry to interrupt, but we're ready for the cake." Conner slowly moves away from me to reveal a surprised Hunter, a slight smile to his lips as he looks between us with his brows raised in question.

I clear my throat and find my voice. "Great, I'll be right there."

Hunter walks away from the door, still open for me, and just as I go to leave, Conner grabs my hand, stopping me just as I pass him and he says, "You can't keep running from me, Ava."

He is right, I'm close to breaking. Hell, I was about to do him on the back porch, but maybe this is the universe telling me not to. That's silly, right? Either way, I know Conner is gonna break me, one way or another.

THE CAKE IS BEAUTIFUL; a rich chocolate mud cake with candles lighting up the top. I say my thanks before blowing out the candles, and I make one wish: happiness. For both myself and my child. But also for Conner. It's a small wish, but it's all I want.

After the cake, we migrate to the living room where they plop me on the large recliner reserved for Logan when he's gaming. Everyone standing around me with cards and wrapped up boxes, cheering about it being present time.

"Oh no, don't tell me you guys got me presents," I tell them as they start plopping the presents at my feet with big smiles.

"Of course we did. Now shut up and open your presents before I do." Mia says with a wink, standing back and crossing her arms over her chest as she and everyone else waits for me to open my presents.

I sit there, my heart racing as I look over the presents at my feet, unsure of what to do first.

"Okay," I say, my voice sounding small as I reach for the smallest box at my feet.

I go through each present, my heart melting each time with the amount of love in this room.

I got three book gift cards from Hunter, a voucher for a full body massage done by Logan, from Logan, which awarded him a smack across the back of his head from Conner. Then Harper got me a leather-bound bullet journal which I've been wanting to try for a while, and Mia bought me a red lacy bra and panties which I refused to show everyone and shoot her a glare, but I'm also thankful. Lucy steps forward and hands me a small wrapped gift, which turns out to be a framed photo of us when we were kids.

I was ten and I had taken her to the park we always go to, she was sitting on the swing and I had come up behind her to take a photo with the camera I stole from Dad. I paid for that later but it was worth it for that day where it was just me and her in our own little world.

I feel the tears fall down my cheeks and quickly swipe them away when Lucy speaks, her eyes also watering. "I found it and thought you should have it. The photo. That was the best day."

I nod, the tears now blurring my vision. "It was." I get up

to quickly embrace her, giving her a quick squeeze before stepping back, biting my lip to hold back more tears from coming. That was a time of so much innocence, before the grown-up world came knocking and demanded me to enter.

"My turn." I blink, surprised when Conner steps forward holding an envelope out to me, a small smile on his face and I shake my head.

"No, you already threw me a party."

"Just open it." He thrusts it forward again until I finally take it, eyeing everyone in the room who watches with curious eyes as I slowly open the envelope and pull out a small slip of paper with rose gold lettering written in cursive.

I squint at the writing before my heart stops as I realize what I hold in my hand.

"What is this?" I ask without looking up.

"An invitation."

Yes, an invitation to his parents' house in a month's time. First of all, who sends out invitations to their son? I guess that is judgmental of me but here I am in front of everyone with an invitation from Conner's parents who want us to join them at their house. I finally raise my head to look at Conner, my jaw firm in disapproval as I hold the invitation up in my hand. "What is this, Conner?"

He expels a tired breath, hearing the anger in my tone. "Look, my parents want to meet you. You're carrying their grandchild after all."

"And I told you I wasn't ready, and you go and do this?" I shake the invitation in his face for emphasis, my anger building. Anger at his impatience, anger at him not caring about my need for time, like he wasn't listening to me or hearing me.

I can feel my blood boiling and I know I'm overreacting. These damned hormones! But I'm upset and he did this in front of our friends.

Feeling their eyes on me is getting to be too much so I bolt from the room and run up the stairs to the sound of my sister telling Conner. "Just give her a moment."

IT TAKES an hour for me to calm down and now I just feel stupid for letting my temper get the best of me, not for how I felt but because of how I reacted. I shouldn't have run away, especially when it was my birthday everyone was celebrating and I don't even remember thanking everyone for the presents they got me or for just being there.

I want to kick myself for being so rude. When I hear the slight creak of the bedroom door opening I shift from where I sit on the bed, getting up slowly and rubbing my palms on my pants when I see Conner enter the room, closing the door behind him. An emotionless expression looking back at me, making me uneasy. I don't like when Conner doesn't show what he's feeling, I prefer him mad, sad, happy, anything that I can read. But this I can't.

I shuffle my feet where I stand by the bed as he leans against the door with his arms crossed over his chest.

"Is everyone gone?" I ask, trying to avoid his eyes, but it isn't until I finally force myself to meet them that he answers me.

"Yeah."

"I should've said goodbye."

"Yeah, you should've." He nods, making me feel worse, but this wouldn't have happened if Conner hadn't given me that damn invitation. "Why are you so mad?"

"I'm mad because it feels like you're not hearing me when I say I'm not ready."

"Why are you not ready? You'll just be meeting my parents."

I throw my hands up, desperate for him to understand.

"Exactly, and what do I introduce myself as? What do I say if they ask how it happened?"

He simply shrugs. "They already know it wasn't planned."

My eyes must be the size of dinner plates as my heart drops into my stomach at his words. My jaw drops for a moment as he pushes himself off the door and approaches me as I lose my shit. "Oh God, you told them?!"

Yeah, there was no way I was going to meet them now.

"Of course I told them! God, Ava." He shakes his head at me. "You've gotta get over it."

"What?" I cross my arms across my chest, raising my chin to meet his face.

"What happened that night, what happened with us. It happened! You're not the first girl to hop into bed with some guy drunk and get knocked up, so don't act like you're the only one."

"You are such a jackass!" I growl, wanting to hit him, even though he was right but it's hard to think about the other girls when it's happening to you. When you're pregnant, you have so much happening in your life and with your body, you don't get any rest, no rest to think about those other girls.

"I'm the jackass? You lose your shit at a party planned for you over an invitation, and I'm the jackass?" He throws his own hands up in the air, shaking his head as his own frustration grows.

Between the two of us, we're boiling volcanoes close to erupting and causing a natural disaster. I look at him now, so different from the man that was turning me on on the back porch earlier. This man is not being nice but he is being honest and a bit harsh. I'm not going to stand here and take him talking to me the way he is. If I do, I may say something I'll regret. I need to leave; I need time away and space.

"I can't believe I ever thought this could work." I shake my head, pushing past him to grab my coat on the hanger behind the door.

His eyes narrow as I shrug it on. "Where are you going?"

"I'll stay with Harper, or Mia, anywhere but here."

"Like hell you are." He growls behind me as I hear the thunder of his footsteps hitting the floorboards, getting closer to me as I fumble with the doorknob and swing it open.

"You gonna stop me?" I call over my shoulder as I rush my way out the door, making my way toward the staircase.

"You bet your sweet ass I am." He growls at my back, closer than I thought he was and I gasp as he suddenly picks me up, tucking his arms under my back and legs. I latch on to him, kicking my legs, and scream.

"Hey! What the hell do you think you're doing?! Put me down!"

I continue to scream with no one coming to my rescue. Traitors! After walking me back to the room and pissing me off even more, he puts me down like I've been demanding. Once I feel the floor beneath my feet, I push against Conner's hard chest, it doesn't budge beneath my touch and I huff as I adjust my shirt.

Conner is in my face, his eyes blazing and hot. Damnit! This is not the time for that! I am mad, I tell myself as he growls in my face, "Now, are you gonna start acting like a grown-up?"

"Screw you," I hiss, my face getting closer to his and a string of curses flit through my mind but before I can say any of them, I feel it. I jump in surprise at the sensation, gasping, "Oh!"

The anger quickly evaporates as I place a hand over the place where I just felt the jab of something kicking me… from the inside.

I've felt flutters before, knowing it's the baby moving

around when I'm trying to sleep but never like this. It knocks the wind out of me.

I move my hand over my stomach, waiting for the kick again when Conner turns concerned eyes to my stomach, slight panic crossing his face, "What is it? Is it the baby?"

I couldn't speak, I could just feel, feel the baby kicking me in the ribs. But she was there, or he.

Without a second of hesitation, I grab Conner's hand in mine. "Give me your hand." And I place it where the baby is kicking, holding his hand there, and I watch his face as he waits.

I feel the kick and so does Conner, his eyes widen and he places both hands on my belly. "Holy shit."

I can't fight the smile beaming on my face as I look up at Conner's equally happy face, like we weren't just fighting and I wasn't about to leave.

"The baby is kicking."

I place my hands over his on my belly and we just enjoy feeling our baby, tears rolling down my cheeks, when Conner speaks. "It's almost like he doesn't want us fighting."

"What if it's a she?"

It may sound crazy but he's right, as soon as I got so mad I was going to leave it's like the baby felt it, like the baby was telling us he wanted us together and we've never been more together than in that moment. With our hands on my belly, feeling our baby. Maybe I'm just grasping at straws but I have to believe that was our baby communicating with us.

"Look," Conner sighs, still holding my belly as he looks down at me solemnly. "I'm sorry. I just thought it would be a good idea. My parents want to meet you and be involved with the baby. They are good people, Ava."

"I don't doubt that. I guess I'm kind of worried what they will think of me," I say, letting him in a bit.

"Well, I can tell you that they don't think less of you."

"How would you know that?"

He laughs, making the baby kick again. "I know my parents."

I consider it, because if we are going to be a family of some kind, I would need to meet his parents eventually. I think I just need more time to process and prepare for it. I was never great with parents, you know, with not having good ones myself. "Let me think about it."

"Alright. It's not till next month anyway."

CHAPTER 21

AVA

The house is quiet now, some of the guys went home for break, but Conner ended up staying here, saying his parents were away anyway. So, it's just been me and him, though we've barely had any time together with our work schedules, but finally we both have a day off so we thought it would be good to give a Lamaze class a go.

Well, actually our doctor recommended it and Conner has been pushing for it. As for me, I'd rather not. What's so hard about breathing and pushing a baby out anyway? Other than the obvious.

Angling my head toward the window, I groan over what is to come as Conner drives past houses and buildings that blur together as we go.

"Do you think they will have those big balls?" I ask him, the silence becoming too much.

"Stability balls?" He gives me a side look and I look back at him, he furrows his brow slightly.

"Yeah."

"Maybe," he says after some thought, not sounding too sure himself.

So even he doesn't know what he has signed us up for.

I roll my eyes, the tension growing in my shoulders as I feel the distance between us and the hospital getting smaller. "You sure we have everything? We can go back," I ask, looking in the back seat and seeing everything we need.

Fuck.

This time it was Conner's turn to roll his eyes. "Ava, we have the yoga mat, two pillows and water. What could we have left behind?"

"How do we know unless we check?"

"I know what you're doing and we are going. We are already late; we have everything and we are going."

I don't feel so convinced but I didn't want to go because if I went, I'd have to deal with the look. You know that look? It's kind of sad, like a poor you look, with a hint of judgment at my willingness to get knocked up accidentally, like that hasn't happened to anyone else.

Back at the house in my own little bubble, I hide from the looks. I look down to avoid them at school now that I've started to show, but here I know I won't be able to hide.

I'm squeezing my fists when I suddenly feel a cool hand over one of my fists. I freeze, but after a second I relax into the feeling of comfort that one small gesture gives me, like Conner can read my mind and is silently telling me that he is here with me. He's always there for me, if he's not at work or class, he's with me. Getting everything I crave, and even listening to me complain, but I still can't give myself over to him completely because I will always wonder: is it all because of the baby?

"It will be fine," Conner promises, with his hand still on mine.

. . .

"WELCOME EVERYONE!" Chirps a too cheery nurse with red hair in a short ponytail, her green eyes wide and bordering on crazy as she shows all her teeth in an intense smile.

Yeah I'm not feeling too compelled to stay now.

The nurse stands in front of the room as Conner and I sit on the floor with other couples in a semicircle, each couple different and with their gear all around them, ready for the lesson. "My name is Nurse Patty and I'll be teaching you all about the beauty of childbirth."

I can't help but scoff at that, wondering what drugs she's on and knowing she hasn't had a kid herself; she was such a small thing. But my response only earns me a sharp pointed look from Nurse Patty, a break in her happy cheery façade.

Quickly putting her smile back in place and focusing her attention on the rest of the class, she says, "Today we will go over what to expect in childbirth, we'll cover everything from complications, the birthing process and how to deal with the pain."

"So you will tell us how to make it not painful?" The question is out before I can stop it, but it's a genuine question.

She just gives me a tense smile and I already know she doesn't like me. Oh well, feeling's mutual. "We will go over positions that will help lessen the pain. We cannot stop it entirely."

"Great…" I slump where I sit, defeated, and roll my eyes.

"And we will even watch a short film showing you what birth is actually like."

Could this place get any better?! And in that moment, everyone in the room groans a bit, and I start to feel a bit of comfort knowing that it wasn't just me.

Nurse Patty continues, her smile more intense than ever as she talks over our collective groans. "But first I'd like to get to know you. How about we start with our colorful couple in the back."

It takes me a moment to realize that she's talking to Conner and me, it's when everyone in the room simultaneously turns to look at us, leaning forward and cocking their heads in waiting that I catch on.

I blink in surprise and my brain starts to short-circuit, my mouth forgetting to control itself as I let out a whole lot of word vomit, sputtering over my words. "Us? Oh, we're not a couple. I mean we are having a baby together but it was a mistake, not that we are not happy about the baby."

Conner cuts in with a charming smile on his face and his hand on my tense shoulder, giving it a gentle squeeze. "What my eloquent partner is trying to say is that this wasn't planned but we are happy about this new journey we get to go on together."

The group goes 'aww' at his sentiment but I knew it was bullshit.

I feel the distance close between us when everyone moves on to another couple, his warm breath tickling my ear as he whispers, sending a shiver down my spine. "Nice job, little lamb."

"Don't call me that," I hiss, making him chuckle.

"What should I call you? Baby mama?"

"Don't you dare."

Our little moment is interrupted when Nurse Patty coughs loud enough to interrupt the couple currently talking and we look up to find her looking at us with a narrowed expression, making me shrink where I sit.

Seeing me slump, she must be satisfied enough to move on to the couple at the end, forgetting the other couple that she'd interrupted. This couple is different than the others. They look a bit older than the rest, with a slight dusting of gray hair at their roots, but they look like the happiest couple in the room as the woman leans back against the man's chest for him to wrap her in a comforting embrace. I fight the need to look at Conner, wishing things were different, but I shut that idea down very quickly. There's no point dwelling on that now.

"And what about you, lovely couple?"

The woman looks back at who I assume to be her husband, looking a little nervous before returning her attention to the group with a gentle smile. "Oh, well this is our first baby. We've been trying for twenty years." She rests her hands over her belly.

"Wow, twenty years! And you finally got there! Well done," Nurse Patty exclaims, her eyes wide.

They share another loving smile, a whole world in that look. "Not without its challenges. Many doctors told us it wasn't possible and just when we were thinking of giving up, God gave us a miracle. Now we are like the oldest couple here."

The group laughs but I can't help but be a bit curious about this couple who appear to love each other more than anyone I've met before. It was so foreign.

"Well I'm glad you could join us."

From there, Nurse Patty went into talking about the procedure of childbirth, what to expect and what could go wrong. Conner paid extra attention and when I looked over, I saw him actually writing notes in a tiny notebook. I didn't even see him bring that in, but it surprised me. I didn't even think to bring one. I figure I'll be too busy in pain to do much of what Nurse Patty is saying, so I guess I'll leave that up to him.

As soon as Nurse Patty announces that we're going to start watching a video of an actual birth, I decide now is a good time for a bathroom break so I discreetly scurry out of the room, earning a questioning look from Conner. I mouth that I'm going to the bathroom and tell him to stay as I increase my pace before he can change his mind and follow me to the damn bathroom.

Once I hear the click of the door behind me, I let out a big relieved breath before making my way to the bathroom, because standing outside the door isn't far enough away from the wretched video of some chick screaming.

I cringe at the sound and continue to the bathroom until the screaming fades to nothing when I reach the door.

It's bad enough that I have to live through the birth, I don't want to witness someone else's. It's like seeing your death before it happens, why would anyone want that? What happened to ignorance being bliss? I think to myself as I push the bathroom door open and quickly step inside.

"Oh!" I hear behind me, making me jump as I spin around to see the older woman from the class. I think she said her name was Heather. She's sitting on the floor by the toilet, her legs out in front of her and a bag of chips in her hand, her mouth already full and her eyes wide from being busted.

"Sorry, I didn't think." I turn to leave to find another bathroom to do exactly what she is doing, because I wish I had thought of it first. A bag of chips sounds really good right now.

"You too, huh?" Her light voice makes me stop, turning to face her.

"What?"

She pops another chip in her mouth, raising her brow at me. "Freaked you out as well?"

I shrug, feeling a little comfort in not being the only one freaked out. "Just a little. I guess seeing it makes it all so real."

"They certainly don't make it as glamorous as they do in the movies."

We both laugh at that, at how much they lie to us in movies, before the room is again filled with nothing but the crinkling of chip packets and the distant hustle and bustle of the hospital beyond the door.

I shuffle my feet awkwardly, wanting to stay but not sure if she wanted to be alone, but all she does is smile an amused smile at me before laughing and holding up the bag of chips, its salty scent teasing my senses. "You want some? I was craving these like crazy."

I smile. "Okay."

I sit down awkwardly with my growing belly, putting my legs out like hers as she sets the bag between us. We stuff our faces and I swear I almost orgasm from the salty deliciousness of the chips. I don't remember reacting this way over food before, and that just makes Heather laugh again.

"So yours wasn't planned?" Heather asks, and a chip freezes halfway to my mouth, but I don't see judgment when I look at her, just curiosity.

"No," I say, trying not to hang my head, not knowing what else to say.

"And that man in there isn't your boyfriend?"

"No." I continue to wait for the look, but all she does is nod as she takes in the information.

"Hey at least he's sticking around. My dad never did for my mom." She shrugs as if that doesn't bother her.

I give her a sad smile. "I'm sorry. My mom never stuck around for my dad, not that he gave her much to stick around for. Gosh, I'm sorry, I don't know why I said that."

She just laughs. This chick is always laughing or happy, I seriously need to get some of whatever shit she's on. But maybe she is just happy. It is possible, isn't it? "It's the pregnancy, sometimes works as a truth serum." When I don't say anything, she wipes her hand on her leggings and reaches over to grab mine, giving it a squeeze. "It'll be okay."

I almost want to cry over the emotions spilling out of me, but I bite the inside of my cheek to hold them back, not wanting to lose my shit completely in front of this woman. I squeeze her hand back. "Thanks."

"Hey." She nudges my shoulder, lightening the mood up instantly with a beaming smile. "Maybe after, you guys could come have lunch with Hank and me?"

"That'll be nice."

She watches me a moment and for a second I think she can see into my head. Her eyes soften and she leans in to whisper, though there was no one else around to hear. "For what it's worth, I think he really likes you."

She didn't need to elaborate who she meant, so I rest my hands on my stomach and laugh. "So much that he got me pregnant."

But she didn't laugh. "And he stuck around and is coming with you to these things."

"Actually he's making me go."

She nudges me again, excited, her smile getting bigger. "See? No guy who doesn't care makes a girl go to these things. Hank wasn't even doing that."

We laugh again, though I couldn't get her words out of my head. I know that Conner feels something, but it could just be for the baby. He could be doing these things for the baby, not because he actually wants to be with me. Would he want to be with me if I wasn't pregnant? He slept with me, sure, but that's not saying much.

We're so caught up in our conversation that we both jump in surprise when the door suddenly opens to reveal the tiny nurse. Nurse Patty looks at us pointedly, like a teacher catching kids smoking in the bathroom. "So this is where you went off to. I see you are going to make things interesting, Miss Daniels."

I meet her look with a smile. "I try, Nurse Patty."

"Let's go back to class, it's time for the breathing exercises."

THE BREATHING EXERCISES ARE WEIRD. She has each couple face each other and pretty much breathe in each other's faces. Luckily Conner doesn't have bad breath but I am all too aware that I probably have potato chip breath. I groan internally, cursing Nurse Patty but Conner never says anything. He does every exercise and helps me when I need it. Each day it gets harder to not be curious about Conner, about being with him, but it just wouldn't be a good idea. But at this point, I'm starting to wonder if I'm protecting my baby or just myself. Before I can fall too hard down that rabbit hole, Nurse Patty announces that it's time to learn some birthing positions to help relieve some of the pain.

I eventually find myself on all fours, with Conner behind me and I can't help but wonder if we did this position that night. Sometimes I wish I could remember, but other times I'm happy I don't.

I suddenly hear Conner chuckle a bit behind me, sounding more like a hiss as he tries to hide his laughter. I look over my shoulder and hiss. "What's so funny?"

He's got his hand over his mouth and his face is slightly red when he asks, with a twinkle in his eyes. "You wearing a pink thong?"

I almost think I misheard him because surely he couldn't know. "What?"

"Because I can see it. Not that I mind the view, but—"

"What?!" I spin around and plant my ass on the floor with a thud, my eyes wide and my heart racing as I look at Conner as he continues to try not to laugh. I want to punch him.

"There is a slight rip in your pants."

"What? How slight is slight?" I resist the urge to check,

not wanting to draw more attention to it than I already have. But I run my hand over the area beneath me and gasp when I feel the ripped fabric of my yoga pants and the smooth skin of my butt.

"I can see your butt."

Just as I am about to lose my shit, my day gets even better when a shadow falls on us and I hear the sharp tone of little Nurse Patty. "Is there a problem over here?"

I turn to look at her, not sure if I want to say anything because she already hates me and I doubt this would help my cause. But I don't have much choice unless I leave, but how can I leave without anyone seeing my butt? Maybe if Conner walks behind me, but I think he has seen enough of my thong. So, I swallow my pride and I say in the softest voice I can, making sure no one can hear. "Do you have any spare pants around here?"

She blinks and furrows her brow before leaning forward slightly. "I'm sorry?"

I bite my lip, feeling uncomfortable as I notice others staring at me with questions in their eyes, but I focus on Patty when I explain, "I've ripped my pants."

She blinks again, but this time in recognition. "Oh, I think I can rustle something up. If you'd like to lead the way to the door, I'll follow closely behind you."

I grab her extended hand and she thankfully positions herself behind me, excusing herself from the class. And just like that, Nurse Patty became my favorite person, whereas Conner was going to get a kick in the face with all the laughing he's doing as I leave the room in pursuit of pants.

ONCE CLASS IS OVER, I'm grateful.

After the mishap with my pants, Nurse Patty was able to rustle me up some surgical pants, the blue ones you see doctors and nurses using. They didn't fit around my belly, so I had to wear them uncomfortably low in the front. Made the rest of class time uncomfortable with everyone looking at me, wondering about my sudden change of pants.

But I didn't tell them. No way!

Conner is no longer laughing thankfully and now it is finally over. For today anyway.

Conner is scooping up our pillows and other belongings when Heather's husband walks up to us with a bag on his shoulder, pillows under his arm and a mat under the other, a smile on his face as he approaches us, eyeing my pants with humor in his eyes. "Snazzy pants you have there. I heard from the misses that we're having lunch."

It's not a question, but I feel Conner's questioning gaze on me, so I just ask the man, nervously, "If that is okay?"

He nods, his friendly smile still in place. "Of course. It's great my wife is meeting others who are in a similar state. She's just gone to the restroom." I was just wondering where she was, I couldn't help thinking she was sneaking more potato chips. Maybe I should go check…

"Hey, I'm Conner." Conner interrupts my plan as he steps forward, awkwardly extending his hand only to realize the man had no hands to shake with. He drops his hand and stands awkwardly at my side.

"Yeah, I remember from the introductions. I'm Hank."

"Nice to meet you." There's a brief stretch of awkward silence, where we stare at each other with no clue on how to proceed and silently beg the other person to say something. That is, until Conner turns to me with a raised brow, asking, "So you've been making friends?" He doesn't sound angry but amused mixed with pleased.

I shrug. "Just a little. You don't have to come."

He scoffs, putting a hand to my shoulder. "And miss spending more time with you? I'd rather die."

I roll my eyes as Hank laughs.

Thankfully, I see Heather walking through the door again and am grateful to be leaving for lunch soon because I am starving.

"So you met in your freshman year of college?" I ask Heather, genuinely interested.

We've been at the restaurant for only thirty minutes and as I dig into my carbonara pasta, Heather and Hank dig into their history, pushed on by my constant questions. I've always been so fascinated by other couples, curious about how they last and stay happy for such a long time. I guess it's because I haven't really seen a long functioning relationship.

Hank and Heather don't seem to mind, because with each question they either laugh at some inside joke I'm missing or they smile at each other. It makes my heart feel warm. Heather answers my question with her husband's arm wrapped around her shoulder. "Yep, he was best friends with my big brother, a year above me and he was just always around."

"Any chance to see her, am I right?" I look at Conner and see him smiling at Hank before looking back at me. The look he gives me is soft and full of so much emotion I have to turn away. I can feel my cheeks heating up as I hear Hank's reply.

"Right."

Clearing my throat, I focus back on Heather. "So you just got together?"

She sits up a bit with a chuckle, Hank smiles at this. "Oh, it wasn't as easy as that. You see, my brother was extremely protective of me, so if Hank and I wanted any time alone, we had to sneak away."

"What happened when your brother found out?" I ask, leaning a bit forward.

Hank was the one to speak up. "You see this scar?" He points to a thin scar running along the left side of his hairline. "Hit me with a lamp when he caught us in bed together."

"Oh geez." I sit back a bit as Heather waves it off.

"Oh it's okay, they made up eventually and we've been together ever since."

Just as they're digging back into their food, I can't stop my curiosity from getting the best of me so I have to ask, "How did you handle it? Sneaking around, stealing moments."

They freeze with food still in their mouths for a moment, then they swallow and look at each other with the same soft loving look I saw on Conner's face. "We just did. If you love someone, you make it work no matter what." They blink, turning back to me as if just remembering that we're still here. "You see Ava, there will always be obstacles in love as well as life, it all just depends on how you handle it."

I guess my parents didn't handle it well, or maybe they weren't in love. I resist the urge to look at Conner because yes, my feelings have grown for him in the past months. He's really stepped up and proven he cares about the baby, but the question remains, would he be like this if it wasn't for the baby? If only I hadn't become pregnant but I couldn't wish my baby away now. It's changed my life, but I love it, it is a part of me. And I wish I wasn't plagued by fear put there by my parents, but I don't think I can help that.

"WELL, it was really nice meeting you," I say as I shoulder my bag outside the restaurant, but before I can say anything else, Heather envelops me in a hug, holding me in her arms awkwardly with our two bellies acting as a barrier, before pulling away and handing me a slip of paper. "Call me if you need anything. I really like you, Ava. I see a lot of myself in you." She gives my shoulder a squeeze and I can't help but giggle.

"That's quite the compliment"

She laughs, leaving me standing outside the restaurant with Conner and what lies between us.

CHAPTER 22

AVA

That night, Conner is cooking dinner for us. The rest of the guys are still gone, it is just us and that knowledge makes me nervous, which is evident as I shift in my seat at the kitchen counter, watching his strong back in his black T-shirt as he stirs the pasta in the pot.

My eyes roam south to his butt which is hugged perfectly in a pair of dark blue jeans and is almost begging me to smack it. Shit, where did that come from?!

I shake my head, silently urging him to hurry with the food so I can hide in my room away from him. Maybe chain myself to the bed so I'm not tempted. Fuck, now I'm imagining Conner chained to the bed! Since when have I ever been interested in kink?

I shake my head again and the movement catches Conner's attention as he turns. "Everything alright?"

Aside from wanting to do you right here, yeah I'm just dandy! Seriously why am I not giving into my urges again? As if on cue, the baby kicks, making me gasp. The sound makes Conner spin fully to face me, concern on his face. "What's wrong?"

Before I can answer, he's around the counter and has his hands on my belly, a crease evident between his brows.

"I'm fine, the baby just kicked again."

He moves his hands around my belly with the gentlest of touches, and as if the baby knows, it kicks again toward where Conner's hand is. This time he gasps, like he does every time he feels the baby kick, his blue eyes shining and a big beaming smile appears on his face. I look up at him and what looks back at me is a look of pure happiness.

I can't help the smile that appears on my face in return and before I know it, we are standing in the kitchen looking into each other's eyes, like a couple of lovestruck idiots.

Is that what it is? Is that what I feel? It could just be lust, or my hormones. But the way my heart is fluttering right now as he smiles down at me, it makes me want to always see that smile. But is that love?

How would I know?

Maybe it's best if I don't know because I can't do anything about it anyway, can I?

Our moment is interrupted by the loud sound of bubbling and we both look over to see the pasta boiling over.

"Fuck!" Conner runs to turn it down before turning back to me, the moment lost.

It isn't until dinner is being served and we are both sitting at the table that he speaks again. "We should start thinking about names."

I swallow my food and cock my head at him. "What?"

"For the baby."

"We don't even know the sex."

He points his fork at me. "Because you don't want to know."

I scoff. "Neither do you."

Conner shrugs and continues to eat his food. "Either way, it might be good to just go through some names. We don't have to pick any now, but at least we can think about it."

I consider it and think that maybe it's not a bad idea. What could it hurt? "Okay. You got any suggestions?"

He thinks, tapping his fork on his bottom lip. "Mildred?"

This time I point my fork at him. "Don't make me stab you with this fork."

"Okay, okay." He raises his hands in surrender before continuing, "Stewart?"

"Okay, that's it. You are not naming our child."

He chuckles, shoving the last forkful of food into his mouth, raising his brows at me. "You got any ideas then?"

I think and only one comes to mind. "Charlie. Works for a boy or a girl."

Conner regards me for a moment then leans his forearms on the table. "Why Charlie?"

I shrug, the memory filling my mind and making me smile. "When I was a kid, I used to love *Charlie and the Chocolate Factory*. The book, not the movie. I would read it to Lucy every night."

I was lost in that memory, a faraway look on my face when Conner asks, "Why that story?"

"It gave us hope."

"For what?"

I didn't know if I was ready to say anything, but I guess if he is gonna be in my life, he will find out eventually. "That one day we could get out." I suck in a breath, bracing myself as I finally tell him the story I didn't want to tell. "Our mom left us when I was eight years old. She went to the gas station, Lucy and I were in the back seat of the car. It was snowing then, close to Christmas. I remember seeing our breaths and worrying if Lucy was warm enough. We waited for Mom to come back."

"She didn't," Conner finishes, his voice a hushed whisper.

I nod. "Yep. She left because of my dad. He was a truck driver, so he was rarely home, but when he was… he would drink. A lot. He would get mean, but never physical. I mean he'd throw things but he'd never hit her or us. I guess she just couldn't take it."

It's quiet and I am left swimming in an anger I thought I buried years ago.

"Why didn't she take you guys with her?"

I shrug, because that is the question I've asked myself for years. "I don't know. All I know is that after that, my father hated me. He never did anything to Lucy, which I'm grateful for, but everything I did was wrong for so many years. It was like I had replaced Mom. Father told me that he hated looking at me because I looked so much like my mom." I feel the tears roll down my cheek and all I want to do is wipe them away. I don't want my father to have this power over me. He didn't win. I left, and soon, so will Lucy.

"Is Lucy okay there now?"

I can't help but smile at the concern in his voice for the safety of my sister, but I wouldn't have left if she wasn't safe. "Yeah, she's his favorite. He's never yelled at her. At the worst, she is ignored. But it's kind of the best as well. It shouldn't be like this but it is. I make sure to check in on her often. We text and Skype."

"You took care of her." His blue eyes soften as he looks at me, and I feel the truth in his words.

"Yeah, I did."

"That's why you are going to be an amazing mom. And I'm so proud it will be to my child." He breaks the tension, reaching across the table to grab my hand and give it a gentle squeeze, rubbing the back of my hand with his thumb and I almost want to purr at the comfort in that one act. "Charlie it is."

Looking at him, I know that I'll never be alone, that he

will have my back, that he will be there for our child. But could it ever be more?

Should I let it?

CHAPTER 23

AVA

Weeks have passed and the guys have finally returned from their hometowns, classes have started back up and everything is in full swing. Conner and I have gone shopping for cribs and baby clothes. Not buying anything yet, but it doesn't hurt to look.

I love the comfort I feel hearing the blasting noises coming from the TV as Logan shoots his video game guns at players and the sound of Hunter and Conner arguing over lives lost in said game.

Standing here in sweats, making beef stew for everyone, I actually feel happy. I can feel my smile beaming on my face as I listen to the sounds they're making, the men that have become my family.

Who would've thought?

"Ava! Control your man. He has no honor." Hunter comes stomping into the kitchen and I laugh, shaking my head at him.

"What has he done now?" I ask, hoping he doesn't notice my lack of correcting him about referring to Conner as 'my man'.

"You just don't know how to take a hit." Conner comes strutting in, answering before Hunter can speak.

"Take a hit?!" Hunter exclaims when Logan enters the kitchen, all the men making the kitchen feel a whole lot smaller than it did previously.

Seeing the growing tension in Hunter's shoulders, I raise my hands to pacify them, speaking in a calm voice, I say, "Listen, if you boys can't play the game like men, then don't play at all."

"But," Hunter tries to argue but I hold up my hand, silencing everyone in the room, until Logan whispers under his breath.

"Damn."

I narrow my eyes.

"Sorry," he mumbles and it's then I realize how much control I actually have in this house. I never asked for it, but the guys just listen to me. It only took me getting pregnant for that to happen. That's a tactic I won't be using again, I think to myself as a knock sounds at the door.

After looking at each other, Conner is the one to answer the door, with all of us peeking from our place in the kitchen.

"Fuck," Hunter hisses when he sees the red-headed beauty on the other side of the door, now beaming up at the father of my child and batting her stupid eyelashes at him.

I feel my body tense as I watch them talk, her body closer to his than I would like, and it is then that I feel it. A big hand on my shoulder and another holding my hand. There I stand in the entry to the kitchen, watching the father of my child talking to a woman I know wants him, a woman it would be easy to be with, and I have my family at my back, practically holding me, letting me know they are there, my pain evident on my face.

I try to swallow it, because what right do I have to be

angry? Except what kind of woman goes after a guy who is having a baby with someone else?

I guess I'm going to find out, I realize, as I watch Conner close the door after letting Vivian in. Vivian takes off her coat to reveal a skintight, low-cut red top with long sleeves. It's sexy, but in a subtle way, unless she bends over, then she may be giving these boys a show.

"Wow, it's so chilly out there," Vivian says, rubbing her arms as she approaches us, Conner following behind her. "Thank you so much for letting me stay."

"Stay?" All of us turn confused looks to Conner to see his expression, a mix of annoyed and apologetic. But Vivian clarifies.

"Oh, sorry. I texted Conner because we have a pop quiz on Monday and I'm really stressing; so Conner, like the hero he is, said he could help me."

"To be fair, I meant tomorrow," Conner comments with a hint of a bite, but Vivian remains oblivious.

"Yeah, but there is no way I can sleep until I understand some of the stuff for the test."

"I'll go get my notes," Conner says before leaving us to run upstairs, leaving me to stare daggers at the girl currently checking out his ass.

That's mine to check out.

I'M surprised there hasn't been a noise complaint with how much racket I'm making. I'm throwing plates in the sink, knives and forks, pots and pans. Getting everything ready for dinner when Hunter comes in, his hands over his ears. "Wow, what is going on in here?"

But I don't answer, I just continue to mimic Vivian's stupid high-pitched voice. "Oh Conner! You saved me!" I growl in my own voice, "Why don't you save yourself." I go back to Vivian's voice. "I don't care that you have a baby on the way, I'm thin and beautiful and can have sex without ruining your life."

"Hey!" I didn't see Hunter move but he somehow made his way to stand in front of me, putting his hands on my shoulders and forcing me to meet his eyes. "Is that what this is? You think you ruined his life."

I bite my lip to keep my emotions in check. "It's nothing. I was just ranting."

He bends a bit at the waist, until his eyes are level with mine. "You don't see it but I do."

"What?"

"The change in him. Yeah, this wasn't planned, but Ava, that guy has wanted you since he first met you."

I start to laugh, but the look he's giving me makes me go silent. "Conner has known Vivian since freshman year. She's been following him around all this time and yes, it's annoying. But don't you think if he was interested he would've done something about it ages ago? He doesn't see her; all he sees is you. Now you can laugh, but he talked about you all the time freshman year. Truth be told, I didn't know it was you until we moved in, but I saw it in how he looked at you. You think this pregnancy created a connection, but Ava, the connection was there long before."

I'm speechless, unable to comprehend the words he just said, unsure of what to do with it.

Seeing my stunned expression, Hunter smiles. "Listen, you don't have to do anything now. But I know the feeling's not one-sided. You wouldn't be pissed if you didn't care, that is your guy in there, the father of your child. Are you really going to let some bitch come in and try to take what is yours? And he is yours."

Giving my shoulder a final squeeze he leaves me in the kitchen, food ready to be served, dirty dishes in the sink and my heart now on my sleeve as I think about all Conner has done since I met him, things with the pregnancy and before, the looks he used to give me and still does, the way my body would react to it. Could Conner's feelings for me be far more than the pregnancy? Why would Hunter lie about that?

I'm staring into the sink, tapping my fingers on the counter when her voice shatters my peace, my shoulders instantly go up to my ears.

"Oh, hi! Conner wanted to know when dinner would be ready?" She comes around to stand beside me, leaning in to say, "We are working up quite an appetite in there."

I grit my teeth against the image she is trying to project as she cocks her head in the direction of the small study that's never used, the same one whose door has been open this entire time.

"Yes, studying will do that," I say, turning away from her to get the bowls out of the cupboard. "And dinner will be ready in a second."

I wait for her to leave but she just stands there, staring at me, her eyes moving over my face and body as if trying to copy me to memory, a slight crease appearing between her brows.

"Yes?" I demand, impatience filling that one word.

"Are you okay?" I furrow my brow at her strange question, until she elaborates, "I heard you had an accident a while back, a fall or something."

"How do you know about that?" I instantly get defensive and Vivian looks taken aback.

"I'm sorry. It's just, I can't imagine how scary that must've been for you. Being alone, helpless, scared."

"Did Conner tell you all this?" I demand, wondering what else he has told her and hating the jealousy that is running through my veins at this moment.

"He mentioned it."

I start to ladle the food into bowls. "You guys talk a lot."

She shrugs, a small smile playing at her lips that I want to slap off. "A little."

"Oh great, dinner's ready." Conner comes in, running his hands through his hair, looking tired and hungry as he eyes the bowls in front of me, the army of men following behind him, interrupting my interrogation.

"Oh thank fuck, I was gonna start eating Hunter." Logan sighs, his hand on his belly.

"Don't say that shit around me. Besides you're not my type." Hunter comments, giving Logan a playful shove.

"I should hope not." Conner says under his breath, coming up to get his food with a warm smile.

"What the fuck are you talking about? You'd be lucky to have me." Logan yells in Hunter's face sounding more serious than anyone should.

I finish dishing up the guys' food and I'm about to dish up my own when another bowl is put in front of me. I look up to see Vivian standing there with a smile, waiting.

I level her with a look and debate telling her where she can shove it, but it's the small smile I get from Conner as he sits at the table, a smile that is grateful and too kind. He is the one helping out a friend, but one look at this chick and I know she is taking advantage of his good heart and that just doesn't sit right with me. But I have to be smart about this. I can't tell her to go fuck herself like I want to, or bitch-slap her, so instead I give her a tight smile and dish up for both of us.

I gather my bowl and make my way to the table and that is when I see Vivian going for my spot.

She reaches for the back of the chair and I watch as the boys stiffen in their seats, alert to what is going on.

"Um, I wouldn't," Logan mumbles loud enough for everyone to hear.

"That seat's taken," Hunter informs her, loud and clear, her brows rise and she turns her attention to Conner, silently asking him what's going on.

"I didn't know it was assigned seating." Vivian comments with a nervous chuckle, but before Conner can say anything, I step up to her, waving a hand.

"It's not. It's fine. You can sit there," I say, making my way to the other side, right across the table from Conner. "I prefer to sit here."

"You do?" Conner asks, cocking his head.

"I do now," I say, giving him the sweetest smile, which earns me a confused look.

Dinner was uneventful, Logan making a few jokes with Hunter, Vivian giggling at anything said by Conner, while Conner's eyes haven't left me. It's not until there is a lull in conversation that Vivian actually speaks, moving her eyes over me, and I watch her eyes widen and light up as her smile grows to a grin, her eyes focusing on my growing midsection. "I have to say, you are just getting bigger by the day! But I bet you're itching to see that bundle of joy."

I see the backhanded compliment clear as day, but the thing is, I will lose my stomach eventually, but she will always be an evil bitch set on moving in on a guy that's not officially my man but still is, if that makes sense. That much I see and my tense smile grows tighter when I nod once. "Yeah."

"Oh, I mean no disrespect. It's really cool you having a kid and all."

"Glad you approve," I comment under my breath, which earns me a chuckle from Conner, his amused eyes twinkling as he looks at me.

"So how was... studying?" Logan asks, purposefully stirring the pot judging by the mischievous gleam in his eyes, which only earns him a scowl from Conner as he growls through gritted teeth.

"Studying was fine."

"Yeah, he really helped me understand."

"So what do you want to do?" I ask Vivian with raised brows and for a moment she just looks at me like a deer in headlights.

"I'm sorry?"

"After school? When you finish college?"

She simply shrugs. "I'm still figuring it out. I'm not set on anything in particular yet."

"May I recommend that you take classes you actually understand?" The table goes quiet and thick with tension. I raise my brows as Vivian's eyes turn to slits.

"Excuse me?"

I shrug, not bothered. "I'm just saying with all the help you're asking of Conner, I would think you might want to take a different class. Besides, you were the one concerned with how he spent his time, remember?"

I see her fists clench on the knife and fork in her hands and the thought does occur to me that she could stab me any minute, but Hunter told me to stake my claim in some way. I guess this is it. This is me staking my claim on Conner, until I figure out what I'm going to do.

But she doesn't stab me, instead, she sits there with her jaw clenched and practically seething before Conner steps in. "What is she talking about?" But the question is aimed at Vivian. Conner twists in his chair to face her, his brows raised expectantly and I can see the panic hiding in Vivian's eyes.

She knew what she was doing when she put that in my head, and she knew what Conner would think if he knew she was putting that shit in my head.

At first, I don't think she will answer him, but the silence around the table remains thick with everyone waiting for her to speak.

With a subtle eye roll, she faces him and I wait to hear what she will say. "It was nothing, Conner."

"Let me be the judge of that."

He waits.

"We were just talking. I ran into Ava at the mall some time ago and I mentioned how worried I was."

"About?"

"About you and how much time this pregnancy was taking from your studies."

I scoff, unable to hold it back.

"Away from you, you mean." Hunter mumbles under his breath with a shake of his head, but none of us comment or look away from Conner and Vivian as Conner scowls at a nervous Vivian.

"You put that in Ava's head? This crazy idea that our baby may be affecting my grades?" His question ends on a growl.

"Conner, I—" Vivian stammers out but Conner cuts her off.

"Well, I will tell you something Vivian." He stands from his chair, tucking it in. "My grades are better than ever; I'm not struggling or drowning. In fact, the most stressful part of my life is having to drop everything to help you."

She flinches as if she'd been slapped and I can't help but feel a little sorry for her, but that may be the baby talking.

Conner moves slowly around the table as he continues to speak, until he finally stops to stand beside me. "And don't think I haven't noticed what you are doing. I've tried to overlook it, wanting to help you. But right now, I'm not sure if you want my help, or something else."

She clears her throat and schools her features, trying to hide the pain and anger I see buried in her eyes. "Don't flatter yourself, Conner."

"Good, because I'm taken with a baby on the way, and I hope you wouldn't go after a man like that and risk destroying a family."

She doesn't answer, but steels her jaw and looks around the table at each of us, until her angry eyes land on me, like I'm the worst person she's ever met, and maybe I am.

So, I say as calm as I can. "I think you should leave."

She snaps back so quickly I'm stunned. "I don't care what you think. This is all your fault, you and that—"

I hold up my hand to silence her, knowing that if she finishes that sentence, I may be the one to kill her. "You can stop there." I scoff, folding my arms across my chest. "You know what, I feel sorry for you."

"So glad I didn't miss this," Logan comments gleefully only to receive a glare from an annoyed Conner.

But Vivian just seems pissed as she narrows her heavily made-up eyes at me. "You feel sorry for me?"

"Yeah, you sat there throwing yourself at him right in front of me. Only a desperate woman would do that."

Vivian stands, outraged. "I'm the desperate one? You sneak your way into his bed, accidentally get pregnant and then get pissy if he even talks to another girl."

I slowly rise from my seat. "I'm getting pissy because you are throwing yourself at him!"

"He wasn't saying no."

"Really?! Because I believe he just did. He's too nice to say this, but I'm not." I slam my hand on the table and growl. "Back off from my man."

"Oh why don't you go stuff your face."

"Wow, jokes about my weight, is that all you got?"

"Enough!" Conner yells loud enough to make the room go silent as he slams his own hand on the table, glaring at Vivian who stands frozen and her mouth slightly agape in shock at his outburst. "Get out."

He says the words so softly I'm not sure anyone else heard him. Vivian blinks, genuine hurt appearing on her face and a part of me continues to feel bad, a very small part. "What?"

At that, Hunter rises from his chair beside me, his large frame tense with irritation, "I believe what my friend is trying to say is, get the fuck out."

Vivian's hurt eyes move past everyone, even me, before landing back on Conner, pleading. "Conner? This is not my fault, she was—"

Conner doesn't let her finish. "She's the mother of my baby and what you said is unacceptable. I sat here and watched you being spiteful to her, and I have had enough. Now I would never hit a woman, but don't make me throw you out of my house."

She turns tearful eyes to me and I hate that I am being made to feel bad when she was going to put all the blame on me. We are both to blame for this. "Are you happy now?" With a huff she turns on her heel and storms out, slamming the door behind her with a bang.

CONNER LEAVES the table without a word shortly after Vivian leaves and I have a feeling he is pissed. About what I don't know exactly, but I need to find out. I need to know where we stand and I am also scared I may have done more damage tonight than I thought.

I stand outside the closed bedroom door and wonder if I should knock or just walk in. I mean, it's kind of my room now, isn't it? Do I need to knock on my own bedroom door? But what if Conner wants to be left alone? I decide it's best to be safe and I knock twice, hearing nothing on the other side. "Conner? I'm coming in."

He's standing by the window when I walk in, his profile

showing him deep in thought, the muscles of his back highlighted by the lamp on his desk, lighting the room in a subtle glow.

"Hey, I'm sorry. I shouldn't have let her get to me." I say nervously, playing with the ends of my shirt.

"Why did you?" Conner asks, still not looking at me, and I hate it.

"I don't know," I lie, and he scoffs, finally turning to look at me, his eyes burning into mine, forcing me to look at him as he slowly approaches me. "Yes, you do. Say it."

I'm speechless as he moves in slow predatory steps toward me, stopping just in front of me and in that moment, I make a choice. I fought for him downstairs, it makes no sense to go back to hiding now. Swallowing my fear, I square my shoulders, looking him in the eye when I say as clearly as I can, "I wanted to fight for you."

He cocks his head. "Fight for me?"

"Yes, don't laugh. She had every intention of putting the moves on you and I wanted to show her that she had to go through me to get you."

He takes a step closer, closing the distance between us, until I can feel the warmth of his body radiating into mine. "Were you jealous, Ava?"

"Shut up."

"I thought you didn't want to be a couple," he says this with his face lowered, whispering soft sexy words in my ear, almost making me weak in the knees. I resist the urge to grab him to hold myself up.

My voice shakes when I finally find words, finally laying myself open for him, emotionally anyway. "I don't know what I want anymore. But I do know that I didn't want you with her or anyone else. I'm sorry if that makes me selfish."

"Hey, it doesn't." He tucks a hair behind my ear. "I don't want you with anyone else either, just me."

I finally lift my head to look into his eyes, to see the truth there, but instead I smell his sweet, woodsy smell, taste him and the taste is so familiar. God I wish I could remember. Conner's lips are on mine in a second, so soft and gentle at first, testing the waters. But when I start to move my mouth against his, my tongue playing with his, I moan into his mouth and I feel his grip on my hip tighten.

Feeling that touch makes something flash in my mind. The feel of his hands, I've felt them before. Everywhere. I remember these lips. I remember all the pieces but not enough to make a full picture. God, I wish I could remember.

Just when I feel like we are a hop and a skip away from moving this to the bed, I feel the vibration of his groan in his chest a second before he pulls away, pulling his taste with him. Feeling the emptiness between us, I long to close the gap, I want more. Conner was not my first kiss, but he was better than Teddy at the sixth grade party... who was the first and last person I had kissed.

Yep, kissing Conner was definitely a different experience, judging by the wetness between my legs and the craving I feel there.

I blink up at Conner in question, wondering if I did something wrong and praying that I didn't. Did he not feel the same anymore? Was I really too big? No, that can't be it, he was into it, wasn't he?

He pulls back to look me in the eyes and his jaw is clenched as he lets out a long breath through his nose. "Now, before I rip off your clothes, I think we should stop."

His voice is tight with restraint.

"Why?"

He looks at me a moment before answering. "Because you still don't know, and until you do, nothing will happen," he says this with his hand still on my hip, rubbing circles into it with his thumb and I can't help but wonder how good that will feel elsewhere.

"But..."

"I won't have our second time be another regret."

I didn't know what to say, would it be regret? I don't feel like it would, but he is right. I don't know what we are or how I feel yet. I know I like him but with a baby involved, its more complicated than that.

Unfortunately, I need to give this some time and some thought.

Seeing the confirmation on my face, he gives a small smile. "I'll give you time to think, and you let me know when you're ready."

He surprises me by leaning down and placing a gentle kiss on my forehead, which is full of so much emotion it stuns me. He rests his lips there for a couple of seconds, as if he doesn't want to move away. He does care about me, he does so much for me and it's about time I did something for him, something selfless to show that I care.

When he turns to leave, almost making it to the door, I blurt out, knowing just the thing to do for him. "I'll go with you."

He stops, turning to face me with a brow raised in question. "What?"

I smile a small smile when I answer, "To your parents. I'll go with you and meet them."

His smile grows and his eyes light up at my news but he simply gives me a nod and says with gratitude in his eyes, "Good night, Ava. I'll be back up later."

"Good night, Conner."

And that is how he leaves me, for the first time I really want to touch myself, because God knows he won't, yet.

CHAPTER 24

AVA

Well it's finally that time.

Summer Break.

The house is quiet today when we leave. Hunter is with Mia at their parents' house, and Logan has gone home for the weekend. So, it's just Conner and I which makes things tense, about as tense as they are in the car right now as we head down a long road leading to his parent's place.

It hangs in the air, our kiss. I see it in the way he keeps looking at my lips that he wants it just as much as I do, but I need to see how it goes this weekend because over the past few weeks I haven't seen Conner much. That left me lots of time to think about what is holding me back and the thing is that I don't know anymore. I have so much going on in my head with the baby and Conner. It's all jumbled together so now I can't make sense of it. I do have feelings for him, but is it worth pursuing? I don't want him with anyone else and I can't make him stay with me without being with me. So, I have to make a choice.

I almost jump in my seat when a blanket of warmth consumes my hand. I look down and see that Conner, sensing my inner conflict, has reached over and is holding my hand.

I look up at him, but he's showing no emotion, just focused concentration on the road ahead, but his hand gives me a squeeze and that's when I respond, intertwining my fingers with his..

"We're here," he says as we pull up in front of a beautiful house a few minutes later.

It's yellow with a wraparound porch and a mass of green grass and hills surrounding it, looking like some kind of oil painting.

It is beautiful and so full of memories that I feel like I can see them clear as day. Little Conner trying to climb that giant tree, or rolling in the grass. So many memories and so much more inside I'm sure.

Conner squeezes my hand again, sensing my nerves, and I turn to see the biggest smile I've seen on him since I met him. It knocks the breath right out of me, and I never want that smile gone from his face.

It is carefree.

It is home.

He continues to look at me, waiting for me to say something, so I say the only thing that comes to mind. "It's beautiful."

That makes his smile grow, and I feel it in my chest again.

I take in a deep calming breath and give a small smile when I see his eyes move past my head, amusement appearing in his eyes as he nods his head at whatever's behind me. "And here they come."

I turn in my seat, already knowing what I will find because who else could he be talking about?

I see them and I instantly see Conner in them.

His parents.

A small petite woman practically runs up to the car, a

giant smile taking up most of her beautiful face, with a mass of black curly hair blowing in the breeze. But it is the man at her side that makes my breath lodge in my throat. He looks so much like Conner, with his blue eyes and brown hair, except he has a beard that makes him look older. Maybe Conner could grow a beard, I think to myself as they approach the car, hand in hand with big excited smiles beaming on their faces. An element of warmth and love emitting from them and making me want to join them in a hug.

Weird.

Before I know it, I hear the driver's side door close and see Conner walk around the car with his arms wide.

I follow his lead and force my numb legs to work, I swing open my own door and hop out as Conner's mom is swallowed up by Conner's big hug. She's beaming as she holds her son close, sighing happily. "Here's my baby boy!"

She steps away and Conner's dad steps forward to slap a big hand on Conner's shoulder. "Please, don't embarrass the poor boy."

But it is the look on Conner's face that makes me hesitant to step forward, fear that I would be intruding on this beautiful happy family. It was something so foreign that I only ever saw on TV growing up. The happily married couple with their loving son. It's beautiful to witness and I feel blessed to see an element of freedom and relaxation on Conner's face, like he is at peace as he smiles at his family before him. "Happy to be home, Mom."

"And we are happy you are here." She blinks, as if remembering something before asking with a furrowed brow. "Where's your special lady?"

"Oh, Mom, Dad," Conner returns to me, still standing awkwardly by the car like a creeper invading their loving moment, and pulls me into his side, wrapping an arm around me and leading me closer to his family. "Meet Ava. Ava, meet my parents, Melanie and Jack."

It's hard to miss the pride in his voice as he introduces me. I'm not used to that and I guess I was expecting to feel shame because that's what I'm used to. I'm used to cruelty and abuse, not the love and care with which Conner regards me, it's a welcome change.

I briefly look down at my belly, which has grown so much, fearful of meeting their eyes and seeing their disappointment. In their eyes, it probably seems like I trapped Conner. If only they knew the truth,, but how do I explain that? Yeah, we kinda got drunk and a little careless, but you know, shit happens. I doubt that would go over well.

"Hello, sweetheart." I feel their eyes on me and then I hear Melanie's soft voice, speaking to me in a tone similar to how she spoke to him. So gentle and full of affection. The sound of it stuns me enough that I snap my head up to look at her as she smiles at me, her husband's smiling beside her, both of their brilliant smiles shining in their eyes. "So happy to finally meet you." She reaches out to grab my hand, her hand smaller than mine and less swollen as she gives it a gentle squeeze, as if trying to relieve some of the tension building within me.

"Yeah, I was starting to think he made you up." Conner's dad comments with a wink, making Conner chuckle.

"I've just been busy, Dad."

"Nice to meet you, darlin'." Jack says.

I smile a small smile at both of them, unsure of how else to respond, and I force the words from my mouth. "Thank you for inviting us. It's nice to finally be able to put your faces to your names. Conner talks about you a lot."

That makes her smile grow. "Hopefully all good things."

"Well let's not just stand out here. I got steaks that need cooking."

"And that's our cue," Conner says, stepping away from me with our bags in each hand as he leads me into the house decorated with various wall paintings, up a flight of stairs and to the room at the end of the hall.

We open the door, and Conner drops our bags, leaving me to stand in the doorway to take in the tiny room that smells exactly like Conner.

His old room, I assume, is simple with a big bed against the back wall, a desk littered with books, and a dresser. No posters or trophies, nothing to say anyone lived here.

"It's simple, I know. I took a lot of my stuff to college with me," Conner tells me, reading my face.

"So, we will be staying in here together?"

He smiles. "Unless you want me sleeping out in the barn with the horses."

"There's a barn? With horses?" I can't help the smile, any nerves I have over sharing a room are suddenly at the bottom of my priority list.

Conner laughs, throwing his arm around my shoulder and leading me out of the room. "I'll show you while we're here."

"Can I ride one?"

He laughs again. "Not a chance in hell."

AFTER BEING SHOWN around the house, Melanie leads me into the kitchen where food lays on every surface. Colorful vegetables are chopped on a cutting board and food is boiling in a pot on the stove, but the kitchen has a sweet smell to it. A glance at the oven shows cookies baking, which answers that question.

The smell is warm and inviting, like the rest of the house, and I wonder what it was like for Conner to grow up here, to wake up and come to this kitchen every morning to have breakfast before school. And then I get a flash of my child doing the same thing and I can't help but wonder if it is possible for Conner and I to create this life for them.

Conner's mom is cutting the vegetables and refuses my help, saying she just wants someone to talk to, but so far she is the one doing most of the talking.

No longer listening to the many ways you can cut a carrot, I migrate over to the window over the sink, gazing out at the expanse of land surrounding the house, the rolling hills and lush trees. But my eyes don't stray from Conner, standing outside by the grill with his dad, laughing and chatting in a carefree way I never get to see.

The way his eyes twinkle as he laughs, I don't want to look away, I'm entranced by that twinkle until I distantly hear his mother's voice stop, making the room go silent.

I blink, turning to face her, fearful I've been caught not listening. She's looking at me, with a twinkle of her own in her eyes, this one mischievous and I know that I missed something, so I ask, "Sorry, what?"

Putting down her knife and wiping her hands on a dishcloth, she makes her way around the counter to me, her smile moving from me to my belly and I can't help but feel a little self-conscious. It's hard to miss, but this is the first time she has even looked at my belly or even acknowledged it.

"How far along are you?" she asks when she reaches me.

"About five months now."

She regards my belly before asking, looking a bit nervous as she timidly holds her hands out toward my belly. "You mind if I ...?"

Unsure of how else to respond, I nod and that brings a pleased smile to her face, "Go ahead."

Melanie gently places her hands on my belly, moving them around before keeping them on the front of my belly, where I am the biggest.

It doesn't take long before the baby kicks, making us both gasp and I know she feels it too, only it doesn't scare her away. Instead, she moves closer so that her face is in front of my belly, as if she wants to speak to the baby, or maybe she hopes to see through it to the baby if she gets close enough.

I expel a breath after the kick, placing my own hand on my belly beside hers. "She's been doing that a lot lately."

Conner's mom gives me a beaming smile as she looks up at me, asking, "It's a girl?"

"We don't know. I kind of want it to be a surprise. Sometimes I call it a girl, sometimes a boy, sometimes it." I laugh.

She gives my belly a soft loving look before stepping back. "Conner used to kick me all the time too."

As the moments pass, I watch as her smile shifts and softens to a look of concern as she continues to stare at me, her eyes moving over every part of my face and I fear what she can see when she breaks the tense silence I feel growing, asking in the softest voice. "How are you feeling really?"

I had my response ready, I was going to say I'm fine and that everything is fine, but being here with this woman makes it hard to lie. It's usually pretty easy to say everything is fine because that's the response everyone wants. No one really cares if you are hurt or upset, only about the effect it has on them. But this woman has a softness and a warmth to her that makes me want to wrap myself up in it, to let it in, makes me feel like she actually wants to know, so I give her the most honest answer I can. "A little scared. Unsure."

"Is that about the baby or my son?"

My head snaps up at her response, my eyes wide in surprise as they are met with a pair of knowing ones, alight with knowledge and wisdom. I was never great at hiding my feelings and today is no different, but the look in Melanie's eyes tells me that she sees all that I am feeling and all that I am thinking.

For a second, I feel the urge to lie, to deny it, but that's all I've been doing and I am starting to feel tired. I'm also thankful that someone sees it. The way she looks at me, with no judgment and nothing but acceptance, I decide that to argue would be pointless.

I expel a tired breath, letting my shoulders slump and my head hang forward until my hair falls in waves around my face.

I look up to see her giving me a soft motherly smile. "I see the way you look at him, similar to how I look at his father, even after all these years. But there is a fear to your look. I'm not sure where it comes from but it's there."

I finally ask the one question I had burning within me. "How did you know he was the one? That he would stick around?"

She scoffs, amused as she drops the dishtowel on the counter beside us, her gaze moving to the window to look out at the men outside, still chatting and laughing about something. "I didn't. You can never know these things. But I knew how he made me feel, how he treated me. He was there when it mattered and even when it didn't." She finally looks at me, placing a small hand on my shoulder. "Talk to me."

"I'm scared of him leaving or finding someone else, but I also don't want the baby to be the only reason he's with me."

"What makes you think that's the case?"

I look down at my feet, the shame taking over, making it harder for me to continue to look at her. "Because we weren't together before. I'm sorry, I shouldn't."

She cuts me off, holding my hands in both of hers, giving them a gentle squeeze, forcing me to look back at her. "Don't be sorry. Ava, I believe that everything happens for a reason. And I know my son, if he didn't want to be with you, he wouldn't, even if you were pregnant, he would still support you but he wouldn't look at you the way he does."

When I look out at the boy that has changed my life, that has changed me, I find him looking at me, his expression caught between a smile and a concerned frown. He worries about me; he is always worried about me. I don't have a lot of people that worry. Only Mia, Hunter, and Lucy. That's all I had growing up and now, because of this man, I have so much more, I think to myself as I put my hand on my belly and rub soothing circles.

Melanie continues to talk. "That boy is like his father. He will do anything for his family, and he will love them more than anything."

"I'm just scared," I whisper as I continue to look out at Conner, worried that his mother didn't even hear me.

"I understand," she says, finally pulling my attention away from Conner to focus on her as she looks into my eyes, making sure I'm hearing and understanding her. "It's a big leap, but think of it this way, how would you feel if Conner said he met someone else?"

I instantly clench my fists until I hear a crack, thinking of all the Vivians out there who will want Conner and who might get him if I don't get over my shit and make a fucking move.

Hearing the cracking of my knuckles, his mom smiles. "Exactly."

THE SUN IS STARTING to set by the time dinner is ready. The long table on the back porch is set with steaks, sandwiches, and bowls of salad. Jugs of water and juice sit in the middle and the table is lined with plates.

Melanie and I have already taken our seats across from each other, with Jack on the end. Conner plops himself down beside me, taking my plate and continuing to pile it with food.

I smile when he places it in front of me and proceeds to eat his food while his parents whisper in each other's ears, lost in their own world as if we weren't here. Some may consider it rude but I couldn't help but watch them, wondering if that was possible for me, possible for Conner and I.

I was hopeful.

I see movement at the corner of my eye and incline my head to see Conner leaning into me, so close that I can smell his woodsy sent and feel his breath brushing my face when he whispers, "Saw you talking to my mom, anything interesting?"

Seeing his curiosity, I pause, slowly smiling, "It was enlightening."

His brows crease as his curiosity grows and I feel my smile grow as I think about everything his mom had told me, somehow making me want to let down my walls and let him see me.

Our little moment is broken when we hear the front door close, the sliding door leading outside open, and see a tall man walking through the house. This man is tall and lean with black tousled hair, but his blue eyes match both Conner's and his dads. He looks a little older than Conner. Stubble coats his jaw and his hair is a little longer than Conner's. He has on a band T-shirt and a pair of black jeans. But I can definitely see Conner in him so he must be related.

The man finally notices us and blinks in surprise as he walks out to us, running his hand through his hair, messing it up more. "Sorry, I didn't know we were having company."

"Sorry, we thought you had plans." Melanie gives a nervous laugh.

"They fell through."

"No matter. Grab a plate," Jack says, waving a hand at the food.

It is then that I notice how Conner's posture has tensed and his fists are clenched as he frowns at the man. "When did you get back?"

"Hello to you too, brother." He looks at Conner pointedly, sensing the hostility from his brother. Well, that explains the relation. "A couple of weeks ago."

"For how long this time?" Conner comments and this time, his brother tenses and shrugs with a tense smile.

"I don't know."

I shift in my seat, feeling so uncomfortable, like I'm in the middle of something I shouldn't be. The movement only draws his attention to me, making the brother look at me, smiling. "Sorry for my brother's manners, I'm Riley."

"Ava."

"So you're my brother's special lady?" Riley cocks his head at me.

"You told him about Ava?" Conner turns to his parents, irritation evident in his words, but it is Riley that speaks again.

"Well, it's hardly a secret."

"That's hardly the point."

"What the hell is your problem?" Riley exclaims, until a big booming voice shatters the chaos into silence as his father yells.

"Boys!"

The silence lasts only a minute until Conner leans over the table to get into Riley's face. Riley glares at him as Conner growls, angrier than I've ever seen him and I really don't know what to do or how to react but it makes me wonder what happened between these two brothers. "My problem is that you leave town without so much as a good-bye, we don't hear from you for five years and now you think you can just come back here like nothing happened."

"Are you angry at me for leaving or leaving without saying goodbye to you?"

"Fuck you."

"Boys!" their mom yells this time, standing now and glaring at both of them, warning them not to speak. "That is enough. Yes, Riley is back and yes we will welcome him with open arms because that's what family does. I will not sit here while you two antagonize each other."

"I'm sorry, Mom. But I need to go." Conner takes my hand and we both rise from our chairs, food not even touched yet.

"Conner." But before Melanie can finish, Riley rises from his chair.

"Bro, sit down, I'll go."

"See, that's the problem."

"Seriously, you want me to leave, yet you get pissed if I go? Do I ever win?"

"No, you don't." He growls through gritted teeth before looking back at his parents. "Sorry, but I need a minute."

But before he could pull me out, I offer an awkward smile to his parents. "Dinner was lovely, Mr. and Mrs. Sanders." And I say to Riley, feeling Conner's grip tighten slightly on my hand as I do. "Nice to meet you, Riley."

"Pleasure was all mine. Maybe I will see you again during your stay here."

"Don't count on it," Conner growls before we make our way up the stairs to our room and he closes the door behind us. It isn't until we are in the room that I decide I've had enough. I want this man, but I won't be pulled around like a rag doll, especially not being pregnant. I rip my hand from his grip. "Stop pulling me. What is your problem?"

"Just give me a minute, Ava." His fists are clenched and his shoulders are bunched up around his ears. A part of me wants to go to him, but I also know the importance of space so I do as I'm told.

I sit on the bed and wait until finally, Conner plops himself down on the bed beside me.

"Now tell me what the fuck that was," I demand, hating seeing Conner like this and not knowing how to fix it, feeling helpless and useless.

He remains quiet and unmoving for another minute.

"Conner!"

"You don't understand, Ava," he says, not looking at me. "Riley and I are not like you and Lucy. We've never been close."

"That much was obvious."

He runs his fingers through his hair, finally looking up but still not looking at me. "Five years ago he left. He didn't say goodbye, he just called us one day and said he was in England. We thought he was at a friend's place but he was in England. We didn't hear from him for five years and now he comes back expecting everything to be okay." He scoffs, shaking his head, but this time I don't see anger, I see pain. I see the pain of the boy who lost his older brother when he needed him. He felt abandoned and that is something I know a little about.

"You missed him."

"No, I didn't," Conner says sharply. "I'm pissed because of how he just left, I'm pissed because of how it broke Mom's heart and I'm pissed he didn't even talk to me."

"Why did he go?"

"He got a chance to play with this band. I've never heard of them and judging by how he's back, turns out no one else has either."

The pain is there, despite how much he denies it. "Maybe you should talk to him, tell him what he did hurt you and your family."

"He doesn't listen."

"Try."

He looks at me a moment before returning his attention to his hands in his lap, shaking his head again. But it's in that moment that I truly see the pain, the need he has for his brother, why he lives with so many guys. He craves the brotherly bond he was robbed of. He seeks it in his friends but that will never be enough. He still has so much pain from his brother and all I want to do is take that away. "Let's talk about something else. You and Mom seemed to get along fine. What we're you talking about in the kitchen?"

Maybe one day I will tell him, I think to myself as I smile. "Girl stuff."

"Anything you can tell me?" he asks with a raised eyebrow.

I just shrug. "She just helped me sort out some pretty tough stuff."

"Yeah, she's good at that."

"I like her, both of them actually."

"I'm happy to hear that. They liked you too."

Watching him as we sit in silence, I think of everything his mother told me, appreciating the man beside me, always there and quick to invite me into his world, to let me in. I know that I would regret it forever if I don't take a chance.

My decision made, I reach over and take his free hand in mine and rub circles on the back of his hand, letting him know I'm here.

Now I just need to find a way to tell him.

* * *

I COULDN'T SLEEP that night.

My mind racing with thoughts of Conner with another woman, with Vivian and girls like Vivian, holding my child.

I toss and turn until I finally give up on sleep, my baby kicking me as I sit up in bed, looking over at a peacefully sleeping Conner, itching to touch his hair, or his face, but instead I turn away, needing some space and time. Needing to breathe for a second and gather my thoughts.

My rumbling stomach signals where I must go.

I put on my robe and creep my way down to the kitchen.

I turn a corner, flicking the light on only to have my heart jump up into my throat at the sight of someone sitting at the kitchen counter.

My breathing starts to calm when I see Riley sitting at the counter with a carton of chocolate chip ice cream and a spoon hanging from his mouth, his eyes wide like a deer in headlights when he sees me.

I put my hand to my chest, "You scared the hell out of me." I hiss, which earns me an amused smile, so similar to his brother only his has a darker edge to it, less playful.

"Sorry. Couldn't sleep?" He eats another spoonful and I grab my own spoon, plopping myself down beside him, ready to dig in.

"You could say that." But before I could even get a scoop, Riley moves the carton out of reach.

"Oh no, has anyone ever told you to not mess with another man's ice cream stash."

I level him with a glare, holding my spoon at him like a knife I'm threatening to stab him with. "Anyone ever tell you not to get between a pregnant lady and a carton of ice cream?"

I watch as he mulls this over, considering before finally sighing and reluctantly putting the carton between us.

"So what's up?" He sees my hesitation. "You can tell me, we are practically family." He gives me a wink and I scoff.

"You sure about that?" I raise my brows, devouring a huge scoop of ice cream.

"You mean the performance at dinner?" He waves his hand dismissively. "That happened before I even left."

"Really? Because Conner seemed really hurt."

"That seemed like hurt to you?"

I look him in the eye, putting my spoon down on the table. "Some people show hurt in different ways. Conner is angry yeah. You are his brother, his big brother. He needed you and you left."

"You got any little siblings, Ava?"

I furrow my brow at the question. "Yes. A little sister."

"Do you live with her?"

I sigh, seeing where he is going with this, seeing the sharpness in his eyes as he watches me register his point, a slight curve appearing on his lips in a sly smile.

He cocks his head. "I didn't think so. What happened all those years ago is more complicated than Conner or you think." He hisses his words before dropping his spoon on the counter with a metallic clang and turns away to leave.

Watching his tall retreating back, I consider letting him leave, but I think back to the lost look in Conner's eyes and that is what drives the next words out of my mouth, stopping Riley in his tracks. "Maybe you should talk to him. He's angry but he's also hurt. You say it's more complicated? Fine, explain it to him. He's smarter than you think and he's not a kid anymore."

"Ava"

But I cut him off, "Conner will be a father soon and I hope you will man up and be the cool uncle this kid deserves. The same kind of uncle Conner can turn to when the kid and I become too much. He doesn't know it, but I think he will need you. So please, consider speaking to him. If not now, then soon."

He stays with his back to me a moment, the muscles in his back tense, until he finally turns to me, his face soft and thoughtful, a small smile playing on his lips when he says in a soft low voice. "You know, you're different than the girls he used to date."

I bristle at the thought of those woman and the memory of my dream. "Oh?"

"You actually care about him. Enough to call me out on my bullshit. Let's hope the kid gets your spunk."

* * *

CONNER'S GONE with his mom to the farmer's market for dinner.

I wanted to go but I had my mind set on one particular thing.

I set my sights on the red rustic looking barn, sitting perched in the middle of the rolling hills, lush green grass surrounding it.

I walk through the wide doors, hearing the chorus of nays from the horses in the stalls. I look over each horse, fascinated by the strong, majestic and graceful creatures, amazed to be seeing them in real life.

Now I've seen plenty of horses on TV and movies, but I've never seen one up close, and I have to say that I am not disappointed.

I approach one that appears to be the calmest of the lot, standing there watching me with her big dark eyes. This one is black all over, the physical embodiment of black beauty, her coat so shiny and soft, begging me to touch it.

I reach the stall, raise my hand to pat her, showing her my hand so I don't spook her and move gently and carefully to stroke her hair.

There is a peacefulness to this creature, one I welcome after the chaos that has been my life.

"You found a friend." The man's voice spooks me and I turn to see the warm smile of Conner's dad, Jack.

I smile as he approaches, standing beside me outside the horse's stall. "She's beautiful." I comment, mesmerized by the creature.

"Yeah, we just picked her up a week ago."

"What's her name?"

"She doesn't have one yet."

I look at him in shock, "What?"

His smile only grows when he leans in a bit to whisper, "We found her in the middle of a storm a week ago. She has a large gash on her leg, see there?" He points and I follow his finger to see the white bandage on her back leg, stained with blood.

I gasp, covering my mouth with my hand, "What happened?"

He shrugs. "I suspect either another animal attacked her or she got hit by something. I haven't been able to inspect it that closely. My wife had to wrap the bandage because she's the only one she will let near her. Had me worried sick the whole time, but when my wife sees someone in need—" He shakes his head but his eyes are full of a love I so desperately wish to see aimed at me one day, from someone I currently can't get out of my head. It is a love that is so foreign but beautiful all at once. "That woman drives me crazy. But she has a big heart and I think the horse can see that." I smile at how beautifully he speaks of his wife when he leans in again. "You wanna know something? Horses are an excellent judge of character. So, it's great to know my son's with someone a horse likes."

"Thank you, I think."

"It's a good thing. I'm proud, but I can tell you're scared out of your mind."

I scoff, laughing. "Of course I am, why wouldn't I be?"

"You have no reason to be. If it's the baby, I know you will be fine. You have a lot of people who love you and will be there to help, my wife and I included because we will be the best grandparents. Unless your parents want to battle us for the title?"

The mention of my parents is like a bucket of cold water in the face, waking me up to the reality of what I was raised around in comparison to Conner's fairy tale, the same fairy tale I want for my child.

I feel my smile melt from my face and I see it reflected in Jack's eyes, his brows furrowing at me as he cocks his head. "What's wrong?"

I ask myself if I should even say anything. I mean, it doesn't really matter to them, right? But the care in his eyes, similar to his son's, makes me think of my father and how it would have felt to have this same look given to me by him when I was a child. Would I still be in the same situation? Probably. Should I even tell my dad? No. When I left I swore I would never see him again. When I can, I will take Lucy away from there too and leave him to rot.

"Ava?" I blink, realizing I hadn't responded to Conner's dad. His expression was a concerned frown now.

"Oh, sorry. No, my parents wouldn't want the title." Though I force a smile, Jack stares at me a moment, thoughtful as he takes in every inch of my face, before sighing and nodding.

"Ah, I see." Is all he says, and by the softening look in his eyes, I know he sees, maybe not everything but enough to understand that my parents are not in my life.

"Well, it's lucky we are not our parents, aye." Conner's dad breaks the tense silence with a chuckle and nudges me slightly, grinning. And it makes me think, could this be my new normal?

CHAPTER 25

AVA

It's been a week since we left Conner's parents' house and I have been on edge ever since, with thoughts of Conner holding our baby with another woman at his side, at our kid's graduation with his new family and it makes it all too clear how badly I want to be a part of his family. I need to do something or say something, but how? Do I come right out and say, yeah I wanna be with you and have a family with you? I'm all in with you? Or do I just kiss him again? Jump his bones? What, damnit, what?!

Well hopefully Mia can give me some words of wisdom tonight because tonight is the night that we finally give in.

For months, Mia has been going on and on about this karaoke bar in town, called *Bruiser's Bar.* Karaoke night is once a week on Friday night and that just happens to be tonight.

So, after months of asking everyone, we finally cave, hence why I am frustratingly trying to apply mascara without poking my eye out.

Finally done, I take a step back to look at myself in the full-length mirror, happy with the new clothes I got for my changing body. I have on dark blue maternity jeans because nothing screams sexy like maternity. I have on a white top with thin straps, the top hugging my growing breasts (more like trying to stop them from busting out) only to flow down over my belly. I finish the look off with a black leather jacket and black boots. My dark hair is hanging in wild curls and I have more makeup on than I thought I could apply myself.

Tonight has to be the night.

"Ava! You coming or what?" I hear Hunter yell from downstairs. I glance at the clock, realizing we may be a bit late, but I'm sure Mia will arrive at the exact same time, or be anxiously waiting for us thinking we ditched. It's anyone's guess, honestly.

I check myself in the mirror one more time before snatching up my purse and making my way downstairs, hearing the boy's antics as I descend.

"If she's not going, I'm not going." Logan whines, clearly unhappy about going.

"You're going." Hunter growls.

"Fine, but I'm not singing."

I smile as I watch Logan and Hunter bicker like an old married couple, but it's Conner who makes my breath stop in my chest when I see how he's looking at me.

His dark hair, longer now, is stylishly messy. His clothes are casual, black T-shirt and blue jeans, but he can always make that look fancy. His hands are in his pockets and his heated blue eyes are on me, moving over my body and I swear I can feel it like a literal touch.

I shiver when I reach the landing and smile. "Hey, sorry I took so long. It's a little difficult to dress with this in the way." I point to my belly and laugh.

"You look—" He croaks the words out, making the guys chuckle as they watch us now, quickly clearing his throat before he continues, sounding normal again. "You look beautiful."

The words are soft and gentle as they touch my heart and make my belly flutter, but that could be the baby, who knows?

My smile widens. "Thank you. You too."

It's at that moment that Logan decides to throw his arm around Conner, whispering in his ear loud enough for everyone to hear, "You are so screwed."

If I have it my way, yes he is.

We pull up to the bar and it is crazier than I expected. The bar is crowded with people; the floor is littered with tables and chairs in front of the stage. Weirdly enough, there is only a small square for dancing which is disappointing for a karaoke bar. Booths, packed with people, line the walls on either side and a modest stage sits at the front of the room with a microphone and monitor.

A gangly red-headed guy is currently belting out a Shania Twain song, while the crowd is either laughing at the guy, or immersed in their own conversation, their voices blending in with his, despite the microphone.

A pair of small arms encircle me from behind, startling me until I hear her. "I can't believe you made it!"

"Of course we did." I smile down at Mia who is practically bouncing with excitement.

"Come on, I got us a seat."

We follow Mia through the crowd when I feel a hand taking mine. I look back only to see Conner looking back at me like this is normal. So, what do I do? I continue to hold his hand through the crowd, trying to bite back my smile at the glares I'm getting from other girls we are passing.

Yeah, that's right, he's mine … kind of.

He will be anyway. Wow, that makes me sound crazy.

Mia and I plop down in our seats and the guys announce they are getting drinks. We give them our orders and Conner leaves with the guys, throwing me a wink over his shoulder as he gets swallowed up by the crowd.

It is the distinct sound of someone clearing their throat that makes me face forward, realizing how long I was watching Conner.

I turn to face a smirking Mia, her head cocked to one side, but before she says a thing, I ask, "Where's Harper?"

"She'll be here later. What I want to know is what's going on with the father to be?" She inclines her head to where Conner disappeared and I shrug, knowing I need to talk to her, but unsure of how to say it.

"We've been getting closer."

"Closer as in …" She waggles her eyebrows, making me laugh and also cursing how far off she is.

"No. I mean, we kissed, but..."

"I'm sorry. Did you just say that Conner kissed you and I'm only now finding out about it?"

I shrug again. "It just happened once, but …"

I can't figure out how to finish my sentence, but Mia, always knowing how to read me, does. "Something happened. You looked at him and saw him differently. He's become more to you."

I nod slowly. "In a way, yes. I don't want to complicate things, but this whole thing is complicated and the idea of someone else being with him…" I shake my head, hating the sick feeling I get from the thought.

"Makes you wanna punch a bitch?"

I laugh. "Exactly."

"So tell him."

"I don't know how. Every time I think about it, my mind comes up blank. I can't find the words."

Mia looks at me a moment before shrugging again. "So sing about it."

Sounding so serious, it makes me scoff until I realize she's serious. "Mia, this isn't *High School Musical*. I can't just sing about my problems."

"You know why I love music?" I shake my head. "It is a form of communication. People can cry about a breakup or loss, or confess their love through music, through lyrics. If you can't find the words, maybe try using someone else's."

"What are you girls talking about?" Conner says, returning with the guys and our drinks.

"Nothing." Mia and I both say in unison, as my mind mulls over what she said.

Surely it's a stupid idea.

Definitely.

I'M ANXIOUSLY WAITING for the elderly lady to stop singing 'These Arms of Mine', knowing I'm next and waiting for my name to be called. The guys don't know what I'm doing and honestly I'm questioning it myself.

No one seems to notice my panic. The guys are either talking to each other or cheering on the grandma onstage. Mia's attention is on the stage as she beams in her seat, though her hand is tucked into mine under the table, giving it a reassuring squeeze and trying to drain the nerves from my body, but of course it doesn't work. It helps, knowing she's there, but the nerves are still there. Nerves over the crowd I am about to humiliate myself in front of, nerves over the guy that could break my heart in the next ten minutes, nerves over the fact that I could ruin everything with just one song.

A glance to my right shows Conner looking at me with his brows furrowed in question, seeing me tense and nervous. I give a shake of my head and a smile, letting him know I'm okay and that it's nothing to worry about.

It's not until that moment that my heart sinks when I hear the applause as the woman walks offstage, knowing my time is up.

I don't hear anything else but my name as the announcer calls it. My ears are ringing and Mia is still squeezing my hand as she urges me to my feet. My legs feel numb as I make my way to the stage, reaching the microphone in time for the announcer to lean in and ask, "You okay?"

But instead of answering, I look out at the lights shining down on me, taking in the cheers from my friends. I seek them out and quickly find Conner's curious eyes as he watches me up here, questions in his eyes but always love.

Since I've known him, he's never looked at me with hate or disgust. Always some kind of appreciation or affection, but right now looking back at me is something more than I've seen. And that is when I know I'm ready to lay it all out for him in the best way I can, because that is all he's done for me. He's been open and honest and it's about time I do the same.

So, I nod and the music for Katy Perry's "Dark Horse" starts to play. The lyrics appear on the screen, but my eyes remain on Conner as I sing to him.

So you wanna play with magic
Boy, you should know whatcha falling for
Baby do you dare to do this
'Cause I'm coming at you like a dark horse.

. . .

I CONTINUE TO SING, watching Conner's face, frozen in shock but starting to soften into a smile the more I sing, understanding what I'm singing, what I'm telling him.

When the song finally reaches the male's solo I don't even bother to sing it. Conner smiling at me is too much and I feel like I need to close the distance. So, without an inch of fear for the first time in a long time, I step off the stage with the microphone, move my way through the crowd to the father of my child who is still sitting with our friends, the same friends who are clapping and cheering, grinning from ear to ear.

When I finally reach him, I start to sing the final chorus, running my hand through his thick dark hair and stroking my thumb on his cheekbone, smiling as I tell him how I feel through that last chorus and belting out my last note.

The room explodes in applause when I stop, my eyes only focused on Conner who is smiling up at me, his eyes soft with adoration before he finally takes my hand from his hair and holds it in his big hand, finally rising from his chair, leaning his head down so our foreheads are touching. "So what are you saying?" His voice is low and gravelly and just barely audible in the chaos in the bar.

I answer honestly, "I'm all in. With you and the baby. This might sound crazy but I want us to be a family. A real family."

His smile grows. "You have no idea how long I've waited for you to say that."

His lips are on mine, his hands are on my hips pulling me to him and when I wrap my arms around his neck, I distinctly hear the crowd cheer louder than before, but it's all a muffled blur to me as I focus on Conner's soft warm lips on mine, we're moving together as if it is the most natural thing in the world. I feel my body start to heat up and my panties are wet between my legs, urging me to pull this man closer, needing to feel his warmth and strength against me.

He's suddenly gone and my body cries out for him, for more. I blink up at him as I watch him catch his breath, his smile bigger than ever. Pulling me close, I think he may kiss me again, but instead, his mouth moves to my ear, whispering, I can feel his hot breath on my ear and neck. "I think we should go home. Better not to give these people a show."

I nod and we leave without saying goodbye to anyone, but we hear their laughter at our backs, they know exactly what is going to happen.

I'M SHIFTING in my seat beside Conner as he drives us home, thankful he didn't get a chance to drink and equally thankful we all took separate cars. His hands are gripping the steering wheel so tight and the air is thick with the tension that grew between us over the past months.

Neither of us say a word. His eyes are focused on the road as he drives through the streets to our home, whereas I couldn't take my eyes off him.

His shirt is hugging his sculpted body in just the right way, making me think of the muscles I've seen beneath it when he tried undressing in front of me in the past. His lips are tense but still appear soft and begging to be kissed.

"You keep looking at me like that and we won't make it home." He growls, his voice sounding deep and gravelly.

His words only make the tingling between my legs grow and I shift again, cocking my head at him. "Is that a bad thing?"

He simply laughs a sexy deep laugh, shaking his head. "When I make love to you, it won't be done in a car. We already did this drunk. I want to do this right."

I feel the smile grow on my lips as my heart begins to flutter and I think to myself, how could I have hated this man before? "Hurry up then."

We reach home in under five minutes. We get out of the car and make our way up the drive in silence, not touching yet.

The house is dark and silent, our thick sexual tension filling each room as we enter and make our way upstairs. It was like we didn't need words, we knew what we wanted and we had waited long enough, I've fought it enough.

My body feels like it's on fire, so in tune with the space between us, our arms just a breath away as we move up the stairs, until we reach our bedroom. Because that's what it is now. It's not his room or mine. Tonight, its ours.

But there is something about the space that feels familiar. Yeah, I've been living here, but it is different tonight, like déjà vu. Walking ahead of Conner as he hangs back in the doorway, my back to him, I move my fingers over the end of his bed frame, the cold making my fingers tingle and shocking an image to my mind.

Flashes of imagery dance across my mind in that moment.

Flashes of me and Conner, similar to the dream I had those months ago, making me think it wasn't really a dream.

Conner laying on the bed this time and me straddling him, leaning over him so my face sits above his, my long hair falling on either side of us. Conner whispering as he strokes my cheek. "You don't wanna do this."

"You don't want me?" I remember saying this as I grind on him, making him groan.

"Oh, I do. But you don't want this."

I cock my head. "How do you know? What makes you think I don't want you?"

"Because you hate me?"

"No. I don't hate you. You drive me crazy, though."

"So you want to sleep with me?" he asks, sounding confused.

"Listen, if you're not interested, then—" But I don't get the chance to get up, for Conner puts his hands on my hips, holding me down on his hard cock.

"I didn't say I wasn't interested. I just don't want you to regret this."

"Why don't you let me worry about that?" I whisper just as my lips touch his and my hips continue to grind.

I blink at the memory, followed by others of gentle touches and of Conner's lips near my ear as he whispers, asking if I'm okay.

It was then that I realized that I wasn't just a random girl he picked, but I pursued him. And the whole time he was thinking of me, careful with how he moved, worried he was hurting me. It was exactly how I wanted my first time to be, minus the alcohol and accidental pregnancy. No, actually I don't regret any of it.

Without turning around, I allow myself to feel everything as I say, "I know you know I was a virgin that night."

"Yes. Ava, I'm so—"

"No," I tell him, finally turning around to see him still in his place in the doorway, looking nervous and unsure. "Don't apologize. I was angry, I'm not going to lie. But I think I was angrier that I didn't remember, not that it happened, not that it happened with you. Because standing with you here and now, I wouldn't take back a thing. Being with you that night changed my life in so many ways." I feel the lump growing in my throat as I let my emotions go, my eyes starting to water. "And I will always be thankful for you and that night."

"I only wish it could've been more special for you."

I finally close the distance between us, cupping his face in my hands, loving the rough stubble tickling my palms. "It was special. It was the start of a new journey." I pause, bracing myself for my next words. Swallowing the lump in my throat, I say, "I love you, Conner."

His hands go to my hips and he takes a step closer until his abs are touching my belly, making the baby move. "I love you, little lamb." He gives me a cheeky wink, making me smile.

His blue eyes start to darken as they move up and down my body and I feel the mood in the room shift as he says in a low voice, "And at least now we can try again. I can give you the first time you should've had."

I cock my head, giving him a sexy smile. "And how would that go?"

He smiles back. "Like this."

Before I can take a breath, he swings me up in his arms and I can't help but wonder how the hell he can lift me, but the thought instantly dissipates as he lowers me to the bed, pressing his body to mine as he hovers over me, his lips on mine, our hands exploring every surface.

I run my hands through his hair, wanting to pull it, so I give it a tug which makes Conner groan. He reciprocates by biting my lip, the sting creating a delicious tingle throughout my body, and I thrust my breasts up into him, needing to be touching him everywhere.

Conner sees the pleading in my eyes and he says against my lips, "You want me to touch you?"

I thrust my breasts toward him again as my answer but he shakes his head, pulling back from our kiss.

"I need you to use words."

"Yes," I beg, thrusting my breasts again, feeling an ache there, among other places, that desperately needs relief or I am going to scream.

"Where?"

The list is endless for where I want his mouth, his hands, his cock. My mouth is practically watering at the thought. "Everywhere."

Conner's smile grows into a grin and he starts to kiss my neck, making my eyes roll into the back of my head. "Here?"

"Yes." I gasp, grabbing his hair and holding him there until he starts to move his mouth down, pulling the straps of my top down and springing my breast free.

"Holy fuck." He groans seconds from putting his mouth on them.

I cry out in a mix of pain and pleasure, the ache between my legs becoming so much that I can't help but thrust my pelvis up to get some relief. But it's not enough. I need more. I don't need teasing or foreplay. I need to be fucked by this man who's been driving me crazy from day one.

"Get off me," I tell him, taking matters into my own hands, he's off me and off the bed in a second with a look of concern on his face, but then I'm up and grabbing him by the shirt, making him look at me and seeing how serious I am. "Get undressed and on the bed. Now." I finish with a shove that lands him on said bed with a chuckle.

I don't even recognize myself right now, but I don't care enough to think about it too much. All I'm focusing on is the sexy man undressing clumsily in front of me.

I follow suit and before I know it, Conner is leaning back on his elbows, his large erection up and ready, begging for me. Conner's heated gaze touches every part of me and I watch as his breathing increases, his brow quirks up at me as he waits.

"So now what?" he asks, a teasing lilt to his voice which makes me smile as I crawl my way up to him.

"Now." I straddle him, feeling the heat of his cock against me. "I get you all to myself."

CHAPTER 26

CONNER

I roll over, completely drained of energy but each thought that enters my mind is of Ava. Of how she felt and sounded last night, of what she did, what we did.

I feel myself getting hard as I think about it, stretching my arm to her side of the bed, wanting more contact only to be met with an empty mattress.

I open my eyes to see that yes, she is gone.

I frown at the empty space, wondering where she is and hoping she didn't run, hoping she doesn't regret last night. But that worry is put on hold when I notice a slip of paper sitting under a picture frame on my bedside table.

I get up out of bed, groaning from my tired muscles and reach for the paper, reading Ava's pretty handwriting.

Conner,

Last night was amazing. I wish I could've stayed for round 2 but my boss called. I'll be at work until 3pm, then I'll be all yours ;)

. . .

Ava (In case it wasn't obvious lol)

I FIND myself both hating her boss for robbing me of round two, but unable to keep the smile from my face.

She doesn't regret it. She wants to do it again and damnit, she will get it again. But I want this time to be different. Last night was desperate and almost rushed, not that I'm complaining, but for round two, I want to spend a bit more time on her.

I get dressed, thinking of what I could do for her and make my way downstairs, being met with the usual bickering between Logan and Hunter.

They stop talking when I enter the kitchen, Logan is sitting at the counter and Hunter is buttering his toast. Huge smiles spread across their faces and I can't help but continue to smile myself.

"Here's the man himself!" Logan cheers, spreading his arms out to his side.

"Doing the walk of shame," Hunter comments as I plop myself down next to Logan.

"Nothing shameful about it."

Logan leans in. "So, how was it?" Only to get slapped upside the head by Hunter. "Ow!"

"You don't ask him shit like that."

"What? We talk shit like that all the time."

"Not about Ava." Hunter pushes his point by pointing his butter knife at Logan in warning.

Logan thinks about this before nodding. "You're right. Ava isn't like those girls."

I smile, thinking of her as I say, "She's special."

The room is quiet for a time as the guys smile at me, soft genuinely happy smiles, when Hunter says, "I'm happy for you, man. I'm happy for Ava, too. You both are like family so

I think it's cool you guys are finally owning up to your feelings."

Logan chimes in, nudging my shoulder, "Yeah, I mean I'm not going to try that method. Getting a girl knocked up." He shivers. "But it definitely worked for you."

I laugh. "Thanks, I guess."

"Never mind him." Hunter waves dismissively at Logan. "So, what are you going to do today?" he says, taking a big bite out of his buttered toast, almost downing the whole thing in one bite.

"Ava's at work today, but I wanna do something for her."

"Like what?" Both guys look at me.

"Just something special. Something we never got to do."

Logan pipes in, "What, like oral? Ow!"

CHAPTER 27

AVA

"So I heard you finally made a move." Harper says as she practically dances up to the register, where I am still banished.

"You could say that." I give her a sly smile, which makes her smile in return.

"I'm happy you did it before I left. I was getting a little worried."

"Left? What are you talking about?"

I am met with a look mixed with nervousness and excitement as I stand with my hands on my hips, aiming an expectant look at my friend.

"I'm going to Australia, for the internship."

My mind goes blank for a few seconds, unable to think about life without Harper in it. I know it will only be for a short time, but I was hoping to have her there for my birth, for my baby. Of course, I'm happy for her, but a selfish part of me doesn't want her to go.

"You're mad?"

I finally blink, seeing Harper standing there, hunched and nervous as she waits for my response and all I want to do is put that excitement back in her eyes, so I smile. "Mad? No, of course not. Why would I be mad?"

I close the distance, throwing my arms around her as she speaks into my hair. "I don't know. You were the one that told me about the internship freshman year. You should be going."

"Does it look like I can go?" I look down to my belly, holding her hands in mine. "Besides, I think I've had enough adventure this year. Now it's your turn. And you shouldn't be worried about me," I tell her, absentmindedly rubbing my belly.

"Well, I am. You're my best friend and I love you. I'll always worry."

A heavy weight sits on my chest as I think of no longer having this person in my life, at least for a short time. When this baby comes, Harper won't be here. I will feel her absence, like I didn't think I would. Since day one we clicked, different to how it is with Mia. With Mia, I have history, but Harper was just easy. Smiling at her now, I give her hands a squeeze. "I should be the one worrying. You're leaving to live in a foreign country. Anything could happen."

She scoffs, rolling her eyes, but squeezing my hand back. "I'll be fine. It's just going to be a few months. I'll be back before you know it."

"Unless you get a permanent position there."

She scoffs again. "Don't be silly. I actually want to graduate, and I have so much here to come back to." She finishes this by giving me a wink and another squeeze of the hand.

"You bet you do. This kid needs you to spoil them."

"You know I will. So," she says, dropping my hand. "how are things with Conner? Are you guys a thing now?"

"We haven't really discussed it, but I'd say we are. I mean, I pretty much told him that I'm all in, and then we..." I waggle my brows which only makes her giggle.

"So he obviously feels the same."

"I'd say so." Or last night was a whole lot of mixed signals.

"He does. I see how he looks at you, how he always looked at you." Harper's expression softens as she thinks to herself before she speaks. "Like you were the only one in the room."

Before I can even react, my phone pings on the counter beside us, signaling a text.

I pick it up and smile when I see Conner's name with a text.

Conner: You got plans tonight?

"I see that smile. Okay, I'll leave you to your sexting. I got stuff I gotta do anyway. But I'm happy for you. It's about time."

"Thank you," I say to her retreating figure until she is swallowed up by bookshelves, leaving me alone with my Conner texts.

Feeling a flitter of excitement, or maybe that was the baby, I message back with one thing in mind.

Me: Just you ;)

Conner: Me, huh? And what are you planning on doing with me?

Me: Playing out every single fantasy I've ever had of you.

Conner: You fantasized about me?

Me: Are you really surprised?

Conner: No, I am pretty hot.

Me: Modest.

Conner: Always. So, what are these fantasies?

Me: You will find out.

Conner: You're not going to tell me?

Me: Where is the fun in that?

Conner: Fine. You coming straight home?

Me: Yeah.

Conner: Good. I'll see you then.
Me: Yes, you will.

ONCE WORK IS OVER, I drag my tired ass to my car and drive back home, eager to return to bed with my baby daddy and have another go. So many things flit through my mind as I pull up the drive, pulling myself from the car and waddling my way up to the front door.

Slamming the door shut behind me, I call out, "Honey, I'm home!"

I expect to hear the rambunctious bickering of Hunter and Logan, or the noises from Logan's video game, but instead I'm met with a quiet house.

An uneasy feeling settles over me as I wiggle out of my coat, calling out with a shaky voice, "Conner?"

"I'm in the kitchen." The familiarity of his voice settles my uneasiness and I sigh in relief as I make my way through to the kitchen and am met with the delicious sight of Conner in a light blue button-down and black pants, his hair styled similar to last night and I can't help but remember running my fingers through it.

Conner is standing over a pot at the stove and has the room lit with only candles.

I stand in the doorway, mesmerized as I take it all in. "What is this?"

"I cooked us dinner," Conner says with a smile as I approach the counter to plop myself down.

"Yeah but why? And where is everyone?"

Conner shrugs as he checks the sauce. "The guys have other places to be. So, it's just you and me tonight. As for the dinner, I figured since we never really had a first date I'd make us our own first date tonight. Do it right."

I shake my head to myself, thinking of all the things he's

done for me, and he just keeps on going. Looking up at him with a beaming smile, I incline my head when I say, "You're pretty amazing, you know that?"

"Yeah, I'm aware," he says, leaning over and placing a chaste kiss on my lips before turning back to the stove.

"Still modest."

He grins. "Always."

"So what's for dinner?" I ask, peeking over into the pot.

"Spaghetti Bolognese. Simple, but I figure after a long day, you'd want something filling."

"You figured correctly," I tell him just as I feel my stomach start to grumble.

"So how was work?" Conner asks, opening up cupboards and gathering plates and cups.

I shrug, trying to ignore my growling stomach. "It was dull. But I got to talk to Harper, which was good."

"Yeah? How is she? Excited about her internship?"

"Yeah..."

Hearing the uncertainty in my words, Conner levels me with a look that tells me he doesn't believe me. "Really?"

"She is, I'm just worried. This is a great opportunity for her but..."

"You worry," he finishes for me, and I smile a small sad smile.

"Yeah."

"Look, Harper will be fine. You guys can Skype and text. She won't be gone long, it will only be a few months."

"That's what she said," I tell him, scoffing.

"So trust that she will be fine." He reaches over the counter and gives my hand a squeeze, which only works to lift some of the weight off my chest... *some* of it.

I give him a small smile. "I know."

"You will be one hell of a mom."

"What makes you say that?" I ask with a furrowed brow, not expecting those words.

"You care so much about other people."

"That's being a decent human being."

"These days not everyone cares."

"You care."

He holds my gaze for a moment, and for that moment I see pain, the same pain I saw once before. "Not about everyone."

"You talking about anyone in particular?" I know exactly who he is talking about and I watch as he blinks his pain away and replaces it with a smile that doesn't meet his eyes.

"Hey, you wanna try the pasta?"

"Yeah, I'll give it a try." He scoops up some pasta for me to try and I swallow the slippery goodness with ease.

"Oh, it's so good."

"Happy you approve."

With that, he starts to dish up dinner and proceeds to walk both our plates to the dining room. I sit across from him and dig in.

It isn't until I've consumed several mouthfuls that I finally speak, noticing how tense his shoulders have become and I instantly realize why.

"Nice, avoiding the question," I comment, moving my food around on my plate now.

Conner tenses more then he sighs. "Ava, please."

Seeing the pain he always tries to hide, over his brother, drives me crazy because I can't do much about it. I can't exactly lock them in a room, can I? *Can I?* "You can't forgive him? Listen, I don't understand what happened between you two, but I do know you are going to regret it if you don't push past this hurt."

"Ava! I just need some time," Conner exclaims, dropping

his knife and fork with a clang that only makes me jump and the room go quiet.

I say in the smallest voice when he finally looks at me. "Make sure you don't leave it too long, or the opportunity will pass you by."

He sighs a regretful sigh when I return to my food.

Once dinner is finished, Conner leads me to the kitchen again where he pulls out a round chocolate cake from the fridge. My mouth waters at the sight but there is something missing.

I furrow my brow as he places it on the counter beside us and I say with a raised eyebrow, "Wow, it's a… cake without frosting."

"I've got the frosting right here. Thought we could do it together." Conner pulls out a tub of chocolate icing from somewhere I didn't see, placing it on the counter beside the cake.

I squeak when he comes around me, picking me up and placing me on the kitchen counter with ease. I open my legs to allow him in, his heated gaze running over my body and face.

"What are you doing?" My voice shakes when I speak and I resist the urge to pull him closer to relieve the ache growing between my legs.

I bite my lip when I feel him pull at the top of my pants. He growls as he watches my lips and I lift my hips to help him pull my pants off, then I am sitting partially nude on the kitchen counter. This can't be sanitary, but any thoughts of sanitary fly out the window when I see Conner drop to his knees in front of my aching pussy and I moan.

Licking his lips, he says, "I'm going to have my dessert, then I'll give you yours."

"Okay…" I say and finish on a squeal when he starts sucking on my clit, touching and licking just the right spots.

I moan, and run my fingers through his dark hair, pushing his face into me and he growls, devouring more of me.

Just when I think it can't get any better, I feel the delicious pressure of his finger when he starts to fuck me with it before adding another one, pumping them both in and out of me, still sucking on my clit.

My eyes roll to the back of my head and I throw my head back, moaning so loud I wouldn't be surprised if we got noise complaints but I didn't give a fuck.

I'm so close, so close.

Just a little more.

Conner gives my clit one final suck and I scream as my orgasm rips through me, taking everything I have to give and leaving me spent and panting as Conner gives my inner thigh a kiss before giving me a proud wet smile.

I laugh as I wipe at his face. "Oh my god, your face."

"I wear this like a badge of honor."

"I bet you do."

"So," Conner says, placing his hands on either side of me, standing so close I can still feel his warmth. "Dessert?" He inclines his head toward the cake but my eyes are on him, and the hard-on in his pants.

I lick my own lips when I say, "I've got something else in mind."

IT'S two a.m. and I am dead.

I flop onto my back, both Conner and I panting and sweaty after what seemed like a fuck marathon.

Every position, so many orgasms. I think I'm orgasmed out, but let's be real… is that a thing?

Glancing over at Conner, a sheen of sweat coats his muscled chest and his hair is sticking to his forehead, I know I must focus on something else or we will go again.

I think back to what Harper said at work and I decide now is better than never. "So I have to ask..."

Conner catches his breath, looking at me through tired eyes. "Yeah?"

"What are we? To each other?"

Conner pauses for a second before giving a little chuckle, rolling over and pulling my body into his. "I would hope this makes you mine."

"Is that really what you want?"

Looking down at me, he rubs the hair away from my face and starts to stroke my cheek. "More than anything."

"Anything?"

His smile turns devilish and I know we won't be sleeping tonight. "Well, now that you mention it..."

I can just sleep during the day...

CHAPTER 28

AVA

"Hey!" Logan exclaims, making me jump and drop the box I'm attempting to lift. He walks around to stand in front of me, a look of astonishment gracing his pretty face. "What do you think you're doing?"

"I'm helping," I tell him, crossing my arms.

"You have any idea what Conner would do if he saw you doing that shit?"

I roll my eyes. "He won't do anything to me."

"I'm talking about me! If he knew I saw you lifting heavy shit and didn't stop you, I'd be a dead man walking."

"Fine." I sigh, kicking the box labeled 'pillows' to him.

"Hey where does this go?" We hear Hunter ask in a gruff voice. He's been moody all day and no one seems to know why. He turned up with a permanent scowl on his face and remained mostly silent.

Harper answers from where she is huddled over boxes of plates and cups near the kitchen area. "In the box by the corner labeled 'toys'."

Logan's head perks up like a meerkat. "What kind of toys?"

"None that concern you," Hunter growls with enough intensity it draws the attention of everyone in the room, making Logan cock his head.

"Whoa, Hunter. You staking a claim?"

"Don't be stupid." Hunter shakes his head at Logan like he's crazy.

"Oh!" Harper exclaims, crossing her arms over her chest and navigating her way around the boxes to make it to Hunter. "Because one would have to be stupid to be interested in me?"

Logan clears his throat, enough to catch Harper's eye for a second to give a cheeky grin, winking. "If that's the case, I am very stupid."

"Back off, Logan."

"Why should he back off, Hunter?"

As she waits for him to answer, he just scoffs, shaking his head and mumbling something under his breath.

"What did you say? You've been a grump all week. What the hell is your problem?"

"I don't have a problem." Hunter gets in her face for a second and she gets on her toes to get in his. All that was missing was them growling at each other a second before Hunter steels his jaw and storms out of the apartment in a huff, leaving Harper to stare after him, her eyes wide.

I'm about to ask if she is okay but judging by the tensing in her shoulders and the clenching of her fists, it's probably best I don't.

Harper suddenly breaks the tense silence filling the room by screaming in frustration and stomping her way back to her bedroom.

Logan and I both look at each other with matching expressions of shock when he says, "I feel like we've missed something."

I scoff, "Yeah, no shit."

We freeze when we hear thundering footsteps approaching the front door and we both turn, expecting to see Hunter storming back in, but instead, we see a confused Conner walking in with a couple of empty boxes in his arms. His eyes move between Logan and me as he drops the boxes by the front door. "Hey, just saw Hunter storming off, what have I missed?"

"We don't know," Logan and I say in unison, which only gets us another confused look from Conner.

"Okay…" Conner rounds some boxes, grabbing me by the hands and pulling me closer, his thumb rubbing on the back of my hand as he leans in with a mischievous twinkle appearing in his eyes, his upset friend soon forgotten when he whispers, "Hey, I was thinking about what we could do tonight."

The heat that appears in his eyes hints to me what he's talking about, and my mind instantly goes to a dirty place thinking of all the things we could do.

A slow seductive smile appears on my face. "Yeah? I'm interested."

I give him a wink and then we hear the sound of someone clearing their throat, reminding us that Logan is still in the room. Our eyes widen and I feel the redness bloom in my cheeks as we both look at Logan standing nearby, among the boxes, with his arms crossed. He raises an eyebrow and says, "I'm standing right here."

"Sorry," I say, biting my lip and trying to hide the blush but Logan just waves it off.

"No, I mean, I'm struggling to hear you. Could you speak louder?"

Conner releases me, hopping over the couple of boxes separating them easily and slapping Logan upside the head before he even knows what's coming.

I swear, one day that boy is gonna have brain damage from how much he gets slapped.

"Ow!" Logan exclaims, rubbing the back of his head and frowning at Conner's retreating back as he makes his way back to me.

I hold up my hand, unable to hide the gnawing guilt I feel at seeing my friend so upset and not having heard a peep out of her since. Looking back at Harper's bedroom door, I tell the boys, "Hold that thought, I should go check on Harper."

Conner frowns, concerned. "Is she okay?"

"I guess I'll see," I tell him, already making my way to the room.

I don't bother knocking because I've never needed to knock with Harper, so I turn the knob and enter the bedroom I've seen so many times before, but this time everything is everywhere. Clothes lay in piles on the bed and the floor, trinkets have their place on the dresser, and shoes lay stacked in the corner.

Harper herself is standing near her dresser with her back to me, looking at a book, appearing to be lost in thought as she runs her fingers over the page in the book. It seems like a private moment and I feel like I shouldn't be in here, but instead of leaving, I step forward and say in the softest tone, "Hey."

She instantly jumps, slamming the book closed and throwing it in a dresser drawer like it burned her. She spins on her heel to meet my eyes with the fakest smile I've ever seen on her. It is big and toothy and a part of me wonders what it is about that book she doesn't want anyone to know; it is clearly a secret, but I also know it's not my place. "Oh, hey." Only then does she dial back the smile, sighing and melting away the façade, slumping against the dresser. "Sorry about that. My emotions are going crazy lately."

"You're not pregnant, are you?" I comment with a smile when I flop myself on a small available spot on her bed.

Her eyes widen in panic. "God no!" Her eyes widen more, understanding what she just implied. "I didn't mean—"

I chuckle, waving off her distress, because I know Harper didn't mean it and that wasn't what I wanted to talk to her about anyway. "It's okay, I don't blame you. So, what's going on?"

"With what?"

I raise my brows. "With what happened out there. You guys barely speak to each other and all of a sudden you're lashing out at each other."

She hesitates and I see the internal struggle in her until she lets out a tired sigh, playing with the ends of her shirt. "I don't know. He's been a jerk all week."

"Who has?" We both jump at Mia's entrance as she walks in and flops on top of a pile of clothes in the middle of the bed, turning to lie on her side and rest her head on her hand, her blonde hair hanging in a little ponytail.

"Your brother," we both say at the same time.

"You know he has been moody lately," Mia comments, with a crease in her brows.

"See?"

"Did anyone think to talk to him?" I ask both of them, leaning back to rest on my hands when Mia laughs a humorless laugh.

"And get my head bitten off? No thank you."

I cock my head. "You guys aren't curious or worried?"

"I'm curious," Mia answers after a moment's pause.

"I'm worried," Harper says, her voice soft and highlighting her concern.

"Maybe it's just school and the future," I offer them but neither look convinced, especially Harper.

"Maybe," Harper says, but her eyes look elsewhere, somewhere faraway from this room and us. I look at her a moment longer until she finally blinks out of her daze and focuses back on me.

I ask, "What is it?"

"I was just thinking."

"About?" Mia pushes, finally sitting up.

Harper doesn't answer at first, but her face turns sad and lost, a look I know too well from my own mirror at times. It's a moment until she finally speaks, her voice breaking. "Maybe I shouldn't go."

Mia exclaims loud enough for the whole world to hear, hopping on her knees on the bed, "What? Why would you not go? Hot Australians! Do it for me, Harper!"

"What brought this on?" I say in a much calmer tone.

"I've just got so much here," she says, picking up a stuffed bear that I didn't notice sitting on a chair near the dresser, holding it close to her chest. "I'm kind of scared to leave it."

Looking at her, I see the fear she's speaking of and I understand that, but I also see something else, something I can't put my finger on. "Listen, I'm scared about you going too, I'm not going to lie. But you gotta remember that we will all be here when you get back."

"I'm not so sure," she says, looking down at the bear in her arms.

"Well, be sure. Because we aren't going anywhere." Mia climbs over to sit beside me, smiling up at Harper, as am I.

I tell her, "Yeah, so go off, have your adventure and come back and tell us all about it."

With one final look at the bear, she releases it on a sad sigh, dropping it back down on the chair, nodding. "I guess you're right." She gives us a sad smile and a part of me wishes to wash away any concern or fear she has, but there is only one way she can get rid of it. She must go and see for herself that there is nothing to worry about. "I should get back to packing."

"Yeah, I think we all should. Who knows what the guys are getting up to in there," Mia says this at the same time we hear a loud crash and the guys cursing and calling apologizes through the door.

CHAPTER 29

AVA

"So how are you feeling?" I ask Harper while we stand in the middle of the airport, ready for her to leave for her internship. I look at her tense shoulders and scared eyes as she watches the screen showing plane departures and arrivals, her bags sitting at our feet.

Her lips tense in a line, she says without looking at me, "Nervous."

"No need to be," I tell her, grabbing her hand and giving it a squeeze until she finally looks away from the screen to meet my eyes, showing me the mix of sadness and uncertainty there. I've been seeing it for weeks and I can't understand why. It could just be the internship, but I can't shake the feeling it's something else. I don't push for answers because it's been clear that she doesn't want to talk about it. All I can do is just be there for her, despite how much I want to help her.

"Really? Tell that to my stomach," she says, rubbing her stomach with her free hand, nervously looking around us. "What is taking Hunter so long with the car?"

"He will be here. Just relax," I say with another gentle squeeze of her hand.

Harper then gives me a long look before pulling in a deep breath, holding it for a second and letting it go, which appears to lessen the nerves but does nothing to stop the sadness in her eyes. She squeezes my hand back when she says, "Promise to call me while I'm gone. Keep me updated."

"I promise. Just enjoy your time away."

"I'll try."

The sadness I see in her eyes is enough to break me, dropping her hand to put my hands on my hips, raising a brow at my friend, I finally ask, "What happened?"

Harper's eyes widen for moment in shock at my question, followed by a look of confusion as she stammers out, "What do you mean?"

"You were so excited when you told me about the internship, but now it feels like I'll have to push you onto that plane."

She shakes her head. "It's just all becoming so real, and—"

Her words are cut off when Hunter appears beside me, towering over both of us and shattering the moment we're having. "I managed to get a spot nearby, miraculously. What did I miss?"

"Harper's just a bit nervous," I tell him and he instantly cocks his head at Harper.

"About what?"

Harper just gives a dismissive wave of her hand and shakes her head with a small smile that doesn't meet her eyes. "Nothing. I'm probably just being silly. You're right, I should just enjoy myself."

"We will miss you," I tell her, trying to smother the pain I feel in my chest at knowing she will not be here tomorrow or next week or when my baby is born. She will be back, but that doesn't stop the ache I feel as I pull her into me, holding her in a tight hug that tells her how much she is loved here and how much we will miss her. I speak into her hair as she rubs my back, "Too bad Conner couldn't be here, but he had to work."

"It's okay," she says, finally stepping out of the hug, only for her eyes to go directly to Hunter who still stands beside me, his hands stuffed into his jeans pockets and an array of emotions moving over his face until finally settling on sadness, similar to what I had seen on Harper earlier.

His voice breaks slightly when he says, "Be safe."

"I will." She gives him a small smile. Movement catches our attention as we see people start to head toward the terminal, her terminal. She sighs a sad sigh and says with a shaky voice what we all know but don't want to say, "I guess this is it."

Harper gives me one last hug before heaving her bags onto her shoulders and pulling her roller suitcase behind her until she finally reaches the terminal, stopping for only a moment to glance over her shoulder. And just like that, she's looking at both of us with that sad look on her face. I could have sworn tears were glistening in her eyes, but before I can look further, she turns away, leaving Hunter and I standing in silence.

I wait a moment, trying to comprehend what just happened, connecting the dots, before looking over at my friend. I see him still looking where Harper just went. I stare for a moment longer before I notice his shoulders tensing and his eyes slowly turn to me, aware that I'm looking at him with my brows raised as some things finally come into focus.

"What?" he asks me, sounding genuinely confused and I cross my arms over my chest, looking up at him.

"You know you can tell me anything, right? You're like a brother to me."

I drop my arms when he gives me a smile, throws his big

arms around me and pulls me into a hug, holding me a moment and saying into my hair, "Yeah I know."

I wiggle out of his hold, still holding his forearms when I ask, "Are you going to be okay?"

"Why wouldn't I be?" he says, clearly not wanting to talk about what I just saw, or maybe he just doesn't want to own up to it. Truth be told, I don't know what I just saw, but I saw something and maybe this is something that Hunter isn't too aware of yet... maybe.

Deciding to let him off the hook, I shrug my shoulders. "Just asking."

"Uh." A painful groan slips out of my lips as I'm hit with a wave of pressure and pain around my belly, strong enough to knock the wind right out of me as I take a breath and put a hand to my belly.

"What is it?" Hunter's brows narrow down on my stomach as he places his own hand on it as the pain starts to increase.

"Something's wrong," I tell him through deep breaths, trying to hold the panic at bay, all thought revolving around my baby and the pain. It could just be labor but there is something about this pain that didn't feel right.

"What are you—" Before he can finish, the pain hits me so suddenly, my legs give way and I cry out as I fall into Hunter's arms. He catches me easily, holding me up. Looking at him I can see the panic I feel reflected in his eyes.

I tell him, my voice strained from the pain, "The baby. Something's happening with the baby."

"Holy fuck," he whispers, looking around before throwing my arm around his shoulder and holding me to him. "We gotta get you to a hospital."

The trip is a blur of panic and pain. I try to calm my racing heart and breathe through the pain, focusing on my baby with Hunter telling me, "Almost there, Ava. Just hold on."

"Uh!" I cry out when a stab of pain explodes across my back, traveling down to my legs and before I know it, I'm being lifted into Hunter's truck and getting strapped in.

Hunter quickly hops in the truck and starts to drive, my vision is starting to get blurry as I start to go in and out of consciousness. My hand on my belly, I hear Hunter's voice as he starts to call everyone in a panic, everyone but who I really want with me.

"Call Conner." I groan out through gritted teeth as another wave of pain hits me.

His vehicle Bluetooth speaker starts to ring in the next moment and I hear an unfamiliar voice answer and I can't help the wave of disappointment of it not being Conner. "Pet Haven Veterinary Clinic, this is Jay, how may I help you?"

"Where's Conner?" Hunter barks into the cab of the truck.

"I'm sorry?"

"Conner! Where is he?"

"I'm sorry, but Conner has stepped out." The man says sounding calm despite the chaos ensuing.

Hunter, suddenly pissed, smacks his hand on the steering wheel, making me jump, then yells. "When will he be back?"

"He should've been back ten minutes ago, so hopefully soon. Who, may I ask is calling?"

"This is Hunter. I'm a friend and when the jackass returns, you can tell him that his girl is having a fucking baby." He hangs up and proceeds to call more people as well as sending texts through his Bluetooth. Many of them to Conner and each one has yet to be replied to.

"Don't worry we're almost there. Everything will be fine," Hunter tells me, his panic leaking through his words.

I look at him, pain evident on my face. "You don't know that."

"Yeah, I do because you're strong and so is your baby. Everything will be fine."

I don't know who he's trying to convince of that, him or me.

CHAPTER 30

CONNER

Today has just been a long day. I'm feeling it in my back and my feet and I've been sitting all day. But that's what happens when you spend a good part of the morning making your girlfriend come over and over again.

Worth it.

If only the day would go quicker and I could get back home to her. I know she will be upset tonight. I wish I could be there with her today when she takes Harper to the airport, but luckily I convinced Hunter to go with her, so I at least have that comfort.

Now I am in line at a local coffee shop, ordering a chicken sandwich, wanting to just get back to my Ava.

I pay the cashier and take my sandwich, I'm turning to leave the busy coffee shop when I suddenly hear a familiar voice, stopping me in my tracks. "Conner?"

I follow the voice, finding a familiar redhead sitting in one of the booths nearby, a small smile on her face as she looks up at me. "Vivian?"

"Hey," she says, sitting with a coffee before her as I approach her table with a questioning look on my face.

"What are you doing here?"

"Having lunch. You?"

I hold up my sandwich bag. "I'm on lunch break."

"Oh." She shifts in her seat, looking around us before asking nervously, "Would you like to join me?"

She gestures to the vacant seat across from her and I can't help the alarm bells that ring inside my head, remembering what she said to Ava that night at our house. I do miss having my friend but it can't be more than that. She must know that. "I don't think that's a good idea, Vivian."

She sighs, her shoulders slumping forward, looking deflated as she nods. "I know, I know. It's just, I don't like how we left things. We were friends. You know I'm not great at making friends."

I shake my head at her. "The way you treated Ava…"

Her eyes are pleading, looking bigger as she explains, "And I'm sorry for that. I'll apologize to her, please just give me five minutes."

Looking down at Vivian, it was hard to not see my friend, my study buddy sitting there and it was for that reason, the fact that we were friends, that we had a history, that I sat down to give her a chance to explain herself. "Only five minutes."

She gives a relieved sigh, her hands wrapped around her coffee as she whispers, "Thank you."

"So?" I ask, tossing my arms, mentally counting the minutes.

She doesn't speak straight away. She shifts in her chair again, looking around us and looking back at me, trying to find her words before she asks, "How are things?"

I raise a brow. "You only have five minutes. Is this how you want to use them?"

"Okay." Vivian raises her hands in surrender before explaining, "I was out of line that night. So out of line. But I really was worried about you, and I guess I let that concern manifest into something ugly."

"You could say that again."

"And I wasn't fair to you, or Ava. I don't know what happened or what's going on between you two, but it's not my place and I respect that."

I watch her face as she speaks, looking for a lie but all I see is genuine concern and remorse. I nod, showing no emotion when I say, "Thank you."

She taps her cup with her finger, biting her lip before telling me with a small proud smile. "I changed my major. I figured I couldn't keep asking you to help me. Everyone was right, so I did some 'soul searching' and decided to change it to psychology."

I blink at her choice, cocking my head, not remembering her ever mentioning anything about psychology even being an area of interest, but things have surprised me before. "Really? What brought that on?"

She simply shrugs. "I'm fascinated by the mind, it's both strong and weak. Adaptable yet stubborn. I wanted to know more. Maybe I'll make a career out of it, but right now I'm seeing how I do with a few classes."

Seeing Vivian actually make an effort to change makes a smile appear on my face, seeing the friend I knew sitting across from me. "That's great, Vivian. I'm happy for you."

She beams at my praise, sitting a bit straighter in her seat. "Do you think we could ever… be the way we used to be?"

That makes my smile waver, because even though I see my friend sitting there, I can't completely get over what she had said and done to Ava. "I don't know. Things are different now and when Ava has the baby…"

My attention veers when I hear the buzzing of my phone in my pocket. Just as I go to reach for it, thinking it could be work asking where I am, Vivian asks loudly, "How is Ava?"

"She's well."

"That's good."

My phone buzzes again and I realize that I had forgotten to check it a moment ago. Work must really need me, I think to myself as I start to shuffle out of the seat. "Well, I should be heading back."

Vivian starts to pout. "Do you have to? We could just sit here and eat like old times, without the studying."

"Vivian…" I warn her, thinking of work messaging me.

"It's okay, I just miss our friendship."

Seeing her sitting there, looking small, I can't help the wave of guilt that hits me and I internally curse when I plop myself back down in my seat and pull out my sandwich, telling Vivian gruffly, "Fine, but just until I finish my meal."

Vivian sits up straighter again, beaming as she sips her coffee. "Deal."

A SANDWICH and cup of coffee later, Vivian and I are weaving our way out of the coffee shop, Vivian with a big smile on her face which makes me a tad nervous. We leave the shop and stand just outside and she sighs happily as she says, "Well, this was nice."

"Yeah, it was alright." I nod as casually as I can, hoping this wasn't a mistake and that dreamy look on Vivian's face wasn't a sign that she hadn't changed.

"Just like old times." And just as she said those words, I think that maybe things haven't changed, not as much as I thought. But time will tell.

"Sorta." We stand there in silence, with her still smiling at me and me being all too aware of the time. "Well I should be heading back. I'm a bit late now."

"Yeah, sorry about that."

"See ya, Vivian."

She says goodbye with a big wave and I turn to head back to work just as I recall the texts I had gotten earlier.

I pull my phone from my pocket as I head back to work, expecting to see texts from work telling me I'm fired or something. But when I unlock the screen I am not met with texts from work, but texts from everyone else.

My steps slow to a stop as I take in each message.

Hunter: Dude! Where the fuck are you?!

Mia: Are you with Ava?

Logan: Man, this is not cool. Answer your phone!

Hunter: When you want to get back to us, we will be at the hospital. It's Ava.

I almost drop my phone as my heart stops working. Images of Ava in pain or injured, the baby, all of it fills my head in a second and makes my heart rate pick up and an ache grow in my stomach.

Before I know it, I'm sprinting down the street with one goal in mind: Get to Ava.

CHAPTER 31

CONNER

The drive to the hospital blows by in a blur, a panicked haze where every thought I have revolves around Ava and the baby. Is she okay? What happened?

I manage to park my car and sprint through the hospital doors, moving on autopilot until a set of elevator doors open and reveal a new floor. My eyes zero in on the crowd gathered in the waiting room.

Hunter and Mia standing side by side and Logan leaning against a candy machine. Everyone wearing matching concerned expressions.

I watch as their expressions shift to that of disappointment and anger as I step off the elevator, but my mind is too focused on Ava and I don't care to ask anything but, "Where is she?" when I finally reach them.

Hunter stands tall, his jaw tense as his eyes narrow on me, his arms are crossed over his chest and the muscles in his arms are bulging. Meanwhile, Mia stands beside him with her hands on her hips and a haughty expression aimed at me, but my eyes remain on Hunter when he answers in a controlled tone, "She's in with the doctor."

"What happened?"

Hunter takes a deep breath through his nose before he answers, worry dripping through each word. "I don't know. We were at the airport and she just fell, like she was in pain, saying it was the baby."

I feel my heart crack and the ache of it makes me wince as I think about Ava being in pain and scared for the baby. I should've been there for her. Is she okay? Is she in labor? Is the baby okay? "Is she…?"

I don't even know how to finish that question, but I don't need to because Hunter answers with a curt response, "I don't know. They took her back there and we haven't heard anything since." He waits a moment and his eyes narrow into slits before he growls out his next words, "My turn. Where the fuck were you?"

"I was..." I open my mouth, but I can't finish that sentence. The look in my friend's eyes is one I hadn't seen before, actual anger, like he was daring me to say what I was doing, like he knew. I wasn't doing anything bad, I could see how it might look like that. I should've just went back to work. I shouldn't have said yes to Vivian and now, looking at my friends, I know exactly what they are going to say when I tell them.

But before I can open my mouth again, Hunter demands, "And don't say you were at work because we called. They said you went to lunch and hadn't come back. So, I'll ask again, where were you?"

"I was having lunch."

His eyes narrow more, seeing the nerves on my face as I start to shuffle my feet, knowing I'm not telling him everything. He was quick to ask, "With who?"

I move my eyes over each of them as they stand before me

now, waiting with expectant looks. I try to hide any guilt, for risk of them thinking something happened. I do feel guilt, but only because I wasn't there for Ava. So, I straighten my back and look Hunter in the eye and say, "Vivian."

"You what?" Hunter's eyes flare and he lowers his arms to his sides, clenching his hands in fists. Standing to tower over me, Logan shakes his head, but Mia just stares at me, and if looks could kill…

I see the assumptions they are making in their reactions and I quickly hold up my hands in surrender, as I tell them, "It wasn't like that. I just ran into her; she apologized for how she behaved."

Hunter scoffs, "Oh, she apologized? Well that's fantastic if she apologized then, all is right in the world."

Mia steps forward, away from her stewing brother and cocks her brow, suspicion evident in her eyes. "Why was your phone off?"

"It wasn't."

Mia's brows shoot up to her hairline. "So you ignored our texts for that bitch?"

"I didn't… I forgot to check my phone," I stammer out, feeling the weight of their disappointment on top of the stress of not knowing what happened to Ava, the room starting to feel hotter.

Logan, always quick to make a joke, turns a somber expression to me as he runs a hand through his hair, shaking his head at me. "That's bullshit, man. Your woman is in there, probably scared out of her mind and you weren't there."

"Especially when you had her believing you would be," Mia adds.

"Look, I screwed up, but I didn't do anything really wrong."

Mia's jaw drops in outrage for a moment until she quickly recovers, her eyes flaring like her brother's when she approaches me, getting in my face and starts to wave a finger at me, exclaiming, "You serious? Okay, let's look at the facts. You impregnated my best friend and had her believe that you had her back, that you would be there. Right?"

"Yeah, but..."

She throws her hand up, silencing me, before continuing, "And then the moment she needs you the most, she can't get a hold of you because you're too busy with a woman who is obviously interested in you. You chose Vivian over Ava today."

"It's not like that!"

Hunter steps forward, growling, "Oh stop lying to yourself! We all see it. Vivian is an evil manipulative bitch that is set to get her claws in you. She will crush anything that gets in her way. She's just trying a new tactic."

Looking back at how she behaved that night, I knew what he said was true. Vivian was determined and she had a crush. But today at lunch, I believed she had changed, that she wanted to be friends. But thinking about it now, I can't help but wonder if Hunter is right. Slumping my shoulders and feeling like everything I have is slipping away, I squeeze the bridge of my nose and run my hand through my hair. "Look, I'm sorry."

"It's not us you need to apologize to."

"I screwed up. I didn't mean it. I thought she was just trying to make things right." I explain, my throat feeling like it was closing up.

"Yeah, you definitely screwed up."

Hearing his words, I know they are true, but before I can say anything a woman in a white coat holding a clipboard comes walking through the swinging doors.

My friends and their words are quickly forgotten as I practically run to the woman, startling her for a moment as I ask quickly in one breath, "How is Ava? Is she going to be okay?"

I feel the others at my back and the doctor's eyes go to each of us until she asks me, "Are you family?"

"I am." We all hear as a familiar petite girl walks in, worried lines appearing between her brows and eyes, similar to Ava's, looking past me to focus on the doctor. "I'm her sister."

I don't know how she managed to get here. I remembered Ava saying that Lucy didn't have her license yet, with her dad not bothering to teach her and Ava not being there often enough to teach her. She must have caught the bus or something.

The doctor nods then tells me, "Sorry, only family right now."

Without looking at me, she starts to follow the doctor and I can't help but call out after her, knowing she is my only connection to Ava right now. "Lucy!"

She stops, turning to look me in the eye with a look of sadness mixed with disappointment and it is in that look that I realize how much I screwed up, even if I didn't mean to, it still happened. "I'll check on her. I think it's best you stay out here right now."

She leaves before I can say anything else, the doors flapping closed behind her, leaving the rest of us alone and waiting once again.

IT'S BEEN the longest ten minutes of my life, my mind going in a loop over what happened today. This morning was amazing, waking up to Ava, skin on skin and resting my hand over her belly until I feel our baby kick me. That kick was strong enough to wake Ava, her tired eyes finding mine and smiling, knowing I was there. Now here I am, sitting in the cold hard chairs of the waiting room away from everyone with my head in my hands and an unsettling feeling of uncertainty washing over me.

What will happen when I see Ava? Will she smile at me like this morning or was that smile the last one I'll have? If only I knew…

I sigh just as I feel the weight of someone plopping themselves down on the chair next to me. I turn my head to see that it's Logan. His face is unusually serious and worried as he watches his hands clasped in his lap. "You really screwed up, man."

"I know," I say, returning my attention to the floor at my feet, my voice low and broken, feeling and knowing the truth in his words.

"What happened today? Why didn't you check your phone? It's not like you."

I shrug, not knowing what else to say. "I don't know."

Neither of us says anything for a moment, until he finally breaks the tense silence growing between us. "Is it Vivian? Do you actually have feelings for her?"

"God, no!" I exclaim so quickly that I don't even think about it. I don't need to because it is the truth. It wasn't like that with Vivian, not for me anyway and the thought that my friends could think such a thing of me, I shake my head, looking Logan in the eyes when I say, "It wasn't like that, for me at least. She was a friend and I guess I kind of missed that, the normalcy of it. Everything has changed so much, not that I'm complaining. I guess, everything is just becoming real. I'm going to be a dad, man. And… I don't know, I guess I missed the normalcy of just hanging out with Vivian and studying and stuff."

Logan's expression doesn't change until he leans in to tell me, "You know what I'm hearing right now?"

"What?"

"Bullshit," Logan spits through gritted teeth, making me flinch back at his tone, so foreign I didn't know how to react.

"What?"

Logan scoffs, shaking his head before casting an irritated look my way. "Seriously, I would kill to be in your shoes. You have a cool girl that would be fun to hang around and is loyal. She cares about you and is loving. You can tell by how she cares for that baby inside her. How she cares for all us guys. She's a good woman that you landed. Yeah, it's not like you planned to be having a baby and it's scary, but imagine what it's like for her. It's not all about you. It's happening to her too. And you choosing another woman over her, because that's what you did today, was pretty much a slap in the face." He shakes his head again as I try to process everything he's saying, "Man up and realize what you have before you lose it, because I can guarantee that any other guy won't let her go without a fight."

He lets up and walks away to stand with the others, leaving me speechless as I think about Ava with another guy. No, that can't happen. And I know it could because he's right, she's amazing.

It isn't until Lucy comes through the door that I awaken to the here and now, springing up from my chair, pushing past the others until I reach her. "Is she okay?"

She levels me with a look before answering, moving her gaze over everyone behind me, waiting to know themselves. "It was just Braxton Hicks. False labor. Doctors told her to take it easy."

"So the baby is okay?" I ask, fear seeping into my words.

"The baby is fine. They just want to keep her under observation for a night. She'll be fine to head home tomorrow."

I finally allow myself to breathe when Mia asks, "So can we see her?"

Lucy's eyes focus on me, giving me that look again, a look that says I'm in deep shit. I should've seen that coming. "She wants to see you."

With that, she leads me through and down a hallway until we finally reach her room, stopping just outside the door, then she places her small hand on my arm and whispers, "Good luck."— before walking away and leaving me to face this alone.

I should be nervous about what I'm going to walk into, but the urge to get to Ava and be by her side wins out, so I take in a breath and enter the quiet room.

Inside sits a large armchair tucked away in a corner, a small TV hangs from the ceiling and a hospital bed sits against a wall with my girlfriend on top of it with blankets draped over her.

I smile and go to her, seeing her sitting up with her hands resting on her belly. "Hey, how are you feeling?"

I reach to hold her hand but she quickly snatches it away from me, showing me her expression. It was one of sadness and hurt, bordering on indifferent at times.

The look set me on edge, cluing me in to the fact that she may already know what happened, so I quickly try to explain, "Look, I know—"

But I don't get a chance to finish when she asks in the most emotionless voice I've ever heard from her, "Where were you?"

"I was—"

"Don't lie to me."

I wasn't going to lie, but I didn't know how to say it, because based on how our friends reacted to my whereabouts, I'd assume Ava would react about the same, but there was really no other way to say it. "I was having lunch."

She contemplates this. "Your work said you didn't return from lunch. Must've been some lunch."

She knows. Maybe she doesn't know everything but she knows something is going on, I can tell by how she's looking at me, like she's waiting for me to fess up, so I say on a sigh, "I ran into a friend."

"So you had lunch with the friend? Who?"

"Ava."

"It was her, wasn't it?" She narrows her eyes slightly but otherwise, her face remains neutral which almost makes me wish she was yelling and screaming at me.

"It wasn't like that; you need to listen to me."

That's when the mask breaks and emotion filters through, hitting me in the chest as I watch the pain on her face when she holds a hand up to silence me, squeezing her eyes shut and sucking in a breath through her nose. "No, I don't." She opens her eyes and I see the pain I caused her. "There is nothing you can say that can take back the choice you made today."

I try to go to her, but she still holds her hands up, her eyes narrow on me, daring me to go near her and man, do I want to be near her. I want to wrap my arms around her and tell her how I feel and that she has nothing to worry about, but I know it isn't going to be that simple. I still work through the lump I feel growing in my throat and say, pleading, "I know you think I chose Vivian over you, but I—"

"Didn't you?"

"Of course not. I felt my phone vibrate but I just forgot to answer it."

"Because you were with her!" Her voice breaks as she begins to yell at me, pointing an angry finger at me with tears filling her eyes and the sight just breaks my heart that much more. "You were with her when I needed you. I was so scared and all I wanted was for you to hold my hand and tell me it was going to be okay, and you weren't there."

"I'm here now." My voice starts to break and I risk a step

closer to her as I watch her eyes go dull, still wet with tears rolling down her cheeks.

She shakes her head solemnly. "Now is too late."

The words make me wince; I gasp like the wind is knocked out of me and I feel each crack of my heart at her words. I take one more step closer until I am right beside her bed, so close that she has no other choice but to look me in the eye as I beg, "Don't say that, not after everything. We can sort this out. I won't talk to Vivian ever again, I will be constantly at your side, just tell me what I can do to fix this."

I watch her resolve fade slightly to reveal pain, mirroring my own looking back at me, a second before it is replaced with numb disinterest when she drops her eyes to the hands in her lap, saying so softly I have to strain to hear it. "I need you to leave."

"Ava" I almost crumble.

"I need time, time to think and I just can't think around you."

"Ava…"

I try to reach for her hand again in a last-ditch effort only for her to tilt her whole body away from me, saying into the pillow, sounding as broken as I feel. "Conner, please."

How did this day get so messed up? What was I thinking when I sat down with Vivian? I guess I just thought I was having lunch with a friend, and I was, but now here I stand, with the possibility of losing not only Ava but my baby as well.

I walk on numb legs, until I stop at the door long enough to promise Ava. "I will fix this."

CHAPTER 32

AVA

Well, it's been a long and hard couple of weeks.

The first week was the hardest. Every night I stayed up late, trying to avoid going into Conner's room so that I wouldn't smell him on the sheets. I'd fall asleep on the couch and every night, one of the guys would take me to the room because I would always wake up to the smell of Conner, but with no Conner.

I shouldn't feel this pain, this sadness of not having him here. I should be angry about Vivian and what happened. But somehow the pain has grown stronger.

My days have grown darker and I don't even have classes to distract me anymore with classes done for the year.

Now it's just me in this house.

After what happened, I had asked for time and Conner gave it to me. I found out when I came home to find some of his stuff missing and a note telling me he will fix this, like he promised at the hospital.

Everything is just a mess now. Instead of going home, the guys have decided to stay with me during the break. Snow began to fall last week and all we've been doing is watching horror and action movies under blankets with food.

I'm on leave at work so I don't even have that. I just have this existence.

I wrap myself in a woolen blanket and descend the stairs, preparing for another day and waiting for it to end. Everything just seems darker now, like my light has gone.

I place a hand on my stomach and feel a flickering of happiness as I think to myself, "At least I still have you."

"There she is!" Hunter exclaims when I enter the living room, plopping myself on one of the recliners. Hunter has his arms stretched out in greeting as he sits in the other recliner.

We both hear a groan from the couch between us, watching as a disheveled Logan rolls over to face us with a tired and pained expression, dark circles prominent under his eyes. "Man, keep it down, some of us are trying to die over here."

Dropping his arms, Hunter sighs at Logan as he struggles to pull himself into a sitting position, running his hands over his face. "Well that's what you get when you drink too much, you drunk."

"Hey!" Logan waves a finger at Hunter. "I don't do scary movies without alcohol."

I smile at the memory of last night, how we all decided to watch the movie *Truth or Dare* and of Logan consistently finding excuses to leave the room. He needed to get more food, bathroom break, and the very common drink break which mostly consisted of alcohol.

I lean forward in my chair, batting my eyes innocently. "Hey, Logan?" He looks at me just as I change my face to give him that creepy smile from the movie as I ask him, "Truth or dare?"

"Shut up! That movie was fucked up and traumatized my childhood."

"How?" I ask, cocking my head at him.

"I will never think of that game the same way again."

"But Lucy Hale was hot, though," Hunter comments with a small smile.

"Beside the point!" Logan simply waves him off dismissively and I roll my eyes.

"Well, you survived. Thank you for watching it with me," I tell him, feeling the weight of the love in this house. Antics or not, there is love in this house and it shows with everything these men do.

My smile grows when I see Logan pout when he says, "You owe me."

"I'll buy you a jumbo pack of skittles."

That makes him smile. "I love you."

"I love you too." And to sweeten the pot, I add, "And we can watch *Die Hard* tonight."

And that makes him practically salivate. "Marry me?"

We laugh and for a moment, I forget. I forget the darkness and the loneliness, the pain. I forget the absence of Conner.

I feel my shoulders start to slump forward and my eyes cast downward as the silence of the room starts to take over.

The silence grows thick and tense, I can almost taste it. I feel the boys' eyes on me, so I look up just as Hunter asks, concern leaking into his words, "How are you?"

How do I answer that? I'm not good, but I asked for this. So, I answer the only other way I can, "I'm good. Anyone called?"

His eyes grow sad, seeing my pain and my hidden question, "I haven't heard from him."

"Oh." My shoulders slump more and I bite my lip to keep my emotions at bay.

"Ava—"

Hunter starts but I hold up my hand to silence him, forcing the broken look off my face. "No, I asked for time. He's just giving me that. Hey, I'm going to get some food, you want any?"

Hunter's brows furrow as he turns to look out the window taking up the back wall before returning his gaze to me. "You sure you should be going out? There's word of a snow storm hitting us tonight."

"Here, I'll go with you." I hold up my hand again, stopping Logan before he can rise from the couch.

"No, it's fine. I'll be quick and I have my phone on me."

I throw off the blanket I have on my shoulders as I rise from the chair, feeling the strain on my knees and back.

"Okay, just get whatever you want. We're not picky. You want some money?"

"I got it," I tell them as I begin to pull on my big gray coat, scarf, and boots left by the door, bracing for the cold but ready for some distance from anything that makes me think of Conner, some relief from this ache in my chest.

"Ava?" I've been walking in a haze for I don't know how long, my thoughts going into a loop when I hear my name. I stop in my tracks and look around with a furrowed brow only to smile when I see a familiar woman looking back at me.

Her golden hair still hung in waves and her kind green eyes were still bright.

"Heather? Wow, what are you doing here?" I close the distance between us, welcoming her smile with my own and giving her a hug, strange to feel the absence of her belly, but I guess mine makes up for it.

I pull back and she inclines her head to the stroller beside her. "Taking this one for a walk. She doesn't sleep unless she gets a walk."

Looking into the stroller, I cannot believe my eyes. This baby is so small; a puppy would be bigger. Were they meant to be this small? So cute yet so fragile, how do you not get scared of breaking them? "Oh my god! Look at her. What's her name?"

"Amelia," Heather answers with a loving smile as she gazes at the sleeping baby.

"Hello, Amelia," I whisper to her before looking back at Heather.

She only focuses on my huge belly, smiling excitedly as she says, "Look at you. You look like you're ready to pop."

"I am, pretty much."

Her brows crease as she begins to look past me and around before asking, "Is it just you? Where's the cutie?"

And there's the reminder I was running from. Even outside the house, I can't forget. Feeling her words in my chest, I look away, unable to answer, unsure how to answer. He's gone? I was an idiot? He was an idiot? This whole thing is stupid?

Luckily Heather realizes. "Oh." After a moment, Heather puts a gentle hand on my arm, forcing my eyes to hers, a small smile on her face. "Hey, you wanna take a walk with me?"

"I don't want to intrude."

"No, it's okay. It'll be nice to have some adult conversation for once."

I nod, wanting to escape but also loving the company, someone who knows what I'm going through, that can understand.

We walk in silence until we reach a lovely park full of lush green trees and snow blanketing the ground, making it look like a winter wonderland.

I sigh, feeling the peace of this place, not breaking the silence until Heather finally asks, "So how are you feeling?"

I rub my belly. "Tired, heavy, achy. All the lovely things. Like my body is working against me."

She chuckles before turning serious. "I remember that. But how are you feeling, really?"

I hesitate, wanting to tell her everything but unsure of how or what to say.

"Look, it's okay if you don't want to talk about it. I get pretty nosy these days."

"No, it's fine. I don't know. I'm getting by." I shrug.

"That doesn't sound like fun."

"It's not," I say, looking down at my stomach and finally allowing myself to really feel the pain of what happened.

"What happened?"

I go through everything, from how we finally got together to now, talking so quick, I'm not sure she even caught a lot of it or even understood it. But when I finally finish, feeling a tiny bit lighter, Heather nods to herself before asking me, "So how long has he been away?"

"Just a couple of weeks."

"But it feels like forever?" Heather says, knowing how I'm feeling.

"Yeah. I mean, I shouldn't be feeling like this. I asked for this."

She nods. "Yes, you did, but you didn't promise yourself space. You just needed it at the time. If you feel like you don't need that time anymore, then talk to him."

"He hasn't even tried to contact me." My heart breaks at this a little.

"You did ask for space. Maybe he's just waiting for you."

"I'm scared."

"Of?"

Everything.

"Of letting him in, of getting hurt again."

We stop walking and she forces me to look at her, placing

a comforting hand on my shoulder as she gives me a look I'm sure a lot of mothers give their kids. She will be an amazing mother. "I wish I could say you won't get hurt again but I would be lying. We are human beings. We make mistakes, we say or do the wrong things and sometimes that can hurt. But we also forgive. He made a mistake, just like we all do, but now it's up to you. Do you forgive him?"

If anyone asked me that a couple of weeks ago, I would've said no. But now, after this time away from him, knowing life without him, I knew I couldn't do it. I couldn't not forgive him because he had always been there for me. I can't stay angry at the one time he isn't. It was in that moment that the answer was clear and a weight lifted off my chest at the realization. "I do. I miss him."

Heather's smile grows. "Then you already know what you're gonna do."

"Yeah. Thank you." I throw my arms around her, grateful to have met her and to know this woman that has now changed my life. I give her a slight squeeze and she says into my hair, "Anytime."

Pulling back, we smile at each other, feeling the change that just occurred in our lives, at the same time the wind starts to pick up slightly, making me shiver. The storm's coming, I think to myself as I start to say, "Hey I should—"

"Go get your man?"

"Well, I was going to say get home before these winds pick up anymore." But that's not saying I won't be getting my man, if he will still have me. Maybe I pushed him too far. Time will tell.

She looks around, seeing the wind dancing with the trees. "I guess you're right. I should do the same. Here, let me give you my number and we can catch up."

I get her number, thankful for another friend I can share

this journey with, before pulling my coat tight around me and making my way back home, without the food I said I was going to get.

CHAPTER 33

AVA

I can't shake the aching feeling running through my body when I walk up the drive of the house, the snowy winds picking up and almost sending me tumbling over. I hold my belly as I hobble up the steps, using the railing to keep me standing and turning my head against the winds that keep biting at my skin with its nippy chill.

My body is exhausted and my breath is heavy when I swing the door open, running into the shelter of the house and welcoming the warmth of it before closing the door behind me.

"Thank fuck." I hear behind me in a concerned whisper.

I turn around and practically see a stampede coming toward me in the form of Mia and Hunter. Worry tensing their pretty faces when Hunter calls behind him. "She's here!"

"Mia?" She launches at me, wrapping her arms around me before I can even process what is happening.

Giving me one final squeeze, she pulls back and asks, "Where have you been?"

"You had us worried." Hunter explains, crossing his arms.

"We tried to call," Logan explains as he comes up behind them, wearing their matching expressions of concern.

"What?" As they all stand around me, I pull out my phone, realizing I hadn't checked it since I left the house. I had been too lost in my own thoughts and what was happening in my life that I didn't even realize and when I pull my phone out of my pocket, I find that it is dead. "I guess my phone died. Sorry."

"Where were you?" Mia asks, putting her hands to her slim hips.

"I ran into a friend. Sorry, I didn't mean to worry you."

Hunter steps forward. "We heard on the TV that the storm is gonna hit sooner than expected. We were worried you would be caught in it."

"I was gonna go out and find you."

I smile at Logan in gratitude when I tell them all, "Well, I'm fine."

"Thank God! So, what are we doing tonight?" And just like that, my absence is forgotten and Logan is rubbing his hands together as he starts to conjure up ideas about what to do tonight.

"Another movie night?" Hunter suggests.

Logan shakes his head, probably scared of another horror movie. "I think we should mix it up. Play a game?"

"What game?"

"Poker?" Hunter suggests.

"Strip poker?" Logan gives Mia a lighthearted wink which only earns him an eye roll.

And it is then that I put my hand to my belly, when I feel it.

My heart drops into my stomach as Mia says to Logan, "That's not even funny."

"Guys." The words are said through what feels like numb lips and no one appears to hear me.

Logan gives her a sly smile. "It wasn't meant to be. It was a serious suggestion."

"Well, I suggest that Logan doesn't get a say." Both Mia and Hunter raise their hand in agreement as I try again, my concern growing.

"Guys."

Hunter chimes in, "I second that."

"Hey!" Logan exclaims his offense when I start to feel a wave of cramps encircling my belly and wrapping around my back.

Wincing, I finally yell, "Guys!"

They all turn to look at me with a question in their eyes, as they see me standing in the entranceway, my hand resting on the hall table now to keep me standing as my legs begin to shake, and my other hand on my belly as I feel the warmth rolling down my legs when I finally tell them, with a shake to my words, "I think something else is coming tonight."

Realization quickly registers on Mia and Hunter's faces when they look down and see the water starting to pool around my feet and the wetness soaking my jeans.

But it is Logan that hasn't noticed yet when he laughs out, "That's what she said."— only to get slapped upside the head by Hunter. "Ow." When Hunter finally points at the water at my feet, Logan's eyes widen. "Oh shit, you're pissing yourself!"

And he gets slapped again, only this time, by Mia. "Ow!"

CHAPTER 34

CONNER

I start to dig into the first box at my new place, boxes filling the space, making it hard to move, I open the one labeled 'kitchen'. Unfortunately, I don't have much, considering a lot of the stuff is shared in the guy's house, I didn't want to take plates or cups. So instead, I called up my parents and asked if they had any spares and luckily they did. I also managed to spend this last week before moving in accumulating some basic furniture pieces.

It is strange. I'd been living in the house with the guys for a while, so living here has yet to feel like home. But I know it will, one day when I have my missing piece back.

I smile at the thought of her, hating the ache I still feel in my chest at missing her.

I haven't slept well in the past couple of weeks because she hasn't been there. After sleeping next to her and smelling her, feeling her, it's hard to sleep without that these days.

The memory was quickly shattered when a knock sounds at the door. I furrow my brow at it, wondering who it could be. No one knows I'm here, except for my parents, of course.

They knock again as I try to maneuver around the maze of boxes, and I call out as I get closer. "Coming!"

I answer the door and cock my head at who is standing on the other side, smiling at me as she stands bundled up in a green coat and red scarf. Her red hair pinned up out of her face.

"Vivian? What are you doing here?" I look behind her to see her yellow Volkswagen Beetle and wonder how she managed to get here with the roads being closed now. A storm is coming, though it's worse in some areas. Here it's only just a little windy. The storm has yet to come.

Her smile grows. "I came to see you, silly."

"But how did you know I lived here? I only just moved in a week ago."

She shrugs, looking proud of herself, though who could she have asked? My parents? They were the only ones that knew. "I asked around. So, can I come in?" Before I could ask any further questions, she changes the subject.

Thinking of last time and Ava, I shake my head. "I don't think that's a good idea."

She furrows her brow at me, cocking her head in confusion, "Why? Is Ava upset you and I are hanging out again?"

Yes, I think but don't say it out loud. But I have to say that I don't blame her. If the shoe was on the other foot, I'd be furious, I'd be hurt.

Taking my silence as confirmation, she waves her hand at me dismissively, "She will get over it. Don't worry about her."

She goes to put a hand on my shoulder and I step just out of reach, shaking my head as I finally see by the look in her eyes that she hasn't changed. She still doesn't care about Ava's feelings, only her own. "No. I will worry about her. Something you *still* don't understand, Vivian, is that she is a big part of my life now."

At that, Vivian crosses her arms and turns her nose up at me. "Really? Then where is she?"

"She's… she's at home."

"Not with you?"

I nod. "Yeah, because I screwed up. Tell me something, if I told you that there wasn't a chance in hell of you and me happening, would you be standing here right now? Are you really my friend or do you still want more?" I finally ask, and I'm a bit shattered when I see Vivian's eyes widen in panic at my question only to quickly recover but remain silent.

I shake my head as I realize the truth. She never wanted to be my friend, it was always a ploy to get more. "I'm such an idiot."

"Conner—"

I wave my hand to silence her, not wanting to hear it. "No, I trusted you. I took a chance on our friendship and almost destroyed my relationship. My family! Is that what you want?"

I am met with more silence and I am hurt that much more.

My shoulders deflate when I tell her, "Vivian, you should leave."

"But, Conner."

"All I can offer you is friendship. Nothing more. Ever. If that's not enough, then go now."

She stays, thinking for a minute before cocking her head at me with a sad look in her eyes, then she asks, "I never had a chance, did I?"

"No, you didn't," I answer quickly.

She nods to herself, contemplating before giving me one final look as she's preparing to leave, stopping to look back at me one last time, a sad smile on her face. "She's a lucky girl, so is the kid."

I nod, wishing it didn't have to be this way, but I can't

offer her more. I can only offer her friendship and obviously, she was in my life for the wrong reasons. This is for the best.

"It was nice knowing you, Conner," she says before finally turning to leave, the wind picking up more behind her as I close the door, wanting to drown myself in these boxes and organization.

I go back to the kitchen box and make it two pieces in when another knock sounds at the door.

I silently curse as I navigate the boxes once again and contemplate putting a 'no visitors' sign on the door. When I swing the door open I see the next person I didn't expect standing there with a hoodie under his coat and his hands tucked in his jeans pockets.

"Hey," my big brother, Riley says, actually looking nervous as he stands on the front doorstep.

"What are you doing here, Riley?" I look past him, expecting to see my parents only to see Dad's truck in the driveway.

Riley shrugs, pushing past me casually as he enters the house, looking around. "Can't I check on my little brother?"

I scoff, closing the door. "Since when have you ever checked on me?"

He finally looks at me standing in the mass of boxes. "Okay, so I came because Mom and Dad are on my case. Telling me I need to talk to you, make things right."

Of course, I think to myself, "So, you're just here for them?"

"No. I wanted to talk to you, to explain."

"Explain what?" I ask, crossing my arms over my chest.

"Why I left."

"And if I don't want to hear it?"

He just rolls his eyes and points to my new couch against the wall. "Look, just sit down and stop being so stubborn."

"Where do you think I learned it from?" I comment and I

can't help but feel like old times. We would tease each other and push each other but it was all in good fun. Never malicious. Which was why I was so confused when he left.

So I sit. Not because he told me to, but because in some way, I would like to know why he did what he did.

He moves to stand before me, thinking before he finally speaks, "Do you remember when we were kids, learning the ways of the farm? Remember how fast you picked it up? You were a natural with the animals, I'm happy to know you're pursuing it."

He gives me a smile and I hate how happy those words make me feel, like I was craving them. I bite my lip and tense my jaw when I ask, "Your point?"

He sighs, seeing my resistance. "I never picked it up like you. Mom, Dad. You all knew what you were doing and I never really felt like I did, not there. But with music, that was my thing. It was a way I communicated, how I expressed myself. I got transported to a different world when I heard a song, almost like I could be someone else. My point is, the farm was great but it wasn't a place for me."

"But you didn't even say goodbye."

He shakes his head and I finally see the sorrow that sits in his eyes as he looks down at me. "You think I would've left if I did say goodbye? You are my little brother, my best friend, whether you like it or not. If I said goodbye, I know I wouldn't have gone."

"Why did you go?"

"Because I needed to figure things out. I knew I loved music but I wanted to know if I could make something with it. I had an opportunity and I took it. They offered me a chance to play overseas and I felt like I had to take it. It was my chance. I'm sorry I hurt people, but I didn't mean to."

"Was it worth it? Going, I mean."

He thinks for a moment. "It was an adventure. I got to live

a bit of my dream. But no, it wasn't. Because if I knew what I was going to come home to, to you hating me, I don't think I would've gone."

I feel the tension leave my muscles as the weight of this pain I've been feeling for years finally lifts off me. "I don't hate you. I'm pissed at you."

I narrow my eyes at him to emphasize the point which only makes Riley smile the classic big brother smile, and he nods. "That I can live with."

We sit in silence, unsure of where to go from here, when he asks, shuffling his feet nervously, "You think I could come by and see your kid?"

I finally laugh. "Hell, you'll be helping me build the crib."

"Hey, I never agreed to that."

"Think of it as making up for lost time."

We both laugh, shattering the barrier that developed over time, feeling that connection we had when we were kids reform within us, then my phone rings.

I hold up a finger to my brother telling him to hold on for a second when I see it's Hunter calling. I answer and am met with a distant scream on the other end.

"Hunter?"

I hear Hunter over the screams and he sounds panicked as shit. "You need to get the fuck over here now!"

"What's wrong?" My heartbeat starts to pick up in a panic, matching that in Hunter's voice, when I hear Logan call into the phone.

"Ava's poppin'!"

"What?" I ask, thinking I misheard him, but Hunter quickly clarifies.

"She's having the baby, Conner. Now!"

"What?" My body goes numb but my mind goes crazy as I hear the screams, realizing they're coming from Ava. They are vicious screams of pain, screams I will never get out of my head, screams that make me want to go to her and help relieve her pain.

"Yeah, and we called the ambulance, but they are saying the roads are closed because of the storm. They will get here as soon as they can, but man, oh shit, there's so much everything. Mia's on the phone with the 911 operator now."

She screams again, and I ask, "Where are you?" I see at the corner of my eye, my brother is now standing at my side and I feel the concern radiating off him.

"At the house. We can't exactly leave."

"I'll be there as soon as I can." I hang up before anything more can be said. I know enough and I know I need to get to Ava.

My baby is coming.

"It's Ava, she's having the baby," I explain as the words finally sink in and panic starts to take over.

"What? Now?"

I nod, my breaths starting to pick up and the next thing I know, Riley is in front of me, his hands on my shoulders, forcing me to look into his eyes.

"Hey, calm down, everything will be okay."

"It's happening now. I'm gonna be a dad. What if I fuck this up?"

He gives me a quick shake. "Hey! You will definitely fuck this up because that's what guys do, but what matters is what you do next. Now are you going to lie down and cry or are you going to go to your woman?"

"The roads are closed," I explain, unsure of how I can get there.

Riley only smiles, "I'll get you there. I promise."

I nod, throwing on my coat, ready to go to my family.

CHAPTER 35

AVA

"We need to get her to the couch," Mia says as she lifts my feet, her phone pinned between her ear and shoulder, and the guys take my upper body, carrying me to the living room as the next wave of pain hits.

I let out a whaling scream as I feel like my stomach is being ripped open. "Ah!"

I grab on to the closest thing I can and pull only to realize it's Logan's hair as he cries out, "Ow ow ow, that's my hair."

"Okay, let's lower her down, gently," Mia instructs, as the boys lower me to the couch as I continue to scream.

Logan is quick to run away, but I watch as they stand there looking at me and it is then that I actually feel worried.

I'm having my baby right now, with these three idiots! Okay, I know that's the pain talking, but when you're in this much pain, you're allowed to be a bit bitchy.

I send up a prayer when the pain finally subsides again and I allow myself to breathe.

"So what do we do?" Hunter asks, looking a little panicked, but Mia's focus is on me, nodding at what the operator is saying on the phone when she kneels down in front of me, placing a hand on my knee.

Moving away from the phone, she says to me, "Everything will be okay, Ava. I promise."

I grit my teeth as another wave of pain hits, they are getting closer together now. "How can you promise that? How many babies have you delivered?"

"I've delivered several of my sister's baby born dolls." Logan suggests with a proud smile and I clench my fists as I turn to him.

"Logan, come here."

Looking a little nervous he approaches, coming down to my level as the pain starts to intensify and only then do I grab a fistful of his hair and pull, growling at him in a voice that sounds almost demonic to my own ears. "Does it look like I'm having a fucking baby born doll?!"

Fear actually appears in his eyes, "No, it looks like you could be from one of those scary ghost movies, possession and all."

I pull harder and growl again, making him cry out, "Ow."

I let go, Hunter grabs Logan and starts pulling him away as he rubs his sore head. "Yeah, let's get you away from her."

Mia is on her phone, her brow creasing in concentration as she commands the boys, "We need… towels! Someone get me towels!"

Logan is gone in seconds, and comes back with one tiny dishcloth, handing it to Mia.

Mia holds it up, her brow raised. "What is this?"

"It's a dishcloth."

She throws the dishcloth at him. "I asked for towels, this won't do shit."

Hunter enters the room, no one even realizing he left, returning with armfuls of big fluffy towels. "Here."

My pants are off in seconds, not even caring about the guys, they merely look away until Mia lays a couple of towels on me, while using the others.

She mumbles into her phone, her eyes focused on the juncture between my legs before giving a final nod and then she puts the phone down to focus her attention on me as the waves of pain begin to be more consistent. "Okay, she says you will have to push. The baby is right here, Ava, you gotta push."

"Oh fuck!" I distantly hear one of the guys say, a moment before they are both at my sides, their hands in mine. But they aren't the hands I want. This isn't how it's supposed to be. I am supposed to be in a hospital with drugs for the pain, Conner at my side holding my hand.

I shake my head. "I want Conner. I want to tell him I'm sorry. He should be here, it's his baby."

Putting her hands under the towel between my legs, ready, Mia says, "Sorry but I don't think holding it in is an option right now."

Hunter squeezes my hand, telling me, "Ava, Conner has been called. He said he's gonna be here."

"But the roads..."

"He will be here."

"Ava, I think you have to push," Mia demands and I do. I can feel it. I have been feeling it.

"Take our hands. We're here," Logan tells me and I can't help but feel bad for hurting him, but by the loving look on his face, he doesn't care. He's here, just like Mia and Hunter.

It feels like hours, but it is probably only minutes as I keep pushing. My hair is damp with sweat and sticking to my forehead and neck, my vision starting to get blurry and my muscles weak. I don't know how long I push for and I don't know how long until the ambulance gets here, but I do know this is the worse pain I've ever felt in my life.

I grit my teeth and give it one more push but I just as quickly slump against the boys at my back, gasping for breath and shaking my head. "I can't. I'm sorry, I can't."

Just as the words leave my lips a blast of cold air enters the house after a loud bang from the entryway. Everyone stops and follows the sound with their eyes.

"Ava!" A newfound energy finds its way into my muscles as I sit up just a bit straighter, my eyes instantly finding his blue ones as he rounds the corner and sees me.

"Conner." I want to reach for him, but Logan and Hunter both have my hands.

Logan and Hunter quickly move away when Conner runs to me, falling to his knees and pulling me to him, his warmth momentarily relaxing the muscles in my back.

My hand shakes as I cup his cheek. "I'm sorry."

"No, I'm sorry. I don't ever want you to think you are not a priority and I don't ever want you to feel that way again."

I smile, but it is cut short by the pain. I scream and Conner holds me tighter, whispering in my ear, "You can do this."

I grit my teeth again, giving Mia a nod and growl as I go to push. "I can do this."

Mia nods. "Okay, now just one more! You can do it!"

I feel the sweat rolling down my face, making my hair stick to my forehead. I squeeze Conner's hands and grit my teeth and we all scream together as I give one more push, giving it everything I have left in me.

"AAHHHH!!!!!!"

That's when I hear it. The room is suddenly filled with a baby's cry as Mia holds it out of view as she proceeds to wrap the baby up in a towel, the cord still attached.

"Oh my god." Mia gasps, her eyes starting to fill up with

tears as she holds my baby up for me to see, looking so small and fragile in her arms.

"Holy shit." I hear Conner say, but I'm speechless as I stare at the baby.

"You did it." Mia smiles a beaming proud smile at me.

"Let me see her." I hold my hands out and Mia hand's me the baby.

"Actually, it's a boy," she tells me once I have the baby in my arms, smiling as I take in the little bundle.

Covered in gunk, his face is wrinkly but his nose is a cute button nose, and his lips are cute pouty ones. Chubby cheeks and dark eyes look up at me, no longer crying but staring at me in wonder like he knew who I was, that I would always be here so there was no reason to be scared. "I have a boy. A son. He's so beautiful."

"Cuter than his dad," Mia comments, giving Conner a wink and I smile through happy tears before turning to look at Conner.

"You wanna meet your son?" I smile up at him with our baby in my arms, and Conner looks down at the baby with so much love, it is breathtaking.

"I have a son."

I nod, feeling the tears fill my eyes as the wave of happiness overtakes me, and Conner isn't close behind as he begins to cry, stroking his son's chubby cheek with his finger.

He takes a moment before looking at me through tear-filled eyes. "I'm so sorry."

"Me too."

"I love you so much. Both of you."

Smiling, looking down at our baby then back to Conner, I say, "We love you too."

I hold our son's little hand in mine, whispering, "Say hello to Daddy."

Conner's smile grows at the word just as the ambulance finally arrives.

A DAY HAS PASSED, and we finally made it to the hospital.

Despite the home birth, which I didn't plan on having, there were no problems. The doctors were surprised, but all that matters is that our son is healthy and happy.

Everyone has already come to see us. I got a call from Harper this morning, Conner's parents came yesterday and doted on the baby, spoiling him. Lucky kid. Hunter, Mia, and Logan have all dropped by but had to leave to shower considering they each looked like extras in a horror film.

But I can never be thankful enough for what they did for me.

I am pretty lucky myself.

Lucy arrived ten minutes ago, catching the bus, and arriving with a couple of bars of chocolate. My savior!

Now I sit on the bed, with Conner at my side and the baby on my boob for his afternoon feeding, when Lucy asks, "So have we decided on a name yet?"

"Yeah."

I smile when I tell her the name we agreed on ages ago. "Charlie. My special little boy, Charlie."

"Chocolate factory?" Lucy raises a brow, remembering my love for the story.

"Of course."

"How could I forget?" She rolls her eyes before smiling down at Charlie, in awe of him. "He's beautiful, Ava."

"Just like his mother," Conner comments before placing a chaste kiss on my lips and then he continues to stare lovingly into my eyes.

Lucy clears her throat after a moment, "While you're busy, can I hold my nephew?"

Looking down, I see Charlie finish with the boob and work at tucking it back into my gown, nodding and handing the baby off to her. "Yes you can."

She instantly starts to coddle him. "Look at you, little one. You are so precious and I am going to spoil you rotten. I will be your favorite aunt."

"I bet."

"We will watch scary movies and eat all the junk food."

"You what?" Conner's head perks up at this in alarm, making Lucy and I both laugh at the joke.

Conner just sighs, running a hand over his tired face. "I already know this kid is gonna give me gray hairs."

"That'll just make you a silver fox."

"Oh really?" He raises a brow at me, leaning closer.

"Really," I say, closing the distance and puckering my lips for a kiss only to be interrupted by a loud voice as Logan comes storming in, holding the biggest teddy bear I've ever seen. It was his height and blue.

"Hopefully we're all decent in here but we're coming in."

Mia and Hunter come in behind him carrying flowers and balloons saying 'It's a Boy'. But my focus remains on the bear.

"What is that?"

"It's a teddy bear," Logan says, confused by my amazement as Conner chuckles at my side.

"That's not a teddy bear, it looks like your fluffy twin."

"Funny, but Charlie will love it." With that, he approaches Lucy holding Charlie, grabbing the bear's fuzzy hand and giving it a wave.

The room is silent until suddenly, distressed whaling sounds erupt from the baby as he starts to cry in Lucy's arms, probably terrified by the bear.

Logan, defeated, walks his bear to the back of the room,

sitting him on the large recliner in the corner, before returning to us.

Trying to cheer him up, seeing what he was trying to do, I say, "Maybe he will grow to love it."

"Kind of like you," Hunter comments under his breath, but loud enough for people to hear.

"Ha!" Logan exclaims, victoriously pointing a finger at Hunter. "So, you admit you love me?"

Hunter merely rolls his eyes as Mia steps forward with not only flowers she places on the table but a paper bag. "Well, my gift is for the mother."

"Ooh, presents." I hold the bag, opening it up and feeling my cheeks heat at what sits inside.

Mia explains, "These next few months are going to be exhausting and I think it's about time you got around to these."

I hold back from rolling my eyes as I lift all three of the *Fifty Shades of Grey* books out of the bag, knowing this was her evil plan all along. Have me get pregnant so she can give me these, because she has been on my case for years trying to get me to read them. But watching the movies was enough for me to know that Christian was a dick and I didn't want to read about him.

"Oh no! Mia, I'm not reading these."

She points her finger at me. "Mark my words. When you are alone with your kid at night and can't sleep, those books will entertain you."

I sigh, shaking my head and putting the books back in the bag when I feel Conner lean into me, whispering, "Maybe we could try some things from them."

Even though the idea of doing anything with him makes me both hot and tired, I hand him the bag. "You wanna learn something new, you read them."

"Maybe I will." He winks and I shake my head at him, turning to the room full of people I love so much.

"Thank you so much, guys. For everything. I couldn't have asked for a better family."

EPILOGUE

AVA

One Month Later

Even though I missed Charlie, it was nice of Conner's parents to watch him while Conner took us out. I couldn't get much out of him except that it was a surprise, which wasn't anything. I look around as Conner continues to drive around this nice neighborhood until he finally pulls up to a simple little house.

The house is white with a wraparound porch, single story and a large front lawn and a white picket fence going around it.

It's beautiful, but I still didn't understand what we were doing here. Conner smiles at my furrowed expression when he comes around to open the door for me, helping me out of his truck. Looking around, I ask, "What exactly are we doing here?"

He puts a hand to the small of my back and starts to lead

me up the driveway of the beautiful white house. "Well, I never got you a Christmas present."

"What are you talking about?"

"Follow me." I follow him up to the front door, surprised when he pulls out a key and proceeds to unlock the front door.

"A friend of yours live here?"

He smiles. "Something like that." Then swings the door open and leads me inside to reveal an open space. Beautiful modern kitchen, warm and welcoming dining room next to it, then in front of me sits a large cream-colored sofa and a large TV.

The breath is stuck in my throat but I force the words out. "Oh my, it's so beautiful."

Conner continues to smile as he points down the hallway. "You should check down the hallway."

My brow creases, I'm lost as to what is going on and what we are doing here. "Why?"

But I go forth down the hall, walking past closed doors until I reach the one open one at the end of the hall only to gasp and cup my hands over my mouth as I take in the room before me.

It's both white and blue in color, a white chest stuffed with toys and a white crib stands tall in the center with blue blankets inside. A changing table and a name on the wall that makes my heart sit in my throat and tears fill my eyes.

Charlie's name hangs there in big blue letters and the words just fall off my tongue in a gasp. "Holy shit."

"You like it?" I hear Conner come up behind me and I turn to see his smile has grown even more if possible, he's holding up a key. "Because it's ours."

I blink, thinking I must've misheard him. Neither of us can afford a place like this. "What are you talking about?"

Conner explains, "I told you I was gonna fix it that day in

the hospital. I wanted to show you how serious I am about this family we're creating. I want that picket fence life with you, so I found this. Riley helped me with the nursery and my parents helped out, but it's all ours."

I'm speechless as I take in this house with new light, imagining our child running up and down this hall, getting ready for school. Or coming out to that living room to take pictures for his prom. I could see it all and this man in front of me gave me that.

Looking at my tear-filled eyes, he asks, "Do you like it?"

"Do I like it?" I laugh at the idea of not liking it and grab the love of my life, pulling him to me and showing him how much I love it. I put everything in that kiss, how much I love the house, our baby, our new life and him.

Finally pulling back, I ask, "Does that answer your question?"

He grins and I give him one more kiss, pulling back to rest my forehead on his. "No one has ever treated me the way you do, Conner. You drive me nuts sometimes, but I love you so much. I'm so excited about the life we get to have together now."

I grab his hand and hold it to my heart as I watch his grin start to grow into something playful and flirtatious as he leans in. "I think I've got a way of starting it."

I raise my brow at him. "Breaking in the new house?"

"Of course."

"Which room first?"

"Let's start with the bedroom and work our way back."

"First time of many to come."

I pull him in for another kiss, and he picks me up, carrying me to our new bedroom and to the start of the life I never knew I wanted, but was lucky to have.

SOUNDTRACK

We Found Love by Rhianna

About a Girl by The Academy is …

I Want to Hold Your Hand by The Beattles

Unconditionally by Katy Perry

Fighter by Christina Aguilera

Collide by Howie Day

Dark Horse by Katie Perry

The Beast in Me by Bonnie Pointer

Big Girls Don't Cry by Fergie

When You're Gone by Avril Lavigne

Someday by Nickelback

Love Me Like You Do by Ellie Goulding

NOT READY TO LEAVE THE GANG YET?

Keep your eye out for Mia's story
COMING SOON

COMING UP

HOOKING UP SERIES

Hooking Up with Mr Wrong

The Non-Hook Up

A Hook Up to Remember

The Secret Hook Up

NOTE TO THE READER

Thank you for reading *Hooking up with Mr Wrong.* This story has evolved so much over the years and I'm so proud of what it has become. I hope you laugh, swoon and fall in love with the same characters that stole my heart.

If you're new to me and my books, I love to keep in touch with my readers and fellow writer friends. So, if you want to stay in touch, you can...

Sign up for my newsletter and receive bookish content such as deleted and bonus scenes, teasers of future books and bookish ramblings of some amazing books.

Follow me on Instagram and take part in the Indie Bookclub where each month is dedicated to a new indie book with a discussion each week that leads up to a bookish discussion with the author at the end of the month. I also show snippets of my process and any books I'm writing. You may also catch a glimpse into my daily life as I share with you how I manage to maintain a somewhat balanced life.

Follow me on Facebook and gain some insight and snippets of future projects where I may leave plotting decisions to the readers ... just to keep things fun ;)

ACKNOWLEDGMENTS

Well, this book was a long time coming. I had dreamt of this day for years and now here it is, but I could not have gotten here on my own. Gosh, where do I start?

I thank my mum for filling my childhood with stories to help my imagination grow, I also thank her for putting up with my craziness and being the drill sergeant when I needed it. You played a big part in this, mum and I will love you forever.

I want to thank my fiancé, Levi for being my person and believing in my dream as much as I did. I cannot wait to marry you.

My aunty Fiona played a big role in this story as she suffered through so many phone calls with me crying about plot holes, talking me down off the ledge and giving me the kick in the butt I needed to finish this book. Truthfully, it probably would not have been written without her.

I am blessed with the most supportive family and I love them all so much.

I always said I'd do this when I finished a book, so here it goes. I'd like to thank my high school principal Dr Phil

Reeves (I don't know his first name). He was the first to read anything I'd written and the first to put writing in my head as a career option. I remember when he said to my mum on graduation day, "No matter what she does in her life, make sure she keeps writing." And that's what I did. Being a teacher myself, I hope to one day inspire one of my students the way you inspired me.

I am also blessed to be a part of an amazing online writing community, full of people who took the time to read my work when I was just starting out. You helped to shape this story into what it is today and I thank you for all you have done <3

Thank you to all those who made this possible.

XXX

ABOUT THE AUTHOR

Ellouise Liston is the author of New Adult romance novel, *Hooking up with Mr Wrong* and resides in Sydney, Australia. Best known for always needing a healthy mix of humour and heart racing romance in every book she writes. Ellouise writes romance while influencing young minds as a high school English Teacher. When she is not busy with writing and teaching, she can be found reading, binge watching Netflix or spending time with her fiancé and fur-baby, Shep.

Printed in Great Britain
by Amazon

75212322R00193